BEING EMILY

Also by Anne Donovan

Hieroglyphics (2001)
Buddha Da (2003)

BEING EMILY

Anne Donovan

CANONGATE

Edinburgh · London · New York · Melbourne

First published in Great Britain in 2008 by
Canongate Books Ltd, 14 High Street,
Edinburgh EH1 1TE

3

British Library Cataloguing-in-Publication Data
A catalogue record for this book is available on
request from the British Library

ISBN 978 1 84767 044 1

Typeset by Palimpsest Book Production Ltd,
Grangemouth, Stirlingshire

Printed and bound in Great Britain by Clays Ltd, St Ives plc

www.canongate.net

BEING EMILY

THROUGH IN THE livin room Patrick was paintin the fireplace while Mona and Rona practised their line dancin. *Silver bells and golden needles they won't mend this heart of mine.* Step two three, cross two three, turn. *It's threads, no bells*, says ma da, weavin his way through their routine.

Mona and Rona are twins. At first the doc thought it was gonnae be triplets and Da wanted tae call them Mona, Rona and Shona. Mammy says she's thankful for small mercies — ah'm no sure if she means havin two babies at once insteidy three, or if it's the name. The neighbours doonstairs have a dug called Shona, it's a sheltie.

Patrick's on the nightshift at the bakery, and when he gets hame the back of six he's wired up, cannae sleep for hours. That's when he paints the fireplace. He's done it three times

1

— first white but that was too borin, then dark red, but Da said it hurt his eyes. Noo he's tryin a marbled effect wi lilac and pink through the red. When everybody else gets up, we have cornflakes and Patrick has bacon, egg and tattie scones, then he goes tae bed and we go tae school. Except this was the first day of the summer holidays so we werenae.

Ah was at the sink in the kitchen, washin the dishes wi *Spirit of Haworth* propped up behind the taps, practisin bein Emily Brontë. Ah'd read that she baked the family's bread and learned German at the same time, book in fronty her. Since then ah'd developed a new interest in housework, so long as you could dae it while you were readin. Up till then ah thought if you were gonnae be a poet you had tae float aboot in a dwam or lie on a couch all day.

I wander'd lonely as a cloud
That floats on high o'er vale and hill

If you're a poet it's dead important tae know how tae use apostrophes when you miss out bits of words to make it scan. Last year ah wrote a poem for the school magazine that started: 'I wander'd 'mongst the flow'rs fair'.

Mammy put a knife in the soapy watter.

Watch you don't get that book all wet, Fiona.

D'you think ah could start bakin our bread?

Your brother brings hame three loaves fae his work every day. If you've spare time on yer haunds there's plenty other jobs round the hoose.

Usually ah skived aff at this point but since ah'd discovered Emily, ah just smiled and said, *Okay, Mammy.*

Da was pointin out the windae. *Oh my God — would you look at that!*

Mammy and me followed his finger but all ah could see was Mrs Flanagan next door hingin out her washin in her yellow velour tracksuit. It looks as if she's stuffed it wi newspapers, lumps and bumps jigglin round as she bends and pegs.

What?

Can yous no see thon pig, over there, just up above the roof . . . look at its wings flappin.

Very funny.

First time ah've heard Princess Fiona here volunteerin tae dae a tap round the hoose.

Well, be thankful. Everyone is gonnae have tae pull their weight this holiday. Ah don't know how these weans have tae get six weeks aff anyhow.

The first day of the summer holidays Mammy always does her spiel aboot how they're far too long and we get intae lazy habits. Da sloped aff tae his work efter the first sentence. Ah trailed ma haund in the soapy bubbles, cairried on readin ma book. Miss Hughes had lent me it for the holidays. She was ma English teacher last year, first year of secondary, and she was the wan that got me interested in Emily.

Ah done the hooverin wi the book in wan haund then went and made the beds wi it stuck up on the headboard. Patrick's room's dead neat and when he started work he bought hissel a new downie cover – navy blue wi a cream stripe through it. When ma granny was alive she'd say he should join the forces he's that tidy and Mammy'd get really mad at her.

They have tae fight, you know – it's no a fashion parade.

It's a good life for a boy. He's that good wi his haunds too, he'd learn a trade.

Have another cuppa tea, Gran, said ma da. *Patrick's no really the type.*

Patrick never said anythin, just went on wi his jigsaw or

3

his model makin or whatever he was daein wi his long fingers. He looks dead different fae the resty us; fair straight hair and skin that pale and thin you can near see through it, while we're all brown and curly-haired. *Like tinks*, ma gran'd say when she was in a bad mood.

Patrick appeared at the door.

You finished? Ah want tae go tae bed.

Our room's a guddle of Barbies and scrunchies, My Little Pony and Animal Hospital toys, hauf of them broken or twisted fae bein left on radiators or ootside in the rain. The wardrobe door was hingin open and a long red scarf ah'd started knittin in Primary Seven and never finished, still on its needles, trailed out, wrapped round one of the twins' pleated navy school skirts. The three beds are hunched thegether wi only a few inches between them. Ah don't know where they'd of put Shona if she'd arrived. Mona's bed has a Princess Barbie cover, Rona's has a Horse Riding Barbie cover and mines has a purple and lime green Groovy Chicks one with a shiny blob on it where ah spilled some glittery nail polish. Mammy was really mad at me.

That cover's split new, Fiona.

She'd scrubbed it for ages but the stain never came aff. Ah quite liked it but; at night when the twins were asleep and ah was readin in bed, the mark glinted in the light of the torch.

Ah climbed over the other two beds and sat on mines, the wan nearest the windae. Emily would of liked the purple background; purple was her favourite colour and she had a frock that was purple wi lilac lightnin patterns on it. She had a room of her ain but, a toty wee wan just big enough for a bed; she'd sit there in the cauld of winter wi her notebook on her lap, writin *Wuthering Heights*. *Wuthering Heights* is the best book ah've ever read, but Emily was a poet too and ah'd learned some of her poems aff by heart.

No coward soul is mine,
No trembler in the world's storm-troubled sphere

Fiona, are you finished?
Nearly.
Will you bring the washin through, hen?
Mammy stuffed the washin in the machine afore she went out tae her work. She does part-time in Boots, starts at ten three days a week.
Don't forget tae take that washin out when it's done. She opened the fridge and put in the mince she'd just cooked. *That's for the night. And make sure the twins eat fruit for their lunch.*
Although the twins were in the next room ah knew they were makin the silent vomitin noises they always done when the word fruit was mentioned.
And keep them quiet while Patrick's sleepin – take them tae the swing park. You could read your book while they're playin.
Aye that'll be right. See, she thinks the twins are wee angels and when Mammy's around they nearly always are, but the minute she's out of sight they turn intae monsters. You can almost see the change comin over them as she puts on her coat, like the way you smell thunder in the air afore the storm actually breaks, then when the door closes behind her the devils dance out their eyes and they start. The number of times she's come hame tae an upside doon settee, earth fae a plant spilled all ower the carpet, and turnt tae me and said, *Fiona*, in that voice. *How could you let the twins make such a mess?*

5

And they're climbin up her legs like squirrels, cuddlin her and sayin, *Mammy, you're hame.*

They're nearly as bad wi ma da, but he puts on that helpless look and Mammy says *Bobby*, but no in the tone she says *Fiona*, mair like, *well what d'you expect, he's a man.*

As usual, the second the door slammed Mona started haulin the cushions aff the couch in the livin room. *We're tigers and you're our prey.* She growled and clawed at me.

Let's go tae the swing park, ah said.

Don't want tae go tae the swing park. Want tae kill wur prey. Rona bit ma leg through ma jeans.

Hey, pack it in. Ah've got Smarties for yous.

The twins'll dae anythin for chocolate and Patrick'll dae anythin for a quiet life so he gies me money tae buy sweeties.

Gimme, gimme.

After we've been tae the park.

At the swing park the twins climbed up the chute the wrang way while ah read ma biography of Emily. Her brother and sisters and her all lived in this hoose on the edge of the moors; they went out for long walks and made up their ain imaginary world. Their brother Branwell got a box of toy soldiers so they each picked wan and made up stories aboot it, wrote them doon in wee booklets.

The wumman next tae me on the bench said, *Are they your wee sisters?*

When ah looked up Rona was hingin upside doon fae the chains on the swing and Mona was shovin a toddler aff the baby chute. Ah shut ma book.

C'mon, we're gaun hame.

How?

Dinnertime. Anyhow, it's startin tae rain.

*   *   *

6

Later in the efternoon, ah got out paper and felties and scissors. Ah cut the paper intae squares and folded them so they were like wee books, then sat Mona and Rona doon at the table.

Are we playin a game? said Mona.

We're gonnae write stories about your Barbies.

But we've got stories about them. In the Barbie comic.

Ah know, but new stories, wans we make up wursels.

The twins have got loadsa different Barbies but they each have a special favourite they drag aboot wi them. Rona's is called Bendy Barbie because, due tae some accident, she has a big bit missin fae her leg and it bends round as if she's double-jointed. Mona's is called Bubbly Barbie cause she's always greetin.

Ah'll dae the writin. You just tell me the words tae put doon.

The twins looked at each other then Rona said, *Okay.*

Ah'll start, ah said. *It was the first day of the summer holidays.*

Bendy Barbie went tae the park, said Rona. *She was playin on the chute.*

Ah printed the words, dead neat.

Along came Bubbly Barbie. She pushed Bendy Barbie aff the chute. Mona whacked Rona's Barbie wi hers. *Bendy Barbie started greetin so she was Bubbly Barbie noo.*

Are you sure this is what you want in the story? ah said.

Rona hit Mona's Barbie back, then the two of them started batterin each other. Just then Patrick appeared in his stripy jammies.

What's this — Blue Peter?

A zebra, a stripy zebra. Tigers kill zebras! shouted Rona.

She and Mona stood up on their chairs, started clawin at Patrick and growlin.

Then suddenly a miraculous change came over the twins' faces. They smiled sweetly, sat doon and started tae cuddle

7

the dolls. They must be like dugs, can hear things humans cannae, for the next second there was Mammy.

Clear that stuff aff the table, would you, Fiona?

The twins rushed to switch on their music.

Just because we're married
Don't mean we can't fool around.
Let's walk out through the moonlight
And lay the blanket on the ground.

Should they be listenin tae that? said Da, who'd just come in the door.

What? said Mammy, stirrin the mince.

Never mind, said ma da.

Efter tea Mammy took the twins tae their line dancin. They're the youngest in the class but they're stars. For the displays they wear cowboy hats and waistcoats wi shiny fringes; it's like watchin wan person, as they step and birl, turn and clap, spot on the beat.

It was dead quiet without them. Patrick, ma da and me sat in a row on the couch. There was a decoratin programme on the TV and a guy in an orange tee shirt was witterin on aboot paint effects. Patrick watches this every week and Da just sits in fronty anythin that's on the box. Ah looked up from ma book.

Da, what's consumption?

Consumption no be done aboot it?

Da?

Whit, hen?

It's the Brontës. There was six of them at the start and the two big sisters died of consumption. Whit is it?

It's a disease.

8

Ah know that — whit kind of disease?

Some kind of pneumonia or that. They'd all kinds of diseases in they days we don't really get noo. Your granny had scarlet fever when she was wee. My God, would you look at the colour he's puttin on that wall.

Pistachio, said Patrick.

You'd need tae be well pistachio-ed tae paint yer livin room like that.

Ah could hear Mammy and the twins outside. If ah got out the road quick ah'd miss their bedtime. Ah slipped through the close, away tae the far endy the back court and hunkered doon at the wall. Mrs Flanagan's washin was still out, her enormous great drawers and her man's gigantic tartan boxers saggin fae the line. Ah think if ma bum was as big as that ah'd dry ma washin inside. In the bin shelter the Jacksons' grey cat slithered round the edge of a wheelie bin, its tail skitterin against the plastic.

Ah leaned on the wall, took *Wuthering Heights* out ma pocket and opened it at ma favourite bit.

'My love for Heathcliff resembles the eternal rocks beneath, a source of little visible delight, but necessary.'

Patrick came doon the path carryin a plastic binbag.

Mammy's wonderin where you are. Better get inside.

Okay. Patrick, are there any moors round here?

Moors?

Aye. Emily used tae wander aboot the moors.

Ah don't think you want tae dae that. You might get consumption.

Consumption no be done aboot it?

Patrick stood leanin against the washin pole, swingin the bag fae side tae side. The grass was all worn and patchy under his foot.

9

If you like, ah'll teach you tae bake bread.

Really?

Ah'll bring hame some yeast the morra. Mammy's no workin so you won't have tae watch the twins. You can watch yer dough risin instead.

Patrick lifted the lid of the bin and chucked the binbag inside. Then he went out the gate and doon the lane. The last of the sun was vanishin over the roof tops and the back of the buildin looked like a castle, big grey blocks a sandstone risin out the earth. Deep recessed sills. Mammy would of liked a new house wi wur ain garden, but Da loved tenements. *Solid,* he'd say. *Built tae last.* He was a tiler tae trade, done bathrooms and kitchens maistly, but he loved the tiles in our close, the subtlety of their colours, even the wee cracks that ran through them. *They don't make them like that noo.*

Our flat was two up and at the back bedroom windae the curtains were drawn. With a bit of luck the twins would be lyin next tae their scabby Barbies, sleepin like wee angels, breathin deeply and dreamin about line dancin. Ma and Da would be sittin on the couch thegether, watchin TV.

The grass felt sticky wi damp and deep grey settled round the back court. The fluorescent light in our kitchen flickered then snapped on, and Mammy's face was at the windae, peerin out. She spotted me and smiled, made a T sign wi her index fingers. Ah gied her the thumbs-up, lifted ma book, and heided inside.

PATRICK TOOK THE lump of dough ah'd been wrestlin with and kneaded it, pushin the outer part intae the centre, then pressin wi the fleshy part of his palm, just at the base of his thumb, fingers steady and firm. The yella daud, crisscrossed wi creases, smoothed intae a solid mass.

Looks like you're giein it a massage.

Wouldnae like tae get wan fae you then. He kidded on he was attackin the dough.

Ah dunted him in the ribs.

Ow, ow, Mammy she's attackin me.

Don't make a mess, you two — yer Auntie Janice'll be here soon. Mammy bent doon tae the washin machine, hauled the claes out.

Patrick plaited the dough intae a neat shape.

11

Here, brush a wee drap milk on the tap — a wee bit — you're no emulsionin the walls.

The milk dripped aff the brush, left a sticky trail on the worksurface.

Stick it in the oven and whatever you dae don't open it for twenty minutes.

Can you hang these out for me, hen? Looks as though the rain'll keep aff for a while.

Ah wasnae convinced — a big grey cloud was heidin in fast — but ah never said anythin. When it comes tae washin Mammy is the eternal optimist. We've got a pulley but she just loves hangin the washin outside. When she got the new machine last year the guy in the shop tellt her she could get wan wi a tumble drier for the same price but she didnae want it. *Doesnae smell the same if you don't put it outside,* she said.

Auntie Janice arrived in the close just as ah was comin in fae the back court. She's only five year younger than Mammy but looks completely different; short spiky hair wi coloured streaks through it, a nose stud and trendy claes.

Hi Fiona. She gied me a big hug. *How's the poetry?*

Ah wrote a new wan last night. About the wee cat in the bin shelter.

Good for you.

Miss Hughes said you could write poetry about ordinary things as well.

We went upstairs and in the front door. Janice shouted, *Anybody here?* so the twins would have time tae hide. Ever since they were wee she done this same routine but they never seemed tae get fed up wi it. Then she said in a very loud voice, *What a shame. Ah was so lookin forward tae seein the twins. Oh well. Ah'll just need tae eat these sweeties all by mysel.*

All of a sudden she was near knocked tae the ground by what looked like twenty twins chargin fae the livin room. Mammy appeared at the door of the kitchen and they turnt back intae angels.

Don't jump on your auntie like that. And you're no gettin sweeties at this time of the day – they can go in the cupboard for later. Janice, you'll need tae stop bringin them so much rubbish.

The twins followed us into the kitchen.

What's that smell? said Rona.

Patrick's teachin me tae bake bread – he showed me how tae dae the kneadin and everythin.

Yuck, said Mona and they disappeared intae the bedroom to play.

It's just about ready, said Patrick. *Want tae take it out the oven?*

Ah opened the door and there it was, a beautiful golden plaited loaf. Ah lifted it out, turned it carefully ontae the rack tae cool.

That smells fantastic, said Janice.

Fiona's first loaf. You can have some wi your tea. Mammy switched on the kettle.

Wanny the auld guys showed me how tae dae it by haund, said Patrick. *It's all machines at the bakery noo.*

Really? said Janice. *Another illusion shattered.*

Once we were sittin round the table Janice turnt tae Mammy and said, *Will ah tell them now?*

On you go.

Ah'm havin a baby. Janice's eyes shone.

Congratulations, said Patrick.

That's great, ah said, chewin the bread. It was warm and the butter melted intae it. Tasted better than any bread ah'd ever had. *Ah didnae know you had a boyfriend.*

Ah don't, she said.

Sorry. Ah felt ma face gaun red. Should of known better. Auntie Janice was dead independent. Career woman, Da called her. *Lots of women are single parents noo. And you've got a good job and everythin.*

Ah'm no gonnae be a single parent — me and Angela will bring the baby up thegether.

Your flatmate?

My partner.

Ah felt like a right numpty. Couldnae say anythin. Scared ah'd say somethin else stupid. Janice talked about how the father was a friend of theirs but he lived abroad and wouldnae have much tae dae wi the wean.

After we'd had tea Janice and Mammy took the twins out to the park, leavin me and Patrick to dae the washin up.

You're awful quiet, he said. *You okay? About Janice?*

Aye — it's just, ah just never realised.

She's been livin wi Angela for years. They dae everythin thegether.

Aye but so dae Jean and Betty up the stair.

Uhhuh, said Patrick.

You're kiddin. Jean and Betty are about ninety-five.

No quite. Anyway, d'you think folk grow out of it when they get past a certain age?

Naw, ah didnae mean that. Just cannae imagine them . . .

Ah didnae know what ah meant. Never thought about it really. There was lesbian couples on the TV sometimes but that was different, they werenae real, characters in a soap opera or film stars or that. The idea that my auntie or the two wee auld ladies up the stair could be like that. It was just weird.

Patrick finished the last plate, wiped his haunds on the edge of the teatowel ah was usin. *You're no . . . ah mean you don't think there's anythin wrang wi it, dae you?*

14

Ah wiped the sink wi the cloth and hung it on the drainin board.

Mammy seems to think it's okay.

But ma da thought there was somethin wrang about it.

What about the baby but?

What about it? said Mammy. The twins were away tae their beds and the resty us were sittin in the living room, watchin TV, well, no actually watchin it, watchin ma da flick through the channels while we were waitin for *ER* tae come on.

Janice'll be a great mother.

That's all very well when it's toty, said ma da. *But when it grows aulder it'll start askin where its daddy is.*

Loads of weans never have a daddy in the first place. Or they have one that's never around. At least Angela will be there.

No the same, said ma da.

Ah know it's no the same, said Mammy. *But there's different ways of daein things. Janice cannae help how she is.*

Ah kept quiet. Ah was surprised they were havin this conversation in fronty me and ah thought if ah said anything, they might stop. A few month ago they'd never of mentioned sex, even though Mammy had tellt me about it that long ago ah couldnae remember no knowin. And if anythin sexy came on the TV they'd change channels or send me out tae make tea.

Ah never said she could. Ah just think her and Angela should be discreet, no flauntin it.

Da, said Patrick. *Why should they have tae lie about their relationship?*

Ah never said that, you're puttin words in ma mouth. There's a difference between bein discreet and lyin. Ah mean we don't run round the hoose wi nae claes on, dae we?

Patrick laughed. *We don't. But some families dae. Willie Slavin's ma and da have a shower and then walk through the hall wi nothin on.*

How d'you know that?

Harry tellt me. He was in the hoose wan day when Mrs Slavin walked in the livin room, said 'ah think ah left ma hairbrush in here,' picked it up and walked out again, starkers.

Jeezo. Ah think that proves ma point about discretion, said ma da. *Mrs Slavin.*

Could be worse, said Patrick. *At least the Flanagans arenae at it.*

Da turnt the volume up. *Shoosh. It's startin.*

AS WE LEFT the chapel Mrs Reilly slipped a sweetie tae the twins like she done every week after mass. The twins mouthed thankyous and Mammy smiled, placin the sweets in her bag. *For later*, she'd say, but later, at hame, she'd throw them in the bin.

Such a lovely family.

Mrs Reilly wore a knitted beret even on a day like this in the height of summer. She sat in the pew in fronty us. Da was always nearest the centre aisle, then Patrick, me, Mammy, Rona and Mona. When the twins were toddlers it was easier tae have them at that end so if they got girny Mammy could bundle them out doon the side without disturbin the whole congregation.

Nooadays, of course, they were model children. Hair

17

smoothed back in alice bands, wearin identical pink cord skirts and sparkly tee shirts, white frilly socks and patent shoes, they sat demurely through mass, kneelin and staundin and sittin when they were supposed tae, only occasionally takin out their fifty pence piece for the collection and examinin it. They'd made their first Holy Communion in May so we all went up thegether when it was time, me sheltered behind Patrick's blue cord jacket. He attracted attention fae the granny brigade too as he was always smartly dressed, that different fae the other young guys in their jeans and trainers. Patrick didnae buy many claes but the ones he had were expensive. Between Patrick and the twins naebody ever noticed me, which suited me fine.

When my granny was alive we used tae go round tae hers every Sunday efternoon for gammon sangwiches and hard boiled eggs and cake wi pink and yella squares in it. There was a funny smell in my granny's: the pot of soup on the stove, solid wi barley, the ancient cat that ignored the twins' attempts tae get it tae play wi balls of wool, the carpet in the hall that looked as if it was ages wi my granny, all mingled intae one.

Noo she was gone Sundays felt looser. Sometimes Patrick was on the nightshift and went tae his room in the efternoon tae have a nap or lie on his bed, listenin tae music on his heidphones. The twins played in the back court, sometimes by theirsels, other times entertainin weans fae the next close wi cartwheels or dancin displays. Ah went round tae the swing park to meet my pals.

Monica, Jemma and me had teamed up when we started secondary. Ah still mind that first day at St Philomena's, the churnin feelin in my stomach. All the different primaries had been mixed up and in the mad scramble for seats ah was left staundin like a stookie. Jemma rescued me. She appeared out of naewhere and said, *Partner?* Ah nodded and the two of us sat thegether at the front. Ah hardly knew her then, though ah'd seen her around cause she went to the same dancin school as the twins – her class came out as theirs went in. Monica arrived later, waited at the front of the class for the teacher tae find her a seat. Sweet and smiley, that neat and shiny in her uniform she looked as if someone had polished her. When ah got tae know her family ah suspected her mother actually did polish her alang with everything else in their immaculate house. Her parents owned a Chinese takeaway and her ma cleaned the house fae top to bottom, drove Monica to school and went tae mass afore her long day's work.

Jemma was on a swing when ah arrived, swayin gently, tappin one foot on the ground tae stop hersel gaun high.

You're late.

Had tae wash up.

Time your ma got a dishwasher.

Ah sat in the swing next tae Jemma's, started to move, higher and higher, usin ma knees tae power me. Ah loved the squidgy feelin in my belly, felt ah was flyin. Ah kept on swingin, fast and high for a few minutes, then let the swing slow doon till it idled and stopped.

Ah love that feelin you get in your belly when the swing goes dead high.

A lassie in our Alison's class says it's a sin. Jemma's sister was fifteen.

How can it be a sin? You don't go tellin the priest in confession you went on the swings.

It's okay when you're wee. But when you start gettin your thingummies, the feelins you get are sexy.

19

Really?

A nun tellt her.

Ah started tae giggle. *How did the nun know?*

Jemma giggled too, then the giggle became a laugh and the next minute the two of us were nearly fallin aff the swings helpless.

Mibbe it's a . . . test. Jemma could hardly get the words out. *If you want tae become a nun they test you to see if you can control yer sexy feelins.*

The tears were streamin doon ma face. *Aye – when they join the convent . . . they have a row of swings and all these nuns swingin away prayin that they won't feel sexy.*

Jesus Mary and Joseph protect me fae impure thoughts.

Through the blur of tears ah seen Monica wavin at us fae across the road.

Ah waved back. *Don't tell Mon what we were laughin at.*

Later, pretendin to read in the bedroom, ah kept thinkin about this efternoon. Sometimes it was like that when Jemma and me were on wur ain thegether. Monica was lovely but she'd of been really shocked about us laughin at nuns. And somehow, away fae Jemma, ah felt ashamed. Ah knew ah'd need tae confess it next time ah went and it made me feel a bit sick inside tae have to say it to a priest. Even though ah knew ah was really tellin Jesus and he knew anyway, it was dead embarrassin.

And ah kept wonderin about what Jemma had said. Ah'd always thought sexy feelins meant fancyin boys or someone in a band. In RE we'd done a unit called 'Growing Up: Issues of Morality' but it was all about no puttin yoursel in situations with boys that could go too far, kissin and stuff. No one ever said you shouldnae go on the swings. Ah wondered

if ah'd ever had other sexy feelins without knowin. Sometimes if ah woke up at night and needed the toilet, ah'd lie
there for a minute, enjoyin the feelin of my bladder bein full,
wantin tae go but wantin tae lie in the warmth too. Then
when ah got up and peed the nice feelin went. Was that sexy
too? Was any feelin inside you?

Fiona? Mammy came in the bedroom. *Ah'm gonnae get the
twins aff tae bed.*

Okay.

Mammy stroked my hair. *Sorry, hen. Your da's watchin the TV
but if you want some peace you can read in the kitchen.* She smiled
at me.

Ah wanted tae ask her, but somehow the words didnae
come.

Four Years Later

WHEN I FIRST knew Jas his front teeth had wee jaggy bits across their biting edge like a wean's. Serrated. Most folk's teeth wear tae a straight edge by the time they're about fourteen but in sixth year at school his were like mini-saws. I could feel them when we were kissing, hours spent tangling with passion in a quiet bit of wasteground on the edge of the park. We never really done anything much, just kissed till wur lips swelled up. Every time it seemed as if we'd be carried away by it, one of us would pull back or move the other's haund away fae the danger spot and we'd break, talk for a while until the moment passed. Sometimes, lying in bed at night, I'd imagine what it'd be like for him tae put his haunds under my claes, touch my naked skin. In the beds across fae mines were Mona, an unidentifiable lump under her downie,

25

and Rona, wan airm thrown out of the covers, white in the light of the streetlamp.

How did Jas sleep? What would it be like to lie beside him, coorie like spoons all night long?

It seems weird we never spoke about it, since we spent all the rest of our time talking, never ran out of conversation. He never anyway. Always something on his mind; big things, never trivia.

Look at this, he'd say, showing me something he'd cut out the newspaper about fossil fuels. Or he'd start a conversation wi my da. *So what do you think of the situation in Iraq, Mr O'Connell? D'you think we should end the sanctions?*

Da cairried on watching *Countdown* wi the sound turned doon; I knew he was making up words in his heid while he answered Jas.

Havenae a scooby aboot politics son, but these things'll never hurt the government – it's always the ordinary folk end up suffering.

Jas didnae know the meaning of the word casual; everything was important to him and if it wasnae important, what was the point in talking aboot it? Why gossip aboot some daft popstar's lovelife when you could discuss the meaning of life, why watch soaps when you could read about the molecular composition of polymers?

And he didnae just talk about things, he done them. He was aye writing letters for Amnesty or campaigning for something on the school council. Or studying. Or working. Probably the only time he wasnae daeing something purposeful was when he was with me.

I met Jas when I moved to the non-denominational (or – as my da called it – proddy) school in sixth year. I wanted to dae Advanced Highers in English, Art and History and St Philomena's couldnae timetable them thegether. They tried tae persuade me to change one of the subjects, then suggested I go to Burnside just for History but it seemed less complicated tae move school – it was only for a year. And though I'd been dead happy at St Phil's when I was younger, after all the stuff that had happened this past year, I was glad enough tae go where no one knew me.

I met Jas the first day when he came up to me after English and thrust a photocopied leaflet about the debating club in ma haund.

'Is multiculturalism the new racism?'

I went alang cause I'd nothin else to dae efter school on Friday and Friday is a day when you want to have something to dae. I thought it'd be good to get tae know some folk at school but it was just Jas and two of his pals and a couple of fourth-year girls who wanted to get off with the sixth years. And me. Clocked in a dusty classroom wi the desks moved back and stacked upside doon so you could see the chuggie stuck tae the underside.

Jas was electrifying. I wasnae convinced by all he said, but he said it wi a passion that was infectious. He had these beautiful haunds, long and spidery like the winter branches of trees, and he moved them as he spoke, like someone daeing calligraphy in the air. The other guy never stood a chance; he plodded through his well-prepared and well-meaning speech at a steady pace, stopping at regular intervals tae pause, look at us and sum up his point in a deeper voice afore lifting the next index card. He said all the things I'd ever been told about respecting different cultures and religions, about us all co-existing in some happy melting-pot of a city.

But Jas.

I am sick, sick, sick of being a Sikh.

27

He looked round, dark eyes taking in each of us.

Not because I am unhappy with my religion or my culture or my family heritage, but because so-called multiculturalism has stolen Sikhism, has tamed it and made it cute and cuddly. He put on a patronising adult voice, the kind of voice people use when they're trying to humour a three-year-old.

Oh, look at the cute little Asian boy with his hanky tied round his heid, that's because he's growing his hair. It's his religion, you know.

Oh, why don't we all make paper lanterns this week in the Art lesson because it's Diwali? Maybe Jaswinder could tell us about it. Then next week Hassan can tell us about Eid. Then it'll be time to start learning the carols for our Christmas concert.

If I had a fiver for every time I'd told my primary school class about friggin Diwali I'd be a millionaire. But making lanterns every November or drawing pictures of the five Ks doesnae mean they understand anything about being a Sikh — it's just paying lip service to the real diversity of our culture and smoothing over the racism and suspicion that divides us, even those of us who tick the brown boxes in the ethnic monitoring forms we need to fill in in the name of equal opportunities — Sikh and Muslim, Hindu and Sikh.

And I don't have time in the four minutes allowed me to even get started on those of mixed race — those who should be the zenith, the culmination of our so-called multicultural society (if we really believed in it). Yes I am referring to those of mixed race, who, rather than being what we aspire to, far from being the epitome of multiculturalism, are in fact an embarrassment as they can't be done, ticked off on a multicultural calendar by making something symbolic out of coloured paper, or placed in the correct box on the multicoloured form. No, they fit nowhere, not even with their own family.

Efter the debate, predictably, was won by Jas, he and the other guy shook haunds and the fourth-year lassies fluttered round him. I sloped off out the room and heided doon the road.

so. MS HARRIS crossed her legs and clicked the top of her pen. *Today I thought we'd go round the group so each of you can say what topic you're proposing for your dissertation and why you chose it. I'd like you to give us some idea of the areas you intend to explore. Is that clear?*

She looked round us, sat in a circle on scabby plastic chairs. Of course it was clear. Everything she said and done was clear. She spoke wi a precision that was quite different fae the sloppy way the kids done, every other word *like, yeah, dunno, whatever.* But it was also different fae the way the other teachers spoke. They mumbled or tailed away their sentences, turned their back on you while they were explaining things or failed tae make eye contact. Ms Harris was young – 26, 27 mibbe – and everything about her was perfect. The other young teachers were either buttoned up as if they were wearing their parents' clothes or else sloppy like they'd fallen out of bed, but she wore the kind of clothes that managed to look quite cool but perfectly appropriate for a teacher – little cardigans with glittery bits on them, silky skirts that never creased, funky shoes. Even her specs had a designer label. She knew her stuff too – was always prepared, never seemed harassed. Of course the sixth year werenae likely to gie teachers up cheek but some of them could be stroppy in their ain way. And I'd seen her in action in the corridors, gliding through a tumultuous sea of second year, effortlessly calming them with a word.

Naebody said anything. Terrified if we looked up we'd be asked to start, everybody stared at their folder. Ms Harris had gied them out last week at the first meeting of the class; unlike the usual thin school cardboard ones, they were dead fancy, with spaces for lined paper, a pouch for books, plastic pockets for putting pictures and stuff in.

I want you to see this as a very organic process, sixth year, different from the way you've worked before. Don't feel you have to limit your research to critical books or biographies. Maybe a found object, a photograph or poem is what you need to carry around, focus on.

I'd felt excited when she talked like that, imagined mysel piecing thegether a portrait of Emily with all kinds of things I associated with her – heather fae the moors, sketches of her dog – but the day, my bum already numb fae the uncomfortable seat, Kevin next tae me scratching hissel as if he had fleas, I just felt stupid.

Jaswinder, can you start us off?

Jas nodded. *I'm gonnae write about Shelley. Percy Bysshe Shelley, 1792–1822, was everything. One of the greatest poets who ever lived – in my opinion, the greatest – he was a philosopher, a traveller, friend of Byron and other important poets, had several lovers and many children as well as being married to the woman who wrote Frankenstein — and he was a political and a radical thinker.*

That sounds really interesting, Jaswinder. But your dissertation must be no longer than 3000 words so you'll need to focus on one or two aspects of Shelley.

That's the problem — to do that is to limit him, and he never limited himself, he thought these barriers were artificial. 'Hail to thee blythe spirit, bird thou never wert.'

Thanks, Jaswinder. Let's move on. Kevin?

I'm gonna write about three lyrics of the Manic Street Preachers.

Ms Harris touched the bridge of her specs with one perfectly manicured finger. *I can safely say that this will present a different set of challenges from writing about Shelley. Only three lyrics?*

Well you said we had tae focus.

True. Do you think the Manic Street Preachers will provide sufficient weight, though? I want to encourage you not to limit yourself to the conventional literary canon, but you must ensure that your choice of text falls within the parameters of the Exam Board.

Eh?

Alice dunted Kevin in the elbow. *She means the Manics are crap writers.*

That's . . .

Which they are.

Ms Harris said coolly, *I don't actually know enough about them to express an opinion. Perhaps you'd better leave the lyrics with me, Kevin, and I'll get back to you.*

We plodded on round the group. Alice wanted to compare the portrayal of women in the novels of Toni Morrison and Janice Galloway, while Sana was obsessed with Chuck Palahniuk. Danny, Lee and Katie all planned to dae *Lord of the Rings*. I could sense a slight tightening of Ms Harris's lip but her only comment was

32

that choosing popular texts meant you had to work harder to find an original take on them. Two other folk wanted to dae George Orwell and Steinbeck. Then it was my turn.

Emily Brontë.

Ms Harris looked slightly more animated. *Why Emily Brontë, Fiona?*

I've just always loved everything she wrote, the poems and 'Wuthering Heights'.

Have you a specific aspect of her work in mind?

I thought either a sense of place or mibbe her family.

Sounds promising. Can you tell some of the others, who may not be so au fait with the Brontës, what that means?

Well, Emily lived in this remote Yorkshire village – she was the parson's daughter and her mother died when she was really young. She had a brother and sisters and they all wrote and made up stories and plays thegether. The sisters became really good writers – well folk say Anne isnae as good but I still like her – and her brother fell in love with this married woman and took tae drugs and drink and then he died but he could of been a writer too. Emily was a recluse and wandered the moors and . . .

I realised everyone was looking at me and my mind went blank.

Thanks Fiona. Your enthusiasm is evident.

Kevin stuck his haund up. *What kind of drugs did they have then?*

Not now, please – time to pack up. Kevin, can you make an extra appointment to see me?

I shoved my folder in my bag and walked out the room. My cheeks were burning as I heided doon the back stair. Then I heard a voice calling, *Hey Fiona, wait,* and when I turnt round it was Jas, rucksack slung across one shoulder.

Fiona.

Hi.

Where you off to?
Oh, just home.
Got time for a coffee?

There was a wee place round the corner fae the school, no really a café, just a takeout place wi a few high stools at a counter. Legs dangling, sitting side by side, we talked, hardly looking at each other. Maist of the time I stared doon at his shoes, black shiny lace-ups, nice shoes, nothing like the ubiquitous trainers or boots the other boys wore.

See, Fiona, I dunno anything really about the Brontës but when you were talking it sounded so much as if she was almost opposite to Shelley.

I guess – she hated being away fae hame, got sick when she wasnae at Haworth, near the moors.

And Shelley was always travelling – he almost never had a home.

Emily hardly even spoke, except to her ain family. Folk that met her talked about her as if she was like a sphinx or something.

Jas laughed so much he became unbalanced fae his seat.

Cool. Shelley never stopped talking, he wrote polemic and essays. He turned and looked straight in my face for the first time. *But it sounds like they both had this true inner thing – they were pure artists.*

It was the first time I'd heard anyone my age talk like that. Dead serious. He looked straight at me and his eyes were dark chocolatey brown. *That's what I want for my poems. I don't mean I think I can be like Shelley but I want tae have truth in them. Know what I mean?*

I nodded.

Do you write as well, Fiona?

I used tae try to write poetry, when I was younger. But I . . . kind of stopped. Last year.

34

I'm gonnae dae the creative writing option this year — you should try it too — don't let your poetry go.

You're taking Art this year too, aren't you? He was in my class, so obviously he was, but I wanted to keep him talking.

Aye. Photography, mostly. It's that immediate. Real. D'you specialise in anything?

No really — bit of painting, collage stuff. I feel I want to dae something different this year but.

What's your third subject?

History, but History is . . . well I like it but I don't feel the same way I dae about Art or Literature.

Same with me. My third subject is Chemistry. I like it but I don't have that . . . passion for it.

Silence. Jas looked at his watch. I assumed he was fed up wi me, that whatever had attracted him had fizzled out in the reality of talking to me. I was used tae that. No one ever thought I was interesting.

I'm sorry, Fiona. I'd like to go on talking but I have to get to work.

You have a job?

I work in the pharmacy, my family's shop.

He climbed doon fae the stool, stood next tae me, looking smaller fae my perch.

You know I think we should work together sometimes — talking about stuff could really help.

Cool.

And that was us.

After school we'd go for coffee, sit on the high stools, then I'd go hame and Jas would go tae work. Later we'd talk on the phone or go out thegether. At first I said I was meeting Mon and Jemma but after a few weeks it felt daft tae pretend. Jas and me were real.

35

I'd never been in love afore, never even had a crush on anyone really. The rest of the lassies were aye fancying guys or gaun mad over the latest popstar but I never had. When I was aboot fourteen I started tae wonder if there was something wrang wi me, did I have a bit missing? I knew I didnae fancy girls but I didnae recognise the stuff I read in the magazines, the heart stopping, the churning in the stomach. I went out wi boys a few times, usually to make up numbers on a double date, but I never felt anything. When they kissed me goodnight it was less exciting than getting licked by the Jacksons' cat.

The first time Jas kissed me was three weeks after that first coffee. We'd went tae study in the library after school, sitting side by side at the tables near the reference section. We were baith working on dissertations for English. I was poring over *Wuthering Heights*, writing out quotes about nature and he'd Shelley's poetry open in fronty him. I wish someone had taken a photie of us that day; two heids, his hair dark and shiny and straight, mines tangled curls the colour of tea. Notepads and paper spread out in fronty us, his neat spiky writing and mines bigger, looped and flowing. Just happy to sit thegether, every noo and again feeling his elbow nudge against mines as he wrote. Then the moment when we baith turnt to one another and him bending towards me, the soft feel of his lips against mines. Big smiles spreading across wur faces.

That night he put his airm round me as we walked up the road, and he kissed me again in the park, haudin me close this time, tongue in ma mouth and the wee jaggy edge of his teeth on my lip. He wasnae tall, Jas, only three or four inches mair than me, and we fitted that neatly thegether. Then we broke apart and held haunds, walking alang the path while the early evening light faded tae a gash of salmon pink behind the trees.

IT'S THE FRAMING *that makes it.*

Jas taught me about framing. Hours spent in the park taking photies for Art till I knew every leaf, every bud, every change fae moment tae moment.

It started one November Tuesday – my phone went at seven thirty when I was still hauf-dozing under the covers.

Fiona, look out the windae. I drew the curtain and there was a white wilderness where the back court had been.

It'll no last, he said. *Meet me at the front gate of the Botanics in hauf an hour. Bring your camera.*

I gulped doon some orange juice, splashed cauld watter on my face and was at the gate five minutes early, cocooned in a fleece and wellies wi a pair of Da's auld socks stuffed in

37

them. Jas was waiting at the locked gate, stamping his feet and blowing on his haunds.

Nae gloves?

Couldnae find them – anyhow, nae use wi the camera.

A guy in a green council jacket undid the big padlock and as the gate creaked open Jas grabbed ma haund and the two of us sped intae the park.

At first we ran, giggling and shouting at the sight of the whiteness, desperate tae leave footprints on the frozen grass. We ran round in circles, hopped on wan leg, high on being the first folk, the only folk in the park. Jas even tried tae dae a cartwheel but leapt up screamin when he put his haunds on the ice.

We walked by the glasshouses towards the path to the river, starting tae notice the detail; an icing sugar bush wi wan red berry left on it, a swept-up pile of November leaves, salt-crusted wi frost. At first I snapped everything – I'd nae idea how they'd turn out so I took the same ice-veined leaf, over and over fae slightly different distances and angles. Then I slowed doon, started to take my time as Jas done, really look; working out the best angle, the best composition. Sometimes I manipulated the image, moved a brightly coloured leaf intae the centre of a collage of white mulch. Even the dirt looked beautiful, solid brown traced wi ice crystals.

Jas was right but, it wouldnae last. Even afore the trail of students shuffled its way tae nine o'clock lectures, there was a subtle shift; droplets of water appeared, as if the bushes grat for their lost beauty. In an hour it would be gone. I stood in front of an ivy growing fae a sheltered wall; the plant was still green except for wan leaf, which was perfect white. As I looked through the viewfinder, a droplet of water appeared in the centre of the white leaf, like a teardrop.

A great pain welled up inside me, though nae tears broke ma frost.

Everyone kept saying how bad it was for the twins. At their age. In first year at secondary, the age of transition, girls needed their mammy tae help them through all they mysterious womanly secrets. Somehow there was less sympathy for me and Patrick. Folk'd come in the living room efter the rosary, look at Mona and Rona on the settee, hair tied back in matching pink scrunchies, and say, *Just when they need their mammy the maist.*

Barely turning tae take the cuppa tea out ma haund, they'd lift two custard creams fae the plate, shake their heids and sigh.

Ach, lossing yer mammy is a terrible thing.

Lossing yer mammy. That's what everybody said. *I'm so sorry for your loss.*

As if you just went out tae the shops and dropped her somewhere.

I've went back tae every shop but I just cannae think where I left her. Was it in Debenhams or H&M? Still, mibbe someone will find her and return her to me. She has this special identification mark, just at the side of her neck. And when you look in her eyes it's hard tae see if they're blue or green, wee flecks through them.

Naw, she wasnae lost, my mammy, she died. It's us that are lost.

Mammy wasnae a great one for reading stories, usually she left that to my da, but she loved Peter Pan. And in Peter Pan there are the lost boys, the ones that have nae mothers. Peter went back tae his house and looked through the windae and

39

his mother had forgotten about him, put another boy in his bed. When she got to that bit Mammy always said, *Of course that's no true. No real mammy would ever stop looking for her child if they were lost.*

I imagine her, looking doon on us fae her windae in heaven.

All of us, lost.

Da the maist obvious, fallen apart. Dry cracks seemed tae appear in his face, craggy and dark like a rock cliff. Sat there on the couch, had tae be forced tae even have a cuppa tea, couldnae eat for greetin. But then this was the man who sat through *This is Your Life* wi tears streaming doon his face as some second-rate magician was reunited with his ninety-five-year-auld primary teacher. This was the man who wept buckets at Uncle Pete's version of 'And I Love You So' on the karaoke.

Falling apart has advantages. Everybody tiptoes round, looks efter you.

Patrick came back and stayed while the funeral was on, done all the practical things, the organising, him and Janice between them. So the twins were petted and ma da was nursed and Patrick was respected. And somehow I fell through a crack and became invisible. Made cupsa tea, done the hoovering, the washing, made sure the twins had clean claes and there was enough tea and coffee and biscuits in the hoose for the endless relatives and neighbours traipsing through. Every noo and again Patrick or Janice would gie me a wee hug or a smile that showed they appreciated it, that we were in it thegether, the ones that were coping. Sometimes it even seemed as if we felt the maist grief; the twins were too young, Da's misery was self-indulgent somehow. But that kind of thought was short-lived, a bitter twisting of the heart while

40

I washed up for the fifteenth time in a day, a rainbow sparkle of poison that lit up the gloom surrounding me.

Efter the funeral, efter Patrick and Janice went back tae their ain houses, the days shrunk intae deep winter and in the mornings when I walked the twins tae school it was dark. Nights I'd come hame tae unmade beds and a dinner tae cook but that bit was easy. It was the weight that was hard. It's weird how someone can have mair weight in a house they've left than when they were there. There was something light about Mammy, deft and quick, she done everything as if by sleight of hand. How come in her absence there was heavy, suffocating, overwhelming weight? A cloud that needs tae burst and pour its monsoon over the world.

After that day in the park, me and Jas talked about it for the first time. He understood. Mibbe that was one of the things that drew us thegether in the first place, seeing something in each other we could recognise; we were baith orphans.

We sat in the café, side by side at the windae, warming our haunds on mugs of foamy hot chocolate and I told him the story.

One night, about a year and a hauf ago, she and I were in the house wursels. Hardly ever happened cause Da never goes out, but his brother had tickets for something and the twins were in bed. She made us a cuppa tea, and the two of us sat in the living room. She'd seemed a bit different the last few days, mair sparkly and bubbly, but I thought it was just the spring coming – she was always sensitive tae changes in the seasons.

This is nice, Fiona, she said, patting my haund. *A girls' night in.*

Aye.

There's something I want tae tell you.

41

I can still see her face, the shininess of her eyes, the blue changing fae green tae blue and back again.

I'm having a baby.

I was surprised, nae doubt about it. The twins were twelve noo and Mammy was forty-three, ah never thought she'd have another.

That's brilliant, Mammy — when's it due?

December 19th. A winter baby.

Sagittarius.

Ach, don't believe all that astrology rubbish, you're as bad as Janice.

Jas never asked any questions, just sat listening as the story unfolded, how she was fine during the pregnancy, just a wee bit high blood pressure.

And that's just to be expected at my age, she said. *I'll be fine.*

How she seemed tae glow with happiness and I'd catch her in the kitchen daeing dishes, watching bubbles rise fae the washing up bowl.

How she looked when the baby got bigger, carrying it high and proud in front.

How the pains came the day afore her due date and how calm she was as she set aff to the hospital wi ma da, her last words as she went out the door, *Now make sure the twins dae their hamework tonight and mind — put their gym kit in their bags for the morra.*

How she never came back.

Doesnae happen nooadays. Doesnae happen tae a healthy woman who's already had four weans. Doesnae happen in a clean bright modern hospital with highly trained professional staff and all the technology you can imagine. In a Victorian novel, aye, but no on the eve of the twenty-first century.

Mammy died in childbirth. And her baby, a perfect wee lassie, died with her.

Jas took ma haund; the skin felt dry, too auld for someone his age, spoke of years of work carting boxes around and being out in the thin early morning air. I looked intae his face, asked the question without speaking while he kept staring at our haunds, interlinked between the high stools.

My da was struck by lightning. He paused, took a deep breath. *He was sheltering under a tree. A fucking tree. How stupid can you get?*

It was the first time I'd ever heard Jas swear.

Where did it happen?

He was away on a business trip and the guy had taken him out to play golf. He'd never played golf in his life. A golf course in the middle of nowhere and a storm starts and he goes under a tree and gets struck by lightning.

It's . . . terrible. I had no words.

Jas turned to me. *You know I've never said this to anyone else and I probably never will say it to anyone else but I know you'll no take it the wrong way . . . it's the embarrassment of it, the pure riddy you get fae having a dad numpty enough to get struck by lightning. It's such a stupid embarrassing way tae die.*

It grew darker outside. Spits of rain hit the windae.

I stroked Jas's wrist. *I've always been terrified of lightning. When I was wee I'd run and hide in the big press in the hall, squeezed in behind all the auld boxes and suitcases and stuff. The only place in the house you cannae hear it.*

I used tae love lightning storms. I'd stand at the windae and watch them. But no any mair.

Mammy came in the cupboard with me. She'd put her airm round me and explain how lightning couldnae really get you in a ten-

43

ement. *It goes for height, she'd say. It cannae get you indoors. It's only if you're out in the open.*

Yeah, on a fucking golf course.

Jas's face twisted up and I thought he was gonnae start tae greet but all of a sudden a smothered giggle came out.

Mibbe he thought his turban would save him . . . muffle the electricity . . . He was shaking, couldnae haud it in any mair, and I started tae giggle too, then to laugh, the two of us on these stools, laughing and giggling as if it was the funniest thing in the world.

See, said Jas, wiping tears away. *My da was the smartest guy you could meet — always full of information about everything, statistics — I can just see him with this business guy, sheltering.* He put on a mock serious voice. *You see, Mr Parmi, the statistical probability of being struck by lightning while standing under a tree is actually very low and the statistical probability of being killed while wearing a turban is even lower . . . in fact . . .*

Then zap!

Suddenly it wasnae funny any mair.

IT MUST OF been easier in Victorian days. You had mourning clothes and there were rules about how many months you'd tae wear black, then gradually cut back on it; everyone could tell how long it was since you were bereaved. And there was black jewellery you could wear to remember your loved ones. Nooadays you're straight back at school or work and you don't talk. You don't even talk in the hoose, at least we never. Ma daddy couldnae cope wi talking and the twins, well they seemed tae bounce back. It was different in Jas's house, rituals of grieving. A photie of his dad wi flowers and stuff all round it, in a position of honour, as if he was still watching them.

Jas took me hame after we'd known each other a few weeks. I was surprised – boys didnae usually introduce girls to their family unless they'd known them for ages. Hame was a tenement flat, much like ours but bigger, with a couple of attic rooms up a stair fae the main part of the flat. Jas's room was under the eaves – huge, with its ain bathroom. Pale blue bathroom suite. Jas had painted the walls midnight blue wi silver stars and a moon on the ceiling.

My God, it's like having your ain flat up here. Dead posh.

A guy my da knew done it up to let to students – put in a couple of extra bathrooms and showers – there's one in Ma's room too. Then haufway through he'd to sell up and my da bought it, finished the bathrooms and decorated the place for us. We've been here since I was seven. It's dead handy for the shop.

The shop was a pharmacy. Since his da's death his uncle ran it; Jas's ma helped out during the day and Jas efter school.

Jas and me sat side by side on his bed. The cover was blue too, with gold and silver stars and moons patterned over it.

Is your uncle a pharmacist too?

No but my cousin Harpreet, my uncle's daughter, is. And when I qualify, I'll be able to take over. Harpreet's getting married and she wants to have her own business with her husband.

So you're gonnae be a pharmacist? Just like your da.

That's the idea. I already have a place at Aberdeen Uni for next year.

I smoothed a wrinkle in the cover. Somehow I'd assumed Jas would go tae Art School. Or study literature at uni. Or even be a politician, change the world. I couldnae see him in the shop for the rest of his life, giving out prescriptions and stacking boxes of cold remedies on plastic shelves.

What about your art?

He shrugged. *I'd love to . . . but it's a hobby.*

I stood up, walked round the room. Everything tidy, books neatly arranged on shelves, desk clear except for his computer. On the wall above the chest of drawers hung a framed photie

46

of two boys, the older one with his airm round the wee brother. Identical pairs of brown eyes but I could recognise the line of Jas's mouth in the wee one.

Me and Amrik. I was five, just about to start school, and he must've been eleven. He was in Primary Seven and it was so cool having a big brother in the playground.

You had long hair then, I said. Their hair was tied in a topknot under a navy blue cloth.

Like a real Sikh, you mean?

I just wondered if it was a big deal, when you cut it?

We'd never really talked about Jas's religion. I'd always taken for granted his version of Sikhism, just as, I guess, he done the same with me being Catholic.

Jas stood beside me, looked at the photie.

Ever since I can remember I was taught that a Sikh doesnae cut their hair because the body is a perfect creation of God. You have to look after your hair, keep it clean and combed, tie it up – that's how it was when I was wee. Sometimes I'd get slagged about it but no that much because Amrik was always ahead of me, kind of paved the way. Then when he got to about fifteen he started tae wear his hair out, tied it back in a pony tail instead of on top, under his turban. My da was pissed about it but Ma kept the peace. Amrik looked dead cool, like a pop star. And of course I wanted to be like him but didnae dare.

Then it was time for me to start secondary school. My primary class went on a visit and I was the only Sikh boy with my hair up. There were a few snidey comments. Amrik was in sixth year and about to leave so he wouldnae be there to protect me.

The first day of secondary came and I was scared. I left the house looking normal then ducked intae a close on the way, pulled my hair out and tied it back in a pony tail. It was down to my waist. I went to school like that and no one said a word. There were lots of looks

47

and a few teachers thought I was a girl but I didnae care – somehow wearing my hair out like Amrik made me feel strong.

At the end of the day I was all set to put my hair up on the way hame. I walked out the school gate and there was my da, come tae meet me. All the time I was at primary and he never came to get me out of school, was always working, and he had to choose this day. Can you imagine what it was like? I nearly dropped to the ground and his face, well, it was all contorted. I just stood there; all these kids streaming out of school on either side and this guy in a suit and a turban in the middle of them getting shoved every way. I was working out what to say to him when he turned and walked off. Never spoke a word.

I was terrified to go hame, walked about for ages, but I knew Ma would be worried and I figured she'd protect me. If she'd been there nae doubt it would of been different but when I got back Ma had been called away to her sister who was sick and it was just him. He sat on the settee and made me stand in fronty him like we were in a court or something.

So Jaswinder, you are ashamed of your religion?

I'm no ashamed of my religion, I just want tae wear my hair in a pony tail.

First Amrik, now you? What have I done to deserve such children? You're making a big deal about nothing.

So it's nothing is it? One of the sacred principles of the Guru.

But I havenae cut my hair – I'm just wearing it differently.

In a way that does not reflect your religion or your traditions. You might as well have cut it. Oh go away, get out of my sight.

I left the room, eyes blurring with tears. I knew he'd seen me start tae greet and that made me mad. I rushed up to the bedroom, stood in fronty the mirror and pulled the pony tail out. My hair hung in a mass over my shoulders and all down my back. It was like a cape or something it was that long and thick. I opened the drawer, took

48

out the scissors, and almost without thinking, cut it off. It was a mess of course, looked like a bad wig. And all this hair in big clumps round the floor. I lay on the bed and howled.

Ma found me there when she came hame. She put her airms round me, held me for ages, wiped my tears — she was greeting as well. She picked up the hair and put it in a bag — she's still got it in a drawer in her room. Then she blew her nose, said, 'Come on put your coat on,' and took me out to the barbers to have it cut properly. I've kept it short ever since.

So what did your dad dae?

Nothing. It was never mentioned again.

That must of been awful.

I think that was the hardest part. Him looking at me, obviously disapproving. Ma used to ruffle my hair, tickle my neck and went on at me to wear a hat cause I must be cold but he just pretended nothing had happened while all the time carrying this stone round inside him.

What about Amrik?

Oh, he'd left home by then — I think my da had kind of given up on Amrik anyway — no given up exactly, but we always knew Amrik was different and there was nae use in expecting him to behave like other folk. Whereas I had to be the good son. I think what pissed me off maist of all was that I actually was a good son — done the right things, worked at school, helped in the shop — but he couldnae cut me any slack, couldnae understaund how a boy might of felt on his first day at secondary school. If he had, I would never of cut my hair at all.

He put his airm round me. And what would you have thought about that, having a boyfriend with long hair?

I stroked the back of his heid, the place where the silky hair gave way to the jaggy spikes of the cut edge, the smooth-ness of the back of his neck.

Dunno, I said. *Mibbe I might like it.*

Let's go down — Ma will be wondering where we've got to.

Jas's ma had made tea, set it out on the round table in the kitchen. At first I didnae think she looked like Jas, saw mair resemblance between him and the photie of his da, but when she smiled her face crinkled up in exactly the same way as his, and a big dimple appeared in her right cheek.

Jaswinder tells me you have sisters, Fiona.

Twins. They're thirteen.

Lovely. I'd have liked to have a daughter but it was not to be. She shrugged. *But I am blessed with my two wonderful boys. Though of course we don't see so much of Amrik now he is in London.*

My brother Patrick lives in London too.

I mind the night he tellt me he was gaun, just afore the Easter holidays when I was in third year.

D'you have tae go?

You can have my room when I'm away.

I'd rather have you.

Got tae get out, Fiona. This place is daeing my heid in.

Some pal of his had a job in a restaurant doon there and Patrick started aff in the kitchens, making desserts. He'd come up every three month or so, and every time he looked a bit different; smoother, shinier, his hair blonder, his accent flattened out just a bit mair. There was always something new he was intae. First he'd taken a part-time class in design then got intae food styling for magazines.

That one got Da to take his eyes fae the box.

Food styling. Whit in the name of the wee man is food styling?

It's for cookery books and magazines. Sometimes it takes ages to take the photies and the food melts or congeals, so there's things we dae to make sure it looks right in the pictures.

And they pay you for this?

Better money than making desserts in the restaurant.

What kind of world dae we live in?

Gie the boy a break, says Mammy. *You should be glad he's daeing so well.*

Aye, but could you no just have stayed here and done really well being a baker, son?

Da, maisty the folk I worked with are redundant noo.

It's just, when my pals ask me how you're daeing I really don't want tae say my boy's a food stylist.

Patrick had moved on fae that noo, something else in the magazines but higher up, daeing occasional wee bits for TV too. He never seemed tae stick at one job but always had something that was good pay.

I missed Patrick. At first I thought he'd get fed up wi London, but as the months passed there was nae sign of it and I suppose I just got used tae it. I mind one time when he was just off the phone, saying to my mammy, *D'you think our Patrick will ever come hame?* And her looking at me straight and saying, *No hen, I don't think he will.*

How no?

I just have a feeling Patrick needs the space. Glasgow's too wee for him.

I couldnae understaund what she meant – Glasgow seemed huge to me. After all it was the biggest city in Scotland. I'd never been tae London except tae change flights on holiday when we couldnae go direct, but I knew it was dirty and busy and full of traffic and folk all jumping on and off the subway they called the tube.

I mind that was when I realised Patrick had changed, no just his clothes or his job, but hissel – when he used that word insteidy subway. Said something about the tube and my da saying, *Who you calling a tube?* and Patrick hesitating for a minute afore he smiled.

Would you like milk in your tea, Fiona?

Thanks, Mrs Singh.

Here you are. She passed the cup tae me. *But it's Kaur, dear. Some Sikhs do use a family name too but in our tradition, boys are always named Singh — it means a lion. Girls are Kaur, which means princess. So you don't have the same name as your husband.*

I think that's brilliant. I'd never change my name if I got married.

See, Fiona, said Jas. *Sikhs were the first feminists.*

I don't think I'd put it quite like that, though we do believe everyone is equal. Mrs Kaur smiled. *Have a chocolate biscuit, dear.*

IT WAS WHEN I asked Jas tae come for his tea I realised how much things had slipped. He'd been to the door when he walked me hame but just for a minute. Looking round the house, imagining how it would look to him, made me see it clearly. I'd tried tae keep things tidy, cleaned the kitchen and bathroom every week, but compared to the way it was when Mammy was alive, it was a pure midden; corners where dust had accumulated, insides of cupboards in the bathroom sticky with spilled shampoo and ringed fae the bottom of shaving foam cans.

He was due at six efter his work in the shop, so I had time. I spent the Saturday gutting the place, even put bleach round the taps and plughole, scrubbed at them wi an auld toothbrush like Mammy used tae. I had just enough time tae jump in the shower and throw on my clothes afore he arrived.

The twins arrived hame fae their usual Saturday ritual of traipsing round the town texting their pals and meeting up in shops and cafés. Da or Janice or Patrick were always slipping them cash which they spent in New Look or Claire's Accessories and there was usually enough left over for a hot chocolate. It was hard tae believe the twins were still only thirteen – they could easily of passed for two year aulder – and I worried aboot them. I knew if Mammy'd been around there was nae way they'd be allowed to go out the house showing their bellies and wearing skirts that barely covered their bums, but they wouldnae listen tae me. And ma da, well, he didnae even seem tae register it.

Ah'm starvin – whit's for tea? Mona lifted the lid aff the pot. *Yuch! What is that?*

Veggie chilli – there's rice and pitta bread with it.

We don't like vegetables. Rona nearly spat the word out. *Only tomatoes.*

You like chilli.

Con carne, with meat. Duh.

Jas is coming round and he's vegetarian.

We live here and we urnae, in case you hadnae noticed.

Ah can dae burgers for yous – there's some in the freezer.

Cool. Mona flicked her hair back. The twins had wavy hair like mines but you'd never know it as they used hair straighteners about fourteen times a day.

What time's the boyfriend arriving?

Should be here any minute noo.

So like, are you no gonnae get changed?

I just did.

She looked at my baggy jeans and sloppy tee shirt.

54

Sis, you really need tae make mair of an effort if you want to keep this guy.

He likes me like this.

She gied me a pitying look. *He may say that but what men say and what they dae are two different things.*

She followed Rona out the room.

Jas ate the veggie stew — even asked for seconds — but I knew by the slight tightening round his lips that he was being polite. The chilli was mushy and bland and every noo and again there was a hot nip fae the spice somewhere on the roof of my mouth. I wasnae sure what veggie chilli should taste like, had never had vegetarian food afore except for salad or macaroni cheese, but I guessed this wasnae it.

Would you like some yoghurt with it? I asked. It said in the recipe yoghurt could be an accompaniment to the chilli, cooled doon the spicy food.

Aye, please, said Jas.

I jumped up and rummled in the back of the fridge, pulled out a pack of four.

Strawberry, Apricot, Peach or Fruits of the Forest?

Oh . . . Peach, please.

Later, when I discovered it should of been natural yoghurt, I was that mortified I couldnae even laugh, but it's one of the scenes from then that keeps coming back tae me. It seems to sum up who he is, or was, something about the essence of him. He must of thought I was aff my heid offering him fruit yoghurt to put on the terrible chilli, but he never batted an eyelid, tipped the sickly yellow synthetically flavoured stuff over his food and ate it all up.

Later still, when I spent time at his house and realised how wonderful his ma's cooking was — vegetables with subtle

spices, light home-made parathas and minted yoghurt raita –
I realised even more just how well-mannered, how kind Jas
was.

Even the way their food was presented was nice – no posh,
just a cosy family meal, but there was a bright tablecloth and
colourful dishes. The thin plastic covering on our placemats
was beginning to curl up fae the surface and the twins sat
and picked at it through the meal. We didnae have enough
plates that werenae chipped and I spent the meal covering
mines with the edge of my airm. Their kitchen was warm
while ours was draughty. I wondered if this was what it would
of been like if it'd been my daddy, no my mammy, that had
died. And in my bed that night, when I heard him stumble
through the hall, cursing the shoes that someone had left lying,
or the hall table he'd stubbed his toe on, I wished it had been.

He wasnae there again at breakfast. Used tae be just Saturdays that happened. Out for a few beers on a Friday, long lie
tae make up for the early morning starts through the week.
Normal, no like this. I didnae see how he could keep his job
if it went on much longer. He'd worked for this wee company
for ever and the guys'd been dead sympathetic about Mammy,
but they must be getting pissed aff by noo. Every morning it
was just the twins and me, trying tae force them to eat a
plate of cornflakes and drink some orange juice afore they
left for school. They spent that long getting ready in the mornings they didnae have time for breakfast but I'd fill the bowls
for them, stand over them while they chewed a few mouth-
fuls afore gaun back to their room tae tweak their belts intae
just the right angle, redo their ties so there was just the right
length left dangling. I'd clear the dishes then nag them tae get
out on time. I could of left them tae go to school by theirsels

– Burnside was nearer than St Phil's and, with me in sixth year, I just signed in at the office insteady gaun to regi – but I always walked alang the road with them till we had tae go wur separate ways at the traffic lights.

Jas and me had a free period first thing, bagged wur favourite table in the school library, the one in the corner with a view over the playground. There was naebody else in; sixth year could stay hame until they had a class and maist folk did. Jas took out his Chemistry folder and I looked through my notes on *Wuthering Heights*. The librarian checked her post, replaced a few books on the shelf, then heided intae the wee office behind her desk. There was the sound of a kettle being filled and switched on. Jas smiled at me and I squeezed his haund under the table.

You look tired. He traced his finger in a hauf-circle under my left eye.

Couldnae sleep. Da was at it again.

Not good.

I'm getting worried, Jas. That's three nights in a row he's been out this week. And the nights he's no out he's sitting in the living room till all hours.

Is there anyone in your family you could tell?

There's Patrick, but he'd never listen tae him. Anyway, he's in London.

What about your auntie?

Mibbe, but she has her haunds full with Evie.

Did he ever drink too much when your mum was alive?

Only at the New Year. Or weddings. You know.

Jas nodded.

He's so different, Jas. I'm scared.

I thought I could tell Jas everything, thought there were nae secrets between us but the previous night, unable to sleep

57

with the knowledge that my da was in the living room alone, drinking hissel intae a stupor, I'd got up, thinking I'd persuade him tae go to bed, offer to make him a cuppa tea. When I reached the door of the living room and looked in, he was slumped in front of the TV with the sound turned doon on some OU programme about learning Spanish. Flamenco dancers snapped their heels silently, tossing their heids proudly above the subtitles. Da, jerked out of a hauf-sleep, turned and looked at me and I saw such darkness in his eyes, such huge swirling pools of unspeakable emotion that I couldnae bear tae look.

Fiona? His voice slurred like a comic drunk.

I turned and scurried back to the warmth of my bed.

How could I share that with Jas? The sour smell of the room, of my da, who didnae wash or change his clothes as he used tae. I'd found stains on his underwear as I was loading the washing machine, made me feel sick, even as I shut my eyes. I scrubbed and scrubbed my haunds afterwards with disinfectant. But that was nothing compared to the voice that was not him and that hellish look in his eyes.

Jas never drank or smoked. A lot of folk thought it was because of his religion, his culture, and that pissed him aff good style. Sent him intae wanny his rants.

See, Fiona, that's what really gets to me − it's no racism as such, folk arenae racist in the sense that they want to beat you up or call you names, no they're really nice − it's the assumptions they make. Everything you dae is because of your religion or because you're Asian. If I'm vegetarian it's because I'm a Sikh, if I don't drink it's because I'm Asian. Jeezo, last week I'd on an orange jumper and some wee wifie in the shop said, 'Is that a special festival the day son?' and I said, 'No it was a friggin special offer in Topshop missus.'

Sometimes I get it too with being Catholic. Like when I say there's four of us they assume my ma and da never used contraception.

Did they?

What?

Use contraception?

Don't think so, but then how would I know? It wasnae exactly a topic of conversation round the tea table.

Jas laughed. *I mind when I was wee I was in the shop with my da and he was putting stock away and there was this box of johnnies and I said, 'Da can I get some of they big balloons when it's my birthday?'*

What did he say?

He was pure mortified but Ma laughed and said, 'You only get special balloons like that when you are a big man.' He was much shyer than her about things like that. See that's another thing, because she's an older Asian lady folk think she will be very prim and proper and she's no. I hate assumptions!

Knock knock.

Who's there?

Consumption.

Consumption who?

Consumption no be done about they assumptions?

My da's a nice man. That's what everyone always said about him. *Your daddy's such a nice man.* Nice. The cop-out term for anyone you cannae say anything special about. Not a good man. Goodness has depth tae it, good means you think about things, you make decisions about your life, about right or wrong. So does bad. Nice means you bumble along, no giving anyone offence, you're no specially anything anyone can put their finger on, you're nice. No one in *Wuthering Heights* is nice. Good, bad, mad, yes, but no nice.

59

MISS MULHERN TOOK one of Jas's photies and held it up in fronty the class, indicated what was good about it.

Look at the line here, she said, tracing it wi the blunt end of a pencil. *See how it flows.*

If it'd been anyone else they'd of sat, embarrassed intae a big lump, but no Jas. He could take compliments and criticisms of his work as though it was somebody else's, as if it was something apart fae him. If anybody said anything, good or bad, about mines, it felt like they'd lifted a flap of skin, inserted a needle intae me.

Whether it was his attitude or just something about him, naebody else ever bothered that Jas was singled out for praise; he never got slagged like Kieran was when Miss Mulhern raved about his collage.

Jas worked in black and white mainly, stark urban images: litter gathered under a rusty metal fence, flyposted street-lamps. He wrote cards tae explain what he was daeing, set it in context.

When I started taking photies in the park, I found mysel homing in on the detail, but it was the natural world, leaves and branches, that took my attention. Urban too but, scabby and scratched. Sometimes I'd take shots of leaves keeking through rusty fences or dirty footsteps in the snow. I used colour, even moved litter intae the picture to contrast wi the snow or the brown earth.

Miss Mulhern studied them carefully, then said, *There's some nice composition here, Fiona, but try to find your own style.* She looked at Jas. *More edge, maybe, less . . . pretty pictures.*

I picked through the plastic jewellery, bits of Lego and dried up felties wi nae tops on, collecting limbless trunks, heidless bodies. A few of the dolls were intact but maist were relics fae the time the twins were obsessed with *ER* and spent all their time performing operations on them. One had its haunds and feet cut aff, like the victim of kidnappers trying to freak out relatives by sending them a body part in the post. Then there were the makeover Barbies with hair cut in weird styles or painted streaky colours, and one tattooed wi blue biro like a woad-decorated Pictish princess.

I laid them on the carpet beside me. I knew exactly what I wanted to dae with them but I hadnae the technical knowledge tae realise the vision that was so strong in my mind. Jas would know but I was reluctant tae tell him afore it was done. I was scared that if he was involved it wouldnae feel like my work and I had tae dae it mysel. I gathered the Barbie bits thegether and put them in a poly bag at the back of my wardrobe.

The deadline for the competition was the 6th of December. It was one of these young artist things sponsored by a company that sold crisps and the form had a trendy design but with this really tacky cartoon potato face stamped in the corners. Miss Mulhern had persuaded the Heidie to pay the entry fees. She thought it was a good incentive for us to get portfolios thegether early insteady waiting till the last minute afore the exam.

They want a show, rather than just a one-off piece — groups of related work, installations . . . it's a great chance to think outside the box.

What about a group of paintings? Maybe on the same theme? Matt hated Miss Mulhern's insistence that we try out different media. He didnae want to do videos and photography and place his work in conceptual terms. He just wanted to paint portraits and landscapes.

According to the rules you can use any medium, but they're looking for something cutting edge rather than conventional.

She arranged individual tutorials with us and mines was last period on the Friday.

So Fiona, what are you planning — are you going to concentrate on photography?

I was a bit awkward with her, partly because I'd come to the school so recently, and partly because of Jas — I always felt as if I was in his shadow.

The photies are just a starting point — I want to add other images.
Great.
I'd like to use Photoshop.
Sure — computer-aided images are perfectly acceptable.
But I'd need help to learn how to use the program.
She opened her desk diary. *I can book time for you on one of*

the departmental computers — Jaswinder would show you how it works,
I'm sure.

I don't want him tae help.

She looked up. *Sorry, Fiona, I thought you two . . .*

No, it's no that — it's just — I don't want anyone else's ideas.

I'm not very well up on it myself but I can arrange for Mr Lyons
to give you a tutorial — I believe it's pretty straightforward.

Thanks.

If you leave me a copy of your timetable I'll sort out some sessions,
Fiona. I'm intrigued to find out what you're going to do.

After he'd shown me how tae use the program, Mr Lyons let
me go on the computer in his room any time I was free. I
was that absorbed in what I was daeing that, even though his
classes were quite noisy, they never bothered me. He only
paid attention to the exam classes in fourth and fifth year and
ignored the rest of the kids, just set up a still life and let them
draw while he got on with his ain stuff, telling them aff occasionally when they got a bit over the top.

The computer program was easy enough and you could
dae almost anything with it — crop and resize pictures, place
them on top of one another and move everything round —
but it took me ages tae get any images I was happy with. The
pictures I saw in my heid when I looked at the Barbie bits
were completely different when I put them on the screen,
and I tried out every possible variation afore I came up with
anything that looked remotely like my vision.

WE'D JUST TWO hours tae set up our work in a space ten feet by four, like a box with three sides, painted white. Even though I knew which photies I was gonnae use I hadnae decided how to display them. In the end I worked totally on instinct, with nae idea whether it'd be brilliant or a load of posy rubbish.

When time was up we all stood back. Each space looked completely different: Rosie's garishly coloured papier-mâché sculptures of exotic birds with sweetie necklaces tied round them, Jas's stark sleek black and white images, Matt's ethereal abstract watercolours, and mines.

Four big colour photographs hung on the back wall; apparently idyllic winter scenes of snow and ice from the November

64

day in the park, crystallised puddles or delicate leaves rimed in frost, but each with an amputated or mutilated doll superimposed over it. One floated heidless above the trees, another looked as if it had been stamped tae bits in a frozen puddle. And in front of the photographs, on a table covered by a white cloth, lay a mountain of doll parts, each with a Barbie Elastoplast over some part of it. Some had their eyes covered, others their ears, and some wore crossed plasters like a bikini. The title 'Barbie Bits' was printed in pink italics on a card in front of them.

Jas stood beside me, looking intently. After what seemed like ages he spoke. *Awesome, Fiona.*

Really?

Yeah, I'd never in a million years have thought of doing anything like that with those photos.

Hey, Fiona, what have you done? Rosie appeared behind us. *Barbie Bits — wicked.*

Miss Mulhern was making her way along our exhibits. When she came to mines she looked critically as if taking in every detail, then started to nod and smile. *Nice concept, Fiona – good placing of the doll parts and the plasters – but . . .* She looked around worriedly. *Where's your text?*

I didnae know you had tae write one.

There's nothing in the rules to stop you hanging the visual work on its own, but, nowadays, the artist has to contextualise their work . . . too late now, of course, but you can do it for your exam.

I don't see why you need tae explain your art. Turner and all these guys just painted.

That's not really the point, Fiona . . . anyway, the adjudicators are coming.

We stood back while the three judges – two artists and one guy fae the crisp company – looked at the pieces, clipboards

65

in haund, ticking boxes and scribbling on their sheets. They were judging all the entries from schools in the Glasgow area. The winner would get through to the final with folk fae the other regions in Scotland.

Miss Mulhern looked at her watch. *The adjudicators are giving their decision at twelve, so be back here at five to. You could go and see what the other entries are like, get some ideas.*

Jas whispered in my ear. *Let's go and get a coffee.*

The main foyer was a soulless barn of a place, all plastic and metal with posters advertising concerts for has-been bands at extortionate prices. In one of the other halls there was a craft show, and teams of auld dollies in haund-knitted jumpers and lace-up shoes daundered about, carrying poly bags full of cross-stitch kits. Jas and me sat on a bench, sipping coffee out of paper cups.

You know, I think I prefer coffee like this. It tastes better than out of real cups.

Stays hot for longer. But then, paper cups are so bad for the environment.

Afore I met Jas, I'd never thought much about the environment but it was one of his things. I even knew what he was gonnae say next.

It'd be so easy to have recycling bins in here.

He was right, of course, and being with him had made me aware of how folk just chucked stuff out, of the overpackaged products and the way you got handed a poly bag in every shop – I'd even started taking bags to the supermarket mysel. But there was a difference between us. I knew in my heid that throwing a paper cup away was wrong and wasteful, but it actually pained Jas to dae it. I knew that when it was time for us to go back in the hall he'd place the cup in the bin

66

gently and a look of distress would cross his foreheid; Jas could feel the hole in the ozone layer growing even by a particle, could sense the tiniest molecule of carbon monoxide sighing into the air.

I looked at the time on my phone. Ten to.

Finished?

Jas nodded, and I took the cup fae him, put it inside mines as if somehow that made it less bad, then threw them in the bin.

He stood up, held out his haund, and the two of us heided towards the door.

Everyone expected Jas tae win, of course. He'd always been the golden boy of the class, got the school Art prize every year. His photies were perfect; not only were his composition and technique breathtaking, his work had a way of making you feel as if you were seeing an everyday object for the first time. It was true, shot through with Jas's directness, his sense of purpose.

The adjudicators praised his work highly.

Mature, dynamic . . . tonal quality . . . flawless composition. A Cartier-Bresson in the making.

Everyone clapped. A warm feeling rose inside me.

Jaswinder attends Burnside High and the school is to be highly commended for the quality of its students' work. The next entrant, Fiona O'Connell, has not displayed the technical mastery which characterised Jaswinder's work, but her exhibit, Barbie Bits, is a compelling and ehm . . . edgy piece of work with an understated violence. She pushes the boundaries of our perception of childhood, of women, and makes us question our assumptions. The juxtaposition of the doll images over the winter scenes is disturbing and the pyre of broken Barbies is a master stroke.

Jas squeezed my haund. I felt my face flame.

Now to the part which we adjudicators hate. There has to be a winner and it goes without saying that this was a very difficult decision but we are confident we have made the right one. The competition was set up to reward innovative and risky art as well as technical brilliance. So, in reverse order – third place goes to Paula Mason from Anderston High School.

A skinny blonde lassie in a navy blazer went up to get her envelope and everyone applauded.

Second and first place go to pupils of the same school – a tremendous achievement for Burnside High. In second place is Jaswinder Singh, and, for a courageous and innovative work, first place and the chance to go forward to the Scottish finals, go to Fiona O'Connell.

It's amazing how much difference winning the prize made. If Jas had won (and if even one of the judges'd been different, it would of been him, as Miss Mulhern reminded us on several occasions), then his position as best artist in school and my position in his shadow would of been retained. Coming second would of been easier – Miss Mulhern could be nice to me, put me in the box she'd already labelled. Winning knocked out her whole way of looking at things. I'd spent weeks stuck at the computer in Mr Lyons' room and suddenly produced the goods, taking the prestigious prize away fae her star pupil. You could see how it would scunner her.

It made a big difference tae my family. Of course they'd known I was good at art, just like I was good at English or History, but Art was a frivolous subject, no something tae base your life choices on. But the cheque for a thousand quid changed that. Da couldnae believe it, kept shaking his heid in amazement and saying, *You'll need tae take care of this, Fiona,* as if I was gonnae drop it in the street or accidentally tear it up or something. Janice took me out and helped me open a special savings account.

It seems a lot, but when you're a student you'll find it'll be a real help.

The only person it didnae affect was Jas. I worried he'd be pissed aff I'd won the prize, kept watching him for signs of things changing between us, but there was nothing. He was just the same.

THE LAST WEEK of school everyone's in party mood, looking forward tae the Christmas holidays. Hauf the weans have stopped coming and teachers keep the rest quiet with videos and chocolate. As I walk alang the corridor laughter and music spill fae every classroom.

It's Mammy's anniversary.

She died on the 19th of December and it took all Janice and Patrick's determination and organisation to get her buried by Christmas Eve. Sudden deaths cause confusion, sudden deaths mean post mortems, new lairs being opened, but my Mammy's . . . a sudden death where a birth had been expected. Two deaths in one.

Voices on the phone, expecting good news.

A boy or a wee lassie?

What's the weight?

Who does she look like?

Then the voices trailing aff intae silence.

Janice, list in haund, gaun through the details wi my da. Maist of the time he didnae seem tae care or even hear her, but noo and again he'd dig his heels in over something, made things mair difficult for her.

We can get the parish hall for after the funeral, Bobby. They'll do sandwiches.

Geraldine wouldnae of wanted the parish hall.

It's hard tae get anywhere else at this notice just before Christmas — every hotel's booked up with office parties and Christmas dinners.

She hated the smell of stewed tea. She hated they pinnies the wee wifies wear.

Is there any particular hymn you want for the funeral? Father O'Hara's coming round in half an hour.

Star of the Sea. When we're walking out the chapel. And Janice . . . He grabbed her sleeve. *I want her tae have white flowers fae the baby.*

I hated the baby. Hated the wee white coffin placed next tae hers. Marguerite. Da said that was what she'd wanted to call the baby if it was a girl. A pearl.

'Those are pearls that were his eyes.'

Nae wonder Shakespeare used that. Pearls are dead white.

Sitting in the front row of the chapel between Patrick and Mona, hatred rising in me as if all the blood in my body had boiled and risen intae steam, hatred concentrating itsel on that one wee white box, and the person inside who had killed my mammy.

Afterwards folk said how calm I was at the funeral, how I'd no shed a tear, how I'd kept gaun for my daddy, who'd

71

shed enough tears for the whole lot of us, who'd wept and wailed his way through every hymn and every word of the service, who had to be helped doon the aisle, couldnae even take his turn tae carry the coffin.

Only when the familiar strain started,

Hail Queen of Heaven, the ocean star.

Only then did it hit me as we walked doon the aisle after the coffin and I was blinded wi salt water.

I've no been tae confession since.

Jas and me were sitting in the café at lunchtime, rain on the windae blurring the street outside, spinning out two coffees and a chocolate muffin between us.

Is that bad, no going to confession?

When Mammy was alive we used to go every month. You're supposed tae go once a year at least — so I guess, technically I'm still okay till Easter.

Why don't you want to go?

How can I kneel there and tell a priest I hate a baby?

You don't, but.

I do.

I looked at my watch. *We'd better get back.*

I never expected you to be in school the day.

My da thought it was better for us.

What you doing later? Will you go to the cemetery?

Da didnae want to. He doesnae feel that's where she is. He's asked someone fae the chapel to say a rosary with us in the house. Patrick will be here the night and Janice thinks we should all be thegether.

What do you want to do, Fiona?

Hide.

* * *

72

Hail Mary, full of grace, the Lord is with thee.

The furniture was pushed back so we could kneel doon in the living room. Mr Gallagher said the first part of the prayer and the rest of us joined in; Da and the twins loudly, me and Patrick quieter and Janice no saying anything, except *Amen* at the end. As I worked the plastic beads through my haunds, the words of the prayers leaving my mouth on autopilot, I stared at the statue of Our Lady. It was a plaster Madonna hauding Jesus in her airms, and one of the baby's fingers was chipped at the edge.

A few weeks ago Jas and me visited the chapel efter school. He walked round, looking carefully at everything; the crucifix, the wee light that's always kept burning, the altars to various saints. *I never expected all this,* he said. *I've only ever been in a church for school services and it's dead bare.*

That's the Church of Scotland. They don't have statues.

We've got pictures of the Gurus too, but in the Gurdwara it's the word that's important — the holy book.

The Guru Granth Sahib.

Hey you've been swotting up.

I still like the statues but — I guess it's what you're brought up with.

We stood in fronty Our Lady, golden stars round her heid.

Da always lights a candle at Our Lady's altar, carries rosaries in his pocket. But Mammy never liked statues of her — thought she never looked human. No real, like Jesus, suffering on the cross. She wanted pictures of Mary daeing a washing or making a dinner.

The Fifth Glorious Mystery. Our Lady's Coronation and the Glory of the Saints.

Ten past eight. We'd be finished soon, make a cuppa tea,

sit for a while, then it'd be time for bed and it'd be over. We'd all dreaded it so much, this day, and there'd been endless discussion about how we should mark it, what we should dae. *Visit the graveyard,* said Janice. Too depressing. *Go for a meal,* said Patrick. Too much like a celebration. *Stay aff school,* said Mona and Rona. Aye right. No one but Da had been keen on the idea of the rosary but in the end it was the right thing. An ordinary Tuesday evening of an ordinary day, made extraordinary by what was gaun on inside us all. The repetition of the familiar words, the feel of Rona's airm next to mines, the quiet respectfulness with which Mr Gallagher led the prayers. A deep calm descended on the room, and, for the first time, I felt she was still with us.

WHEN SCHOOL FINISHED for the Christmas holidays I went to meet Jemma and Monica in the café near Cowcaddens subway, where we used to come every Friday. They were waving at me fae the table in the windae, big grins across their faces.

Hi, Fiona. Monica stood up and hugged me. *Our favourite table.*

The three of us used tae rush up the road, praying the table in the windae would be free. If it wasnae we'd take another, then move across when the customers left.

You don't mind, do you, Mr Giardini? Monica would say.

For you young ladies, no problem, he'd reply, helping us move our coffees across.

Jemma pointed. *Hey, look at you — don't they have a uniform at Burnside?*

Monica and Jemma were wearing maroon blazers, grey skirts and white blouses. Monica's tie was perfectly knotted, while Jemma's top button was undone and her tie positioned a deliberately casual inch below.

No one wears it.

You're lucky. Jemma sat back and crossed her legs. *Mrs Diamond gied me into trouble for wearing black tights yesterday. I tellt her it was freezing and they were the warmest I had but she just goes 'Not the regulation colours, Jemma. And remember you have to set an example to the younger girls.' Auld bag.*

I prefer uniform. Monica spooned the foam neatly off her coffee. *Then you don't need to worry if you haven't got designer clothes. That's how my parents sent me to St Phil's — it's about the only school left round here that wears a uniform.*

There is a sweatshirt at Burnside, I said, *but no one wears it. Only the wee first years.*

Sweatshirts are gross.

Hello there — it's the third degree.

Mr Giardini always called us the three degrees.

Hi, Mr Giardini.

You've no been here for ages.

I'm at a different school now.

So where is it — the moon? No excuses. You have to come back — these two are lonely without you — two degrees is no use. Now, what can I get you?

Hot chocolate, please.

Jemma pushed her cup across the table. *So, how's things, Fi?*

Fine.

Fine, she says. What about this boyfriend of yours?

He's fine too.

So tell us about him. Some friend you are. We only found out cause Susie saw you with him.

76

Sorry.

I did feel bad. Monica and Jemma were my best friends, had been for years, but somehow, on leaving St Phil's I'd swept them away with all the other things I didnae want to think about. I took a deep breath.

His name is Jas, short for Jaswinder. He's in sixth year at Burnside, in my English and Art classes. He also does Chemistry. He loves Shelley, does photography, and is very nice.

And nice looking, from what Susie said. Jemma grinned. *Small, dark and handsome.*

Well he's not tall, that's true.

What is he going to study when he leaves school?

Mon . . .

It's important, Jemma.

She's obsessed just now. Everybody is. If I hear one more thing about UCAS forms or planning your future I think I'll go daft.

Everyone isn't like you, though. Monica turned to her. *You've always known what you wanted to do and stuck to it.*

Jemma was gonnae be a speech therapist. She saw a TV programme about it years ago and has never wavered. And while I'd no inclination whatsoever to be a speech therapist, wasnae even sure what they done, part of me envied her certainty. When she graduated she'd get a good steady job in the health service – a job that was useful, a job you never had tae justify. Jemma was smart, sensible, got on with folk – she'd be brilliant at it.

So, what is it you're gonnae dae with your life this week, Miss Wu? Brain surgery, nuclear physics or biometric technology?

I spluttered on the hot chocolate. *You made that up.*

No, Monica said, taking aff her glasses and wiping away a speck of chocolate which had travelled across. *I went to an open day and got a leaflet on it.*

77

So what is it?

No, no, don't go there! Jemma waved her arms. *You should see the desk in her bedroom — she has an entire file of leaflets she's picked up at these open days — the only thing the courses have in common is they're unpronounceable, no one's ever heard of them before and you need a brain the size of the Clyde Tunnel to do them.*

Monica smiled. *At least I don't have a mouth the size of the Clyde Tunnel.*

In unison Jemma and I put our haunds to our cheeks — *Ooooooh!*

We all fell about giggling.

Later, at the desk in my room, I sat staring at the forms. For years I'd hoped tae go to uni and study literature if I got good enough grades. Now, I was swithering. Even though I'd always loved art I'd assumed that Art School was only for a few special folk. Winning the competition had changed that.

Last week I'd had my interview with Mr Fraser, the Deputy Head who's in charge of the fifth and sixth year, fills in the references. I felt strange going into his office as I don't really know him — another disadvantage of moving schools when you're in sixth year. But in some ways it's an advantage cause he has no preconceived ideas about who I am, just sees a lassie like every other sixth year, a list of grades and reports on his desk. He doesnae know my sisters or my da or even probably what happened to Mammy. He's no walking on eggshells, feeling sorry for me. And nae doubt he has a hundred other folk to see and wants this over with quickly.

Right, Fiona, let's see — you already have Higher English, Art,

Maths, History and French. Four As and a B. This year you're doing Advanced Higher English, Art and History. He looked up fae the forms. *Where are you applying?*

Well, I always wanted to do English at uni . . . but I'm wondering about Art School now.

Your grades are good all round – really you could do either. You'll need a portfolio for Art School but your teachers'll keep you right on that.

It's just, Art's not very practical, for getting a job.

Doing English at university doesn't exactly guarantee a career nowadays either. You could always teach, though I don't know I'd recommend it.

He pushed his specs up on top of his heid and looked at me.

The other possible option if you want to do English and keep the interest in Art going is to combine it with Art History – do a joint degree.

But that wouldnae actually be doing art.

No, I'm afraid you'll have to make a decision one way or another. He looked at his watch. *But you don't need to choose now. Why not apply for university and Art School, see what you get offered, then decide.*

He handed me some leaflets. *I hear Dundee is very good nowadays.*

I don't want to leave Glasgow.

Really? You definitely don't want to move away from home?

No.

That was the one thing I was sure about.

Everyone in my year was desperate to leave but when I thought about next year, I envisaged mysel waking up every morning in my ain bed, walking towards the big gothic spires of the uni, or taking the subway a few stops to the Art School. When I tried tae imagine getting on a train with a suitcase, even to

79

somewhere no that far away, Aberdeen or Dundee mibbe, opening the door of a wee room in a Hall of Residence, everything went blurry.

Patrick tried to get me to change my mind. He was sleeping in my room and came in tae sort out his things while I was filling in the forms. When I tellt him I was only applying for courses in Glasgow he put doon the shirt he was folding and said, *Why on earth, Fiona?*

How d'you mean?

Why don't you get out?

Don't want to.

Is it because of this boyfriend?

No. Jas has a place in Aberdeen.

I hope you're no being a martyr, thinking you need to stay and look after Da and the twins. They can manage.

It's no that, it's just . . . this is hame.

C'mere. He sat on the bed and patted the cover for me to sit beside him.

Fiona, I know it's scary but there's a big world out there. And this is the time to go, when you're young. Why don't you apply somewhere in London — there's fantastic art colleges there — with that prize on your CV you'd stand a good chance of getting in. I'd show you around, introduce you to folk. You could even come and stay in the flat with me till you made your own friends.

Me and Patrick in a flat. Me gaun to a trendy college in London. Jas could come and stay some weekends. I could still come hame to visit.

Have a think about it, Fi.

I nodded, gathered the folders thegether and left Patrick sorting out his stuff. But somewhere inside I knew I wouldnae take up his offer.

*   *   *

80

Christmas. The second one. Last year we were all rid raw wi grief. Last year no one expected anything except pain.

This year we squeezed round the table in the kitchen, as close as we could so there were nae spaces between us, nae empty place where Mammy should've been, but the gap was as obvious as if we'd left a chair for her. Still, we got through dinner. Patrick had cooked a nice meal of salmon, tatties and veg, followed by a chocolate profiterole dessert, far different fae the traditional turkey roast we'd always had at Christmas. Janice, Angie and Evie came round and that helped. Evie was at the stage where she needed constant attention – laughing, dancing and getting intae every drawer and cupboard – so we were all kept busy.

I thought it would happen on Christmas Day. I thought it'd be my da too, the one that would break, that we'd find him in floods of tears in fronty some sentimental rubbish on TV or lying on their bed hauding her photie in his haund. He wasnae working noo, barring the odd homer, though he wouldnae admit he'd been sacked. *You know how it is, sometimes there's no the work gaun round,* he'd said tae Patrick.

But it happened on Boxing Day, when I thought the worst was over, and it was Mona, no my da, who was the one tae fall apart.

We'd been sitting in the living room, Da flicking through all the crap on TV, when he came across some talent competition. Two lassies daeing a routine tae an eighties pop hit, dressed in what looked like bikinis wi glittery fringes attached to them.

Would you look at that? he said. *And there's the twins can dance far better than them.*

Do yous still keep up the dancing? Patrick asked.

Aye. The Dance School has a show in January. In the SECC.

81

Let's see some of it then.

Aye, right. Mona flicked her hair back fae her face.

I havenae seen you dancing for ages.

Well you should come up mair often.

You're bound to be better than that lot.

C'mon, Mona. Rona tried to pull her to her feet.

Naa. Don't want tae.

C'mon. Let's go and get changed. Patrick — you get the CD.

They returned a few minutes later, in short fringed skirts and sparkly tops. They giggled and nudged each other, missed the start of the music.

C'mon, Mona.

Okay, okay. Patrick, start it again.

This time they went through their routine flawlessly. The fringes swung in unison, the identical heads of straight hair rose and fell as if they were one person. Even the smiles that seemed pasted to their faces were the same. Nae matter how often I'd seen them it amazed me. They finished with a little curtsy and posed for a moment while Patrick, Da and me applauded. Then Mona stumbled and tripped against Rona, falling over. Patrick reached to help her up.

You okay?

Aye, she said. *It's just . . .*

The seam of her skirt had ripped when she fell. Mona held the pieces of fabric in her haunds, staring at them, then sank tae the flair and suddenly began tae sob, great big shuddering sobs that made her shoulders heave up and doon. Rona flung her airms round her.

I didnae understaund.

We can mend it — it's just a skirt.

The words hirpled out. *Mammy — made — it. She — made — it.*

Then Rona began tae greet too, her shoulders heaving in time to her sister's, the pair of them entwined thegether like some classical sculpture of grief.

NAE MATTER HOW still I tried to keep, the seat squeaked at the slightest wee movement. Jas squeezed my haund, breathed in my ear. *Sounds like you need oiled.*

Fortunately the music was that loud and there was so much noise in the auditorium anyway – rustling sweetie papers, girny weans, folk pointing out their children on stage – I wasnae gonnae disturb anyone. It was always like this at the dancing displays but this year the teacher had hired a bigger hall so the buzz of excitement was even greater. All her classes, fae pre-schoolers tae adults, done at least one routine, while some, like the twins, were involved several times. It was gonnae be a long evening.

Not only had Jas volunteered tae come, he'd also got a ticket for his ma. She was two seats along, next tae my da,

84

nodding and smiling as he listed the twins' achievements. Patrick sat next tae Jas. It was the first time they'd met and it gied me a warm feeling to see my tall fair brother shaking haunds with Jas, small and neat and dark. I was sure they'd get on with each other, hoped there'd be time for them to talk properly afore Patrick had tae rush back tae London.

The twins still done line dancing but they'd learned other kinds too. The show was a mixture of everything: wee moppets prancing around dressed as fairies, middle-aged women with top hats and canes tripping through tap routines, lumpy teenagers in skimpy tops thumping about tae hiphop. The audience applauded enthusiastically after every set.

When are the twins on? said Jas, peering at the programme in the hauf-light.

Next — Big Spender. Jemma's in this too.

There were five of them, dressed in fishnet tights and spangly leotards; the dance involved a lot of draping themselves round chairs and wiggling their bums in the air but the twins, wi their deadpan expressions and perfect timing, somehow managed tae make it look almost classy. Jemma looked mortified but got all the moves right and her long legs looked great in the fishnets.

At the interval we went tae the bar, well what passed for one. A barn of a place wi one guy doling out drinks in plastic cups and naewhere tae sit.

What're you having, Mrs Kaur?

I'm fine, Mr O'Connell.

C'mon, no even a wee lemonade or something?

No, really.

What about yous kids — Patrick?

I'll get them Da.

Naw, I'll get them, son. He waved his wallet about and notes started tae drop fae it. Jas and me crawled about on the flair retrieving fivers, while Patrick steered him towards the bar.

Coffees okay for you, Fi? Jas?

Fine.

Da?

Double whisky. Celebrate the twins' show.

Aye, but you don't want to be seeing them double.

We stood in a circle, plastic cups in haund. Da grew even mair talkative.

See, Mrs Kaur, the twins have always been brilliant dancers. Even when they were two year auld.

I can see how talented they are. And they must work very hard. Things which look easy don't come easy.

Aye practisin so they are.

My Amrik is just the same. Sitar never out of his hands. Of course Jaswinder is more artistic.

Our Fiona too. And Patrick.

I couldnae take any mair of this parental pridefest so I heided aff to the toilet. When I returned Patrick and Jas were talking away thegether.

I touched Jas's airm. *Let's go in – the bell's just gone.*

I thought the second hauf was never gonnae end – my bum was numb with the effort of trying tae keep still so the seat wouldnae creak too much. I knew the twins were in the finale so when the curtains opened on a tableau of rockabilly lassies in flared skirts, hair tied back in pony tails, I perked up. 'Blue Suede Shoes' blared fae the crackly speakers and the audience bounced in their seats as the lassies jived and hopped, slid through each other's legs and done acrobatic tricks. Of course the twins were pure stars. Their high kicks were higher, their splits wider, their footwork neater and mair precise, and, as always, they moved as one, even their pony tails flicking at exactly the same angle.

The audience went wild, jumped to their feet tae gie them a standing ovation. The dance teacher came on waving at the crowd to quieten them, then said, *You want more?*

The crowd let out a huge roar and the girls repeated their final routine. Then there was an endless parade of everyone that had been in the show, class by class, for their bow. Finally we heided out intae the mad crowd. Fortunately Patrick had taken charge and ordered two taxis. He put my da and Jas's ma intae one, looking round for Mona and Rona.

Hope the girls don't take too long tae get changed. Mibbe you and Jas could go in this taxi instead and I'll wait for them?

Naw, says my da. *Ah want tae see my wee lassies.*

Da had been like a man possessed during the final number, dancing and clapping and shouting out, and the energy he'd expended and the drink he'd taken seemed tae have hit him all of a sudden, like a wean suddenly felled by tiredness after a party. He shrunk intae a corner of the taxi, leaning on the armrest.

How much has he had? I whispered to Patrick. *Two whiskies at the interval wouldnae of had that effect.*

I think there was a hipflask in his pocket.

Just then the twins appeared, dressed in their normal clothes. The heavy stage make-up on their faces made them look like dolls.

Ah'm that proud of yous. My da lurched forward and tripped, steadied hissel on the handrest, then turned towards Mrs Kaur. *Sorry, hen, sorry.*

Are you all right, Mr O'Connell?

Ah'm fine, just fine. He made tae get up again and this time

87

collapsed on the taxi flair. Patrick and Jas scrambled to help him up.

The taxi driver, who up till now had sat with a deadpan look on his face, listening tae heavy metal music on the radio while the meter ticked away, turned and addressed Patrick. *Now look son, I can put up wi folk having wan too many but if he's sick in ma cab, somebody'll need tae pay for it.*

It's okay, said Patrick. *He'll be fine.* He thrust a tenner in my haund. *I'd better get in with them. You and Jas go in the other cab by yourselves. See you back at the ranch.*

With Jas close beside me as the taxi sped through wet streets, it felt peaceful after the chaos of the night. But my cheeks were burning at the thought of what Jas's ma might think of my da. Jas was quiet, looking out the windae for a few minutes, then he said, *Why did you never tell me Patrick's gay?*

Dunno. We just never talk about it. Did he say something to you?

Hello, I'm Fiona's brother and I'm gay.

I giggled.

Jas put his haund on my knee. *When did he come out?*

He never really did, not at hame. I always thought that was why he left, but mibbe he'd of left anyway. Cannae mind when I first realised. It's hard with your brother cause he's just . . .

Your brother. I know.

We never had any big discussions about it. One time about three year ago some guy he'd been at school with had just got married and there was the usual jokes about who would be next. Later, when we were on wur ain he said, 'You do know I won't be getting married,' and I just said, 'Yeah, I know,' and then we changed the subject.

We were silent for a few moments, then Jas spoke. *I guess you just take them the way they are, the way you never accept anyone else, even your parents. Like Amrik — it's not just his music — it's him that's special. I cannae explain — you'll need to meet him. He does things differently and somehow gets away with it. Other folk think it's because he's an artist, but to me, he's just Amrik.*

WE SPILLED OUT the minibus, glad tae stretch wur legs after being cooped up for what seemed like forever. We'd set aff at six which felt like the middle of the night, and maist of us had slept till the stop in a motorway café for breakfast. Mr Lyons had been driving but Ms Harris took over for the last stage to gie him a break.

The air felt fresh and cold and there were wee patches of white on the surrounding countryside, though the sun shone in a bright blue February sky. A sign in the corner of the car park read 'The Parsonage'. I felt a quiver in my stomach. Here at last.

The trip to Haworth was a big surprise, a fluke. *Karma,* said Jas but I didnae believe in that. The English class were supposed to be gaun tae Stratford to see *Measure for Measure* and *The Tempest* – two nights in a B&B and a visit to Shakespeare's birthplace. We'd paid deposits and the dates were all sorted. Then something went wrang. We never got tellt what it was – mibbe someone screwed up the booking or the grant to subsidise the trip never came through – but one Monday in January Ms Harris sat us all doon and tellt us the trip was cancelled.

Oh naw, Miss, said Kevin. *I was soo looking forward to seeing the plays.*

Getting three days off school, you mean, said Alice.

Kevin pouted. *You just don't understand my feelings about culture.*

I'm really sorry about this, said Ms Harris, *and I'm trying to arrange an alternative visit to Haworth, birthplace of the Brontës.*

Is that the only other possibility, Ms Harris? asked Hassan.

The only other feasible one would be the Lake District – we could see some of the sights associated with the Romantic Poets. But the accommodation would be a little more expensive, and since Fiona is studying the Brontës the Haworth trip would be of benefit.

Jas smiled at me while everyone else seemed to be looking at their feet. I knew maist of them were bored rigid by the very idea of the Brontës, but a trip was a trip.

Kevin piped up. *What about the rest of us, but? Can we no go somewhere we could find out about our writers?*

I don't think the school is likely to subsidise a trip to the US, where most of the novels are set . . . and Shelley travelled extensively in Europe which rules him out too.

What about thon 'Lord of the Rings' place? Could we no go there?

You already spend most of your time there, Kevin.

Whit's she on aboot?

Alice patted his haund. *In a fantasy world.*

Of course, added Ms Harris, looking at Lucy, *We could always go to Wigan Pier.*

Lucy smiled. *I'd rather go to Haworth, Miss.*

I'd assumed it would be a dead gloomy place. All the books went on about how it was that remote and isolated and the villagers were all dying aff of cholera. But as we heided up the steep main street I was amazed at how cutesy it was, loupin wi tearooms and souvenir shops.

The Heathcliff Café, the Brontë Tearoom, Jas muttered. *I wonder if they dae Branwell Buns?*

Wi laudanum insteidy raisins? I giggled.

Haw Miss, can we stop for a can of juice?

Later, Kevin. We have a booking at the Parsonage at eleven thirty. It's just up here.

At the top of the street the tourist stuff petered out. We took a turning intae a wee lane that ran along the side of the churchyard, and all of a sudden there it was. Bigger than I'd imagined – prettier too, wi neat windaes recessed in the pale stone.

We huddled intae the narrow hall. On one side was the parlour, but you couldnae get right in as it was blocked aff. I fumbled wi the rope as Jas and me stood looking round the bare space, reading wee labels on the bits of furniture, maist of which wasnae really their furniture, just like something they would of had. Then I seen it, black shiny surface wi the stuffing spilling out.

Jas, I whispered. *Jas, that's it.*

What?

The sofa Emily died on.

Oh so that's the sofa Emily died on. Kevin's voice was loud in my ear. *It looks very comfy.*

Get knotted, ya tube.

Miss, she's calling me a bad name. Miss, Miss.

Opposite was the auld man's study, the desk where he wrote his sermons and the piano Emily had played. I pointed it out to Jas.

A lot of lassies learned cause they were gonnae be governesses . . . but Emily was really good.

Jas and me waited in the back kitchen tae let Kevin get round the top flair afore us. I knew her bedroom was there and I couldnae bear tae have him wittering on in my ear when we seen it.

Narrow camp bed. Plain white walls with wee drawings on them, fae when they were weans and used tae play wi Branwell's toy soldiers, make up stories and magazines. One windae, looking out on the graveyard.

Imagine looking out on that every day.

And night. Quiet neighbours but.

I'd seen photies of the graveyard afore but nothing could of prepared me for it. Layer on layer of gravestones falling over each other; stringy trees, staunding gaunt as though they too had consumption, guarding the plain stone church beyond.

Must of been dead creepy at night, the wind moanin.

And didn't Branwell walk up every night from the pub? Nae wonder he took stuff.

But she loved it here, Jas. She hated to be away, got homesick — and no just sad, physically ill.

He took my haund. *C'mon, we've still the museum bit to see.*

Afterwards we ate packed lunches sitting in the minibus, then set aff across the moor.

We won't go all the way, said Ms Harris. *It's too cold. But it'll give you a flavour of what their life was like here.*

It was hard tae imagine what it would of been like for them. Walking alang a neat path wi Kevin daeing impersonations of Emily dying on her sofa behind Ms Harris's back, kinda took away some of the atmosphere. And we never went as far as the waterfall, turned back when the sky threatened rain.

Can't have you lot getting consumption, can we? smiled Mr Lloyd.

Ms Harris gied him a look. *Now, folks, you've an hour to wander around the village, get a coffee or look at the shops. Meet us back here and we'll go and have a look at the steam railway.* She put her haund on my airm. *Fiona, I wondered if you would prefer to go back to the Parsonage. I spoke to the curator and you can use the library there if you like. I know you won't have much time but even a couple of hours . . .*

Thanks.

D'you want me to come with you? Jas took my haund.

It's cool. You go with the others.

In the end I didnae spend long in the library. There was that much stuff I'd nae idea where tae start and anyway maist of it was things other folk wrote about her. I looked at a few manuscripts in her spiky writing, then returned to the museum, stood in the wee room trying tae feel what it must of been like for her, alone with the light of a candle and the ghosts in the graveyard outside, her heid filled with Heathcliff and Cathy.

We had tea in a fish and chip place in Keighley. Everyone was exhausted as we'd been up so early but as usual Ms Harris looked as if she'd had ten hours' sleep.

So, what did you think of Haworth?

Weird, said Alice. *I mean, their lives were soo weird. No wonder their books were so intense.*

I hadn't realised the brother had ambitions to be an artist, said Mr Lyons.

Ms Harris nodded. *Everyone thought Branwell would be the golden one of the family, but he ended up dead at thirty, an alcoholic drug addict, who never achieved anything.*

From what I saw, he wasn't much of an artist anyway. I was surprised how good Emily's work was — her drawings of the hawk and the dog were really sensitive. And when you think how little training she must have had — it's impressive.

I know. Ms Harris turned tae Kevin, who was resting his heid on the table, eating chips sideways. *So Kevin, how was it for you?*

I'll never forget the sofa that Emily died on.

Night, girls. I'm just next door if you need anything. Ms Harris closed the door firmly.

D'you think that's a gentle hint? said Alice.

How d'you mean? asked Lucy.

Telling us she's next door so we won't try and sneak into the boys' room.

As if. Sana peered in a hand mirror. *Why do spots always come in the most obvious places?*

It has been known. Alice pulled her hair back in a pony tail. *But then, Hassan would rather study, Lee has been going with Nicole since they were in Primary Four, Kevin has a mental age of eight, Danny prefers boys.*

Danny's gay? Lucy looked confused.

I'm not sure if he knows it himself yet. But trust me, he is.

Alice, you're winding us up.

Wait and see.

That leaves Jas, said Katie. *Mibbe she's worried about you two lovebirds, Fi.*

95

I could feel my face colouring.

You're just jealous, said Alice.

Dead right, said Katie. *He's gorgeous, clever, polite, mature. For years everybody fancied him and he never went out with anyone — then along comes Fiona and ten minutes later they're love's young dream. I just wish he had a brother.*

He has.

Really. Could you arrange a double date?

He's a lot older, I said. *Twenty-five. Lives in London.*

Even better.

Brothers aren't always alike, said Sana. *Look at mine.*

Yeah, look at them, said Katie. *They're both gorgeous too.*

This is so superficial, said Lucy. *I mean, how would you feel if guys were discussing us like that, just our looks.*

They do, though.

That doesn't mean we should do the same. Personality's more important.

I just wish I'd the chance to find out — no one's ever interested in me.

Aw you wee soul.

What is it like, though, Fiona?

How d'you mean?

Well, you and Jas have been together, what . . . six months?

Aye.

So . . . I mean?

Oh shut up, Katie — you're embarrassing Fiona. Sana put her mirror away. *I'm shattered — put the light out would you, Alice?*

Sure, kids. Nightie night.

Lying awake in the dark, a splinter of light falling across my pillow — even though I was exhausted, I couldnae drop off. Katie's questions kept running in my heid. She assumed, all of them probably assumed, that me and Jas slept thegether. Or at least had sex somewhere – in a car, in the park, in the house when everyone was out. And we never. But it was mair than that – it was that we never talked about why we never. I'd nae idea whether he thought I didnae want to or if he didnae want to or what. There was this invisible unspoken barrier between us. Of course the official line was that sex is only for when you were married, but could it really be that bad if you loved each other? I was sure Jas and me would always be thegether but getting married was something far in the distance. Did Jas believe we could wait till after uni, after we'd got jobs, afore it happened?

I turned on my side, put my cheek on the cool scratchy pillow. It felt so weird – the first time I'd spent the night under the same roof as Jas. A few feet away, through thin walls, he was lying on a bed like this, his cheek on an identical pillow. Lying, asleep mibbe, or awake, thinking of . . . what? My face flushed again at the thought of him, of us. And though the weariness of the travelling, of the day, seeped through me, it was a long time afore my mind could let go enough for me to fall asleep.

IT WAS COMING up Easter, make or break time. If I didnae go this week, it was a mortal sin. Even Da said, *Make sure you get tae confession afore Good Friday, girls.*

It was easy when Mammy was alive. Everything had a routine then, she held it all thegether. Ten o'clock mass every Sunday, confession the last Saturday of the month, slipping intae the dark cool chapel at five o'clock, hoping there wouldnae be too long a queue because if there was we'd miss *Blind Date* on TV. We all went, the six of us, in the same order every month; first Mammy, then Daddy, then me, Patrick and the twins when they were old enough. When Patrick started working he didnae always go with us tae confession but he went tae mass on Sunday right enough, and Mammy always worked out which mass he could go to on Holy Days of Obligation, depending on his shift. Whatever else happened we had tae get wur souls cleaned.

When I was wee I used tae imagine my soul like a cross between a cloud and a honeycomb; it had the insubstantial shape of a cloud drifting across the sky, but when you looked closely it was made of wee hexagonal shapes all joined thegether. It was in your chest, just underneath your simmet, but naebody could see it except God. I thought God's eyes must be like a microscope. Miss Mackay once showed the class pictures of wriggling beasties which live inside your skin but you can only see with a microscope. But that couldnae be right either because the soul was huge, spreading out towards your sides under your oxters. However he did it, God could see your soul and he could tell by its colour whether you were good or bad.

Someone who was perfect, like a saint, had a shiny white soul, like new net curtains. The mair sins you committed the mankier your soul became till it looked like a greasy auld flaircloth, washed too many times. That's if they were venial sins of course. Commit a mortal sin and your soul turned pure black instantly. My granny said if you died in a state of mortal sin you'd go straight tae Hell, a place I found hard tae imagine because it was supposed to be like a fire so hot you were just burning up all the time. That was afore we had the central heating and I could never imagine being too hot. Hell would of seemed mair real if it was like the cold draught doon your back when you were in the bathroom or the freezing sheets when you got intae your bed in the winter.

I didnae think I'd ever committed a mortal sin but was all too aware of the wee grey smudges of venial sins defiling the purity of my soul. Every night I knelt doon beneath the statue of the Sacred Heart and the grey plastic replica of the Lourdes grotto with its figures of Our Lady and Bernadette glowing luminously in the dark, and examined my conscience.

I never got out of bed right away when I was called, I never ate all my cornflakes that the starving children in Africa would of been grateful for, I dawdled on my way tae school, I laughed when James McCluskey wet hisself at gym, I didnae help my mammy in the hoose.

Each day was a catalogue of things done and undone, sins of commission and omission. Every night afore I went tae sleep I prayed that next morning I'd wake up and find mysel a new-born baby again. I closed my eyes tight, imagined mysel in my cot, able tae start all over again and this time I would be perfect. All my sins wiped out. If only I had another chance at life I could make a much better job of it.

It was that simple then. But with her gone, things had got intae a guddle. We still went to mass, but no necessarily thegether. Sometimes Da was too hungover fae the night afore to get up for ten so he'd go tae night mass, creeping guiltily out the house at hauf six. Sometimes we'd sleep in and have to go tae a later mass, twelve o'clock mibbe, which meant the rest of the day limped along as if haufy it had been lost. We went tae confession the last Saturday of the month as we always had – the days were still marked out on the calendar in the kitchen for us – but after a few month that stopped. The twins pretended they went at school and I'd given up on my da. I did go tae confession a few times by mysel. I wanted to talk about how I felt about the baby and my mammy, but I couldnae, and after reciting a list of faults like lossing my temper and being jealous and no concentrating hard enough at mass I'd leave the wee box feeling worse than when I went in. I couldnae believe God would forgive me for sins I hadnae the courage tae confess. So I stopped gaun. But it was Palm Sunday the morra, and next week was Easter. And if I didnae go by then it was a mortal sin.

Anyway, surely it couldnae be that bad. Father O'Hara was a fire and brimstone kind of preacher, using the word hell more often than was considered normal these days, and in nearly every sermon he talked about the necessity for Catholics to produce mair missionaries. Since Catholics in Scotland could barely scrape up enough young men to cover their ain parishes, this seemed unlikely. But in the confessional he was gentle and undemanding, saying softly, *God bless you child*. Da said it was because he was deif and couldnae hear yer sins, but whatever the reason, it'd be better tae get it over with. There was extra confessions on after mass this week and it'd be even busier than normal so he probably wouldnae even know it was me.

But next day, insteidy Father O'Hara bumbling about on the altar there was a new wee priest started at St Clare's. He looked like a sixth-year pupil in his neatly pressed trousers, fair hair cut short round his ears and I kind of assumed he'd be a bit mair modern in his outlook.

Afore the mass started he tellt us that Father O'Hara had went intae hospital for a routine op and was expected to be convalescent for a while. A wave of muttering passed through the congregation then everything carried on as normal. And when the young priest took the lectern and produced a magazine which he waved in fronty him, the parishioners settled doon with interest. Mibbe we were in for some parallels between the life of Jesus and an article on one of the latest beauty treatments – beauty for the soul or some such.

Brothers and sisters, this magazine was given to me on a recent visit to Boots, placed in my bag along with my purchase of razor blades and toothpaste. Usually I would ignore such reading matter but I found myself flicking through it in order to help throw some light on contemporary life. And as well as the expected lamentable interest in expensive products designed to so-call improve bodies and faces that God in his infinite wisdom and love has created, I came across this particular article.

He opened the page and waved it at the congregation.

'Me Time', it's called. Addressed to women, the main thrust of the article is that modern women have no time to relax, are stressed out by the demands of running homes and careers and need to carve out 'me time'. The article is full of suggestions as to how they may do this, some of which, like going away to spas and health clubs, cost thousands of pounds, and all of which involve being selfish.

And that's not my word, that is their word – it's screamed at us in bright pink letters. BE SELFISH – you deserve it. So degraded has our society become that even a magazine handed out in a chemist's shop encourages us to be sinful. Even worse – uses the words of sin as something we should strive for.

Be selfish. Shut your children out of your bedroom and take some 'me time' – chill out with a magazine and a glass of wine. Get a babysitter and go and have your nails done. The most precious gifts of God are not as important as trivial, superficial rubbish.

Would the Blessed Virgin have shut Jesus out of her room to take some 'me time'? Can you imagine Our Lady dumping her child on an irresponsible teenager in order to beautify herself?

Brothers and sisters, it may look as if I am addressing myself to women and giving them a hard time. I am not. If men did not collude in such ideas then the women would not feel obliged to spend time beautifying themselves for they would know that their husbands saw their inner beauty. If husbands worked to support their families instead of spending their money in bars or on toys like expensive cars and suchlike, then women could spend more time with their children. If children were regarded as precious gifts of the Lord then we would have no babies sent to nursery every day from morning till night, no children farmed out to grannies so their mothers could

102

spend Saturdays trawling the shops for designer clothes to look good at a party.

Brothers and sisters, in this season of Lent, just before the most precious and holy time of the church's year, let us remember there is no such thing as 'me time', only 'the Lord's time'.

At the end of mass, I sloped out, trying to make mysel invisible. How could I go tae this guy and tell the truth, and if I didnae tell the truth what was the point in going? I could only pray that God would forgive me anyway.

WAKING TO DARKNESS, under the downie, fuddled, thinking at first it was a car alarm, I almost turned over then realised the sound was inside the house not outside. I jumped out of bed, threw the dressing gown round me and opened the door. In the hall the dark was thicker, the darkness of a fog, and smoke was seeping fae under the living room door.

I'd always thought I was a big feartie who'd panic at the least wee thing. But when it happened I went intae some kind of autopilot. All the things they'd taught us in that third-year safety course fae the guy in the Fire Brigade, suddenly came back to me.

I opened the twins' door and woke them, tellt them to get out the house.

Mona, phone 999 on your mobile. Rona go round the close and get all the neighbours out. And don't switch on any lights!

They were that stunned they just done as they were tellt, though when Rona realised I was gaun in the room tae get ma da, she tried tae stop me. Somehow, though, for the first and last time in her life she seen something in me that forced her to obey.

I rushed tae the bathroom and soaked a towel, wrapped it round my face over my mouth and nose, then opened the living room door carefully, remembering to stay behind it in case of flames shooting out. Instead a sick bitter smell swamped me, making my eyes sting and water. The familiar room was a grey blur, and when I shouted, *Da,* a muffled sound fell intae the darkness. Remembering the training, I dropped doon low – smoke is thinner nearer the ground – and a few blurred shapes became visible. I crawled, feeling along the wall wi the back of ma haund till I reached the couch. It seemed ridiculous that a normal sized room could seem cavernous and that in the middle of a fire there could be so much darkness. I felt ma da's leg, moved up his limp body till I got to his shoulder and started tae shake and shake him. *Da, Da, wake up.*

Mmm . . . whhh . . .

For godsake Da, the hoose is on fire.

He jerked slightly.

Da, you have to help me.

I knew that though I could help him, I couldnae move him mysel but he wasnae waking up properly. Christ knows how much he'd had tae drink and with the effect of the smoke . . . I'd be a liar if I didnae admit that for a split second I did think of leaving him there for the Fire Brigade tae rescue. But I never.

Later on they said that's what I should of done, no put mysel at risk like that. I don't know what force I summoned up inside, never thought about what I was daeing, just pushed him aff the settee on to the flair, grabbed him under the oxters and pulled. At first I felt I wasnae getting anywhere, it was nae use, he was like a big deid lump. I screamed at him, *Move ya big lump move,* and the towel started tae unravel fae ma face. I wound it round mair tightly, took a deep breath and hauled and somehow his body started tae soften; he wasnae moving hissel but he was no longer resisting, no longer deid weight, then suddenly we were outside the living room and when ah turned ah seen two students fae the top flat heiding towards our door and Mr Flanagan puffing up the stairs. They helped me get him intae the close where the air was clearer and next minute there were firemen everywhere and I was sitting on the other side of the street wi Rona and Mona, their airms and legs wound round me like monkeys.

Assumptions. You don't know you make them till after something happens. I suppose if I'd ever thought about it, which I never did, I'd have assumed that after a fire I'd feel glad tae be alive, glad no one was seriously hurt, that the fire was caught afore the whole tenement was destroyed. Actually I felt numb. Shock, I guess, but something else too.

We were all carted aff to the hospital to be checked out. They kept my da in overnight but me and the twins went tae Janice's. Three of us bunked up in Evie's room while she slept with Janice and Angela. Like auld times, the three of us squashed thegether, and somehow the shock of the fire had made the twins a bit softer round the edges, blurred that wire-hard teenage look they'd been cultivating.

Janice lent us clothes. I didnae look too bad in her combats and an old jumper of Angela's but the twins were dead skinny. Plus of course their fashion sense was mortified. Janice had two looks: semi-smart for her social work job and weekend stuff which was edgy for someone her age but, as far as the twins were concerned, might as well have been their granny's.

Check this, said Mona, hoisting up a navy blue skirt and folding it over about ten times round her waist. *Ah look like a nun.*

And ah'm like an auld hippy or something. Rona picked distastefully at a crocheted top.

Good excuse for you to go shopping, girls. Janice rummled through Angela's side of the wardrobe. *Nope, that looks like the best we can do. Look, I'll take you out this afternoon to get some underwear and a few basics, put it on my plastic till the insurance pays out. Patrick's plane is due in at seven. What time's your daddy getting out, Fiona? Did they say?*

We've to phone after 12. Jas is gaun with me to collect him.

Great. We'll hit the shops this afternoon and meet you back here.

I looked at Janice, amazed at her lightness, feeling anger begin to rise. We could of been killed last night and she was wittering about underwear. Then I caught a glimpse of her face as she folded a sweater, smoothing it gently as she would of stroked Evie's cheek. She was biting her lip, hard.

The nurse was Irish, with a thin face and a strand of lank fairish hair escaping fae her cap. *Mr O'Connell? He's ready for you, but Doctor wanted a quick word first.* She looked at me and Jas. *You're his daughter?*

Aye.

Is Mrs O'Connell . . .

My mammy's dead.

I'm sorry . . . I'll just get Doctor.

107

A woman of about forty, wearing a white coat over a green sweater and smart dark trousers, walked out of the ward, holding a chart.

You're Mr O'Connell's daughter . . . she glanced at his notes where I was listed as next of kin . . . *Fiona?*

Aye.

She motioned us intae a corner away from the nurses' station. Jas waited at a slight distance.

How old are you Fiona?

Seventeen.

And your mother is dead?

A year and . . . four month ago.

I'm sorry. Look, your father is fine — pretty frail and weepy but no real harm done after last night.

That's good.

But I'm a bit concerned about his general condition. Seems very thin, run down, not very . . . she looked awkward . . . *not looking after himself.*

My face flamed. *He's just given up.*

I know this is very hard for you. Is he drinking too much?

I nodded.

Since your mother's death?

Aye.

Have you spoken to him?

No.

Is there anyone in the family he'd listen to?

Dunno. My Auntie Janice mibbe.

Look, I'd like to refer him to counselling — see if we can give him some help with the underlying problems. I've given him a letter for his GP. Of course maybe, just maybe, this terrible thing could be a blessing in disguise. A wake up call for him. Make him realise how close he came to hurting his family.

She took my arm. *We also have support services for young people. For you.*

I shook my heid. *I'm fine.*

Da had tae sleep on the settee in the living room at Janice's. The next morning was mental, all of us trying tae find time in the bathroom. Janice was amazing, but.

I'm timing yous all in the bathroom — less than five minutes you get a chocolate croissant for breakfast, any longer and it's porridge instead.

Angie made a face. *And you seriously don't want to taste Jan's porridge.*

The threat of porridge meant that even the twins managed to get out in time but we were still falling over each other, and during the next few weeks I started tae spend mair time at Jas's. We were in the final rundown to the exams — we had to get portfolios and dissertations completed and sent away and I couldnae work at Janice's. On the nights Jas wasnae at the shop, we'd go to the library after school to study then heid round to his about six. Their flat was always like a furnace; Jas's ma loved to have the heating and fires turned up high. Jas and she would always go through the same routine.

Jaswinder, shut the door, don't let in the cold fae the close.

Ma, it's tropical in here.

I've been cooking.

It must be a hundred degrees.

It's a cold night outside.

Have you never heard of global warming?

I loved going intae their kitchen after the chill of the under-heated library. The smell of home-cooked food, the radio tuned to the Asian music station and Jas's ma, pinny over her sari and woolly jumper.

Now you sit down, Fiona. You must be starving after all that homework.

I liked being there, just the three of us. After the first couple of times I began tae relax in her presence; that feeling of being at hame, of being at one with Jas, started tae happen when the three of us were thegether, as if Jas's ma was an extension of us. There was a softness in the way they looked at each other, the affection they showed. He'd put his haund on her shoulder when she stood at the sink, or she'd caress the back of his airm when she got up fae her seat and it wasnae obvious or precious in any way, just ordinary. She was never possessive, seemed really happy that Jas and me were thegether, treated me almost like a daughter, but there was a bond between them that was just there, necessary. Sitting in the warmth of the kitchen with Jas and his ma, the atmosphere was so dreamlike, I'd almost forgotten the reality of my life, so when I opened Janice's door to find angry voices coming fae the living room it took me a minute tae come to.

Da was slumped in an armchair, that hang-dog helpless expression I couldnae bear plastered across his face. I'd only ever seen it once or twice when Mammy was alive but since her death it had become mair characteristic of him than anything else. Janice held a bit of official-looking paper in her haund. She looked round when I came in, pressed her lips thegether as if stopping herself from speaking.

Angie got up fae her seat. *Hi Fiona,* she said. *I'll just go and check on Evie.*

When she'd left, Janice turned to my da and said, *Do you want to explain this to Fiona yourself?*

He looked across at me without meeting my eyes, then shook his heid.

What is it?

Let's sit down. Janice put her airm round me and we sat on the settee opposite my da.

I've been trying to help your da get the flat sorted out, but when I contacted the insurance company it turns out he's let the policy lapse.

How d'you mean?

He stopped paying the policy a couple of month after your mammy died.

There's no insurance?

Janice shook her heid.

I sat for a minute, letting her words sink in, trying tae work out what this would mean.

So . . . we won't get back the stuff that got burned – the furniture and all that?

I didnae care about the furniture and anyway, I knew we'd get by somehow.

Worse. It's not just the contents policy – there's no buildings insurance either. No money to restore the building. She paused.

I still didnae get it. In my heid I was imagining Jas and Patrick helping out, Da getting his pals round tae fix up the woodwork and the rewiring and the plastering and all that stuff – they'd know enough guys could dae favours and we'd all pull thegether. There was the prize money too – we could use that tae replace the basics and anyhow, Janice wouldnae let things fall apart.

You won't be able to go hame.

That's when it hit me. The flat where we'd all been brought up wasnae just a building that could be done up again, it was hame. The love that had been put intae it had made it hame, Mammy'd made it hame, and since she'd been gone it wasnae hame any mair. And it never would be again.

111

Something inside me shattered intae a million icy jaggy glass shards and exploded out ontae that broken man sitting there.

How could you? Mammy would never of let this happen. If you'd died she'd of managed, she'd never of sat there wallowing in self-pity like you, drinking yoursel intae a stupor, letting the bloody hoose go on fire. You're useless, naw, you're worse than useless.

I suppose it was bound tae have come out sooner or later but I wish it hadnae.

I wish it was you that died. I wish you were deid. Janice tried tae hold me back as I ran out the room but I was that blind with rage and grief nothing would of stopped me.

I started tae run, at first in a heidlong rush then gradually my pace settled tae a jog. I was a good runner, no much of a sprinter but steady at middle and long distances, and it was great tae sense the night air nip my cheeks, feel my heart pound and the blood surge round my body. Helped tae block out the mad jumble of thoughts in my heid. At first I just ran, taking streets at random. Naebody paid me any attention; it was only about eight o'clock and I probably looked like a real jogger in my hoodie and trainers. Then I found mysel slowing doon, thinking about my direction. I wanted tae go back to Jas's, to that warmth and homeliness, but I couldnae – I knew where I was heided, though as I got nearer the dread rose in me.

Fae the outside of the building, in the dark, there wasnae much difference. Our windaes were smeared and manky but the lights were on in other flats. I imagined the Flanagans, clocked in fronty the telly wi cups a tea, Jean and Betty knitting away and Suzy on the first flair getting her baby tae bed. The students had nae curtains in their living room and one of them was at the windae, talking on his mobile. I felt sick inside. We'd never be able tae live there again, I'd never make the dinner in the kitchen, sleep in my bedroom.

I fumbled in my pocket and pulled out the keys, walked across the road and let mysel in the close. Even though it had been cleaned, a sooty smell lingered under the lemony disinfectant, and it got worse as I went up the stair. When I reached the landing, the sight of our front door, all padlocked up, hit me. I'd thought I'd be able tae go inside, somehow it seemed that important tae walk through the rooms. But the Fire Brigade or the Polis or someone must have secured the place for safety. I turned and walked back doon the stair, paused a moment afore letting mysel out intae the back court. There was a real nip in the air and the heat I'd built up while I was running through the streets had evaporated, but I made my way to the corner beside the shaughly auld wall, under the bare tree, and sat doon so I wouldnae be seen fae the houses.

All around, as far as I could see, were the backs of tenements, lurking under a moonless sky. A web of windaes crisscrossed their shadowy presence, hundreds of lives mapped out in this wee area. Every now and again I'd see someone come tae their kitchen sink to fill a kettle or draw their bedroom curtain, mibbe looking out for a second intae the blank dark. And above me were the deid windaes of the house that was no longer my hame.

I ENDED UP at Jas's. After sitting in the back court till I was frozen I started tae walk aimlessly, but by now it was late and it didnae feel good to be out by mysel. I couldnae face gaun back to Janice's so I went to the only place that felt like hame to me.

Jas's ma said nothing that night, lent me a tent of a nightie and produced a box of new toothbrushes.

Is this stock for the shop? I asked.

No dear, I just like to be prepared in case of any unexpected visitors.

Jas laughed. *In case an unexpected busload of tourists arrive.*

So cheeky, this boy of mine. She ruffled his hair. *The other, of course, hardly ever speaks.* She opened a drawer, handed me two orange towels. *You'll meet him soon, Fiona — he's coming next week.*

Maybe next week, said Jas. *Maybe the week after or the week after that.*

That's another difference, Fiona. One is reliable, the other as vague as a cloud. But you're tired, dear. Go to bed.

Next day Patrick flew up fae London. As usual, he and Janice took charge, Patrick dealing wi the building society about the repossession, and Janice managing to get the council to rehouse us. Except I wasnae gonnae go with them.

I didnae want to think about where I would live. Mrs Kaur was kind and never pressed me to leave, but I knew I couldnae stay there forever. But right noo, I could hardly bear to be in the same room as my da.

I tried. A few days later Patrick came round and took me tae Janice's. They wanted tae include me in the discussions about what had to be done, but I sat on the other side of the room fae my da like a hedgehog, curled in a ball of hate, prickling every time he opened his mouth or looked in my direction. Every move he made grated on me; the way he pulled on his left ear when he was listening to what was said, the whiny tone of his voice as he sat glued to the chair and never even got up to make a cup of tea.

That night when I got back, Mrs Kaur put her airms round me, spoke gently.

I know it's hard to forgive, but it's sweet too. Just take it in baby steps, dear. The smell of the oil she put on her hair, the softness of her cheek, made me want to say, yes, yes, I will, but I couldnae.

Da and the twins flitted tae the new house the following week and I moved back wi Janice and Angie, sharing Evie's room wi its Winnie the Pooh mural.

Are you gonnae sleep in the bump beds with me, Auntie Fiona? Sure. It'll be fun.

When I'm five I'm gonnae sleep in the top bump.

Are you?

Janice held out sheets and a downie cover. *She's desperate to sleep in the top bunk but I don't feel safe with her up there yet — d'you mind, Fiona?*

I took the sheets. *I'd sleep on the flair, anywhere.*

It won't come to that.

I started to make up the bed. Evie skipped around me.

When I'm five and I sleep on the top bump my baby sister will sleep under me.

Will she?

Janice turned fae the drawer she was emptying. *Mibbe not right away, pet. Babies sleep in a cot first.*

I looked at her. *Janice, are you . . . having another baby?*

I'm not pregnant, yet. But we're thinking about it. I mean we definitely want another, it's just a question of when. I want to save up a bit more before I have to take time off work. She hunkered doon to Evie, rubbed noses with her. *But I cannae promise it'll be a sister.*

That afternoon Jas and me took Evie out for a walk. At the swing park she insisted on going on the big chute which was far too high for her so Jas held her in his lap and went doon too. *See — you've got your own racing car.*

When she teamed up with another wee one on the seesaw, we sat on a bench and watched her giggling away as she went up and doon, rhythmically.

Jas took my haund. *How you?*

Dunno. I feel awful. Everybody's being dead kind. Your ma, Janice. If I could just get my act thegether and stop feeling like this about Da, it'd be cool.

It'll take time. Families are like that.

116

Yours isnae.

Sometimes it is.

You and your ma get on better than anybody I've ever known.

That's just luck, how we are. The way our personalities work.

Me and Patrick are a bit like that.

But me and my da rubbed each other up the wrong way a lot. And Amrik and me are total chalk and cheese. You just learn to live with it. Family is kind of . . . sacred.

A few days later Janice was washing up at the sink while I sat at the table. Evie came rushing in the room and Janice haufturned; her face, as the light hit it at that angle, was Mammy's. Lying in bed that night I couldnae sleep, tossed and turned in the bunk bed above Evie, thinking about Janice getting pregnant again. They said that what happened tae Mammy was a fluke, one in a million, but I was scared. Janice would be forty next year. She looked younger and was dead fit, but then so was my mammy. When I closed my eyes all I seen was the radiance of that face, the one that was both Mammy's and Janice's, expecting, hoping for the future, then dissolving intae nothing.

Somewhere in the middle of this stuff, my eighteenth birthday came and went. Janice wanted us all to go out for a meal, but the way things were it didnae seem that great an idea. Instead I went out with Jas, who gied me a box wrapped in white tissue paper.

Got it in Haworth, he said. *I've been saving it till now.*

It was a glass paperweight with a profile of Emily trapped inside it.

It's lovely. I held it in the palm of my haund, felt its heaviness.

*   *   *

The letters arrived the next week, forwarded to Janice's house. I took them to school to let Jas see them. I found him in the library, folders and books spread out in fronty him, placed three envelopes on top of the pile.

That one first — it's the least interesting. It said my piece hadnae got anywhere in the national finals of the competition.

Shame, said Jas.

Ach, I never expected it.

He read the others; one offering me a place at uni and one at Art School.

Cool. He handed them back. *Have you decided what you're gonnae do?*

Art School. I sat doon in the chair next to his. *It's weird — for years I've wanted to study literature at uni, but somehow, when I read they magic words I'd always dreamed of, it just didnae feel the same. Then I opened this one and it said you've been offered a place at Art School and it was just, this is it. This is right.*

That's what you have to go by, that feeling.

I turned tae him. *What about you, Jas?*

How d'you mean? I'm all settled, accepted my place last year.

You wouldnae think of changing — I mean, is this what you really want or is it because your family wants you to study pharmacy?

Fiona, if I said to Ma I've changed my mind, I really want to study literature or go to Art School she'd support me. But I don't.

He replaced the letters in their envelopes. *Do you want me to stay in Glasgow, is that it? It might be possible to change unis next year.*

It's no that. Jas, I know you love Shelley mair than anything, and there's your photography. You said you don't have that passion for Chemistry that you dae for Art and books and all that.

Pharmacy will give me the life I want, Fiona. It feels right.

The librarian glared at us fae behind her glass screen and

we shut up. I opened my books and pretended to read. Still didnae get it but. Jas always had clear ideas about things, had principles. He'd never get sucked intae studying the wrang course out of loyalty. But I couldnae see why he was so keen on pharmacy except that it suited his family. And I couldnae understaund what he meant about it giving him the life he wanted. Sure it was steady and a good job and that. But Jas wasnae materialistic. He didnae want a fast car or fancy holidays. I wished we'd talked mair then about what kind of life he did want, about the future. I assumed I was part of his plan whatever that was but, like sex, it was something we never discussed. Mibbe if we had things might of been different. Naa, I don't believe that. Probably it would of only made what happened next even worse.

AMRIK WAS A fallen angel. Taller and thinner than Jas, his hair tummled past his shoulders in lank curls; he was only twenty-five but the lines round his mouth and eyes were deep. Oh but those eyes — earth-brown with flecks of gold, eyes to drown in. He was draped over a chair in the kitchen, long legs stretched out in front of the gas fire. Jas's ma placed a cup on the table by his side and tapped his thigh as she squeezed past him.

Watch you don't trip over these big legs, Fiona — always in the way. Amrik, this is Fiona, Jaswinder's girlfriend.

His haund moved vaguely in my direction. *Hi.*

Hi.

Sit down, dear. I'll get you some tea. Jaswinder will be back in a moment — he just went out for a message.

I sat in the chair opposite Amrik. He held the mug in his haund, sipped the tea. I noticed that the tips of his long thin fingers were calloused and the fingernail of his right pinkie was longer than the others. He said nothing and, though I rummled around in my heid for small talk, I found mysel unable to speak.

The door opened and Jas struggled in with a bag spilling over with aubergines and peppers, so full that he was hugging it like a baby. He gied a big grin, dumped the bag on the flair and put his airm round me.

I cannae think back to that day without shame that floods me, makes me close my eyes and put ma haunds over ma ears. Sounds stupid to say it, as if I'm making it up in retrospect, but when Jas put his airm round me and I stood looking at Amrik I felt as though I'd already been unfaithful with him, even though we'd done nothing but sit in fronty the fire thegether, drinking tea in silence. There's a phrase in the bible about how you can commit adultery in your heart; I know what that means. Even if Amrik and me had never ever done anything, I was guilty as soon as I looked at him. When I was wee my granny tellt me about sins of intention, how if you really really wanted to murder somebody and felt all they feelings in your heart it was a mortal sin anyway, even though you never laid a finger on them. And I thought that was daft, how could thinking about something be wrang? You cannae help your thoughts, can you? Thoughts are just things that come and go, they don't harm anyone unless you act on them.

I don't believe that noo. Thoughts are dangerous, and no just because they make it that bit mair likely that you will do something bad. The thought itsel is bad. I mentally detached mysel fae Jas the second his ma introduced me as his girlfriend; there was something, that cauld splinter, an ice crystal the size of a pinheid, that crept in my heart and stayed there.

Looking back on it, I find it hard tae believe I even liked Amrik, let alone loved him. Mibbe it wasnae love, but obsession, whatever that is. I was constantly aware of Amrik's presence, as if static electricity had set up hame inside me, wee tremors prickling under my skin. It wasnae a pleasant feeling, no the warm comfort I'd always felt with Jas. I was hyper, couldnae sit still, kept leppin up fae my seat tae make cups of tea or help wi the dishes. And of course Jas's ma thought I was being helpful which made me feel even worse.

That night Amrik was playing in a local café which had live music. Jas and me had been there quite often – he didnae drink so we never went tae pubs. Usually there were local bands, boys posing and playing thinly disguised ripoffs of their heroes. Everyone talked over them except for their pals, who crowded round the tiny platform, applauding enthusiastically after every number. Tonight Jas led me tae a table near the front.

Amrik's amazing – I cannae wait till you hear him.

I've never heard sitar music afore.

It's a dead haunting sound, no really like anything else, draws you right inside it. I used to listen while I done my homework at the kitchen table. Then when I heard my da coming in I'd rush up and bang on Amrik's door to warn him to stop.

Why did your da no want him to play?

Sitar is not a traditional Sikh instrument. Amrik was always musical but he'd learned the tabla – the drums – at the Gurdwara. My da seen it as rebellion when Amrik wanted to learn sitar. He wanted him to play sacred music – of course to Amrik his music is sacred but no the way my da meant.

A few minutes after eight, Amrik strolled in and made his way to the wee platform in the corner. There was a stool and a mic on a stand. Amrik lowered the mic till it was a few feet fae the flair, dumped his jacket in a corner and sat cross-legged. He placed his sitar carefully across his legs, and, eyes closed, paying nae attention to anyone or anything in the room, began to play.

Discordant and harmonious at the same time, the notes flew and trembled like nervous birds. Amrik appeared to be in a trance, swaying slightly, his fingers coalescing with the keys and strings, as though he were tuned intae something larger, which played through him.

At first the folk in the café continued their conversations, sipped their coffees, ate their tapas and muffins. But gradually, a hush descended on the place, people crept fae their seats tae be closer to Amrik, till everyone was huddled round this one corner. Amrik continued to play without stopping, one tune merging intae another, different moods intermingling; sadness and joy, playfulness and melancholy, but above all a sweetness you could almost taste. When he finished, after what could of been hours or minutes, there was silence. He opened his eyes and I saw the eyes of an angel.

Of course then came the applause and the chaos of a fawning crowd round him. Jas went up tae talk to him, put his airm round him, but I held back, no wanting to be like everyone else. I sat alone at the table in the hauf-dark, staring at cauld foam in my coffee cup.

Two days later, Amrik and me were lovers.
Three days later, Jas and me were finished.

I think that's what I feel worst about now, though at the time I was too swept away tae notice what was gaun on. I wish I'd been honourable enough to finish with Jas, leave, get right out of his life afore I took up with Amrik. I know it's an odd word, old-fashioned, but that's the only one that fits. Folk are always talking about respect nooadays but we've nae idea what it means, the word means nothing.

Honourable.

Tell him it's over.

Simple. I should of done it that night after the gig, walking hame with Jas under the full moon that shone on us as if we were real lovers; it was like blasphemy to walk haund in haund with Jas under that moon. But how do you break up with your best friend?

Answer: You don't. You betray him.

I will never forget that Monday afternoon; the wee room high in the attic, the single bed opposite the windae that looked out at the grey sky. Monday afternoon was the only time when you could be sure their ma was out – she never missed meeting her friends for their Scrabble game – and Jas was on a trip with his Chemistry class. As I walked up the road I kept telling mysel that I had a reason to go round to Jas's; I needed a special set of pens I'd left there on Friday, even kidded mysel I was gonnae return tae school once I'd got them, but when I went up the close and heard the sound of Amrik's sitar drifting fae the flat, I knew fine well I wouldnae.

The first time. There was me assuming it would be with Jas, the man who loved me. Sometimes, lying in bed at night, I'd think about what it'd be like, what he'd say, how we'd be thegether.

I don't remember much about that first time with Amrik, what we done or how it happened, just the afterwards, lying cooried like spoons in the narrow bed, watching the grey sky turn a darker shade of grey. I mind other times, when the lovemaking became a kind of dance with a familiar rhythm.

It's a cliché that musicians make good lovers but Amrik played my body like an instrument, his fingers caressing me till every nerve quivered and I screamed and squealed scales. That was after he moved intae the bedsit, when I didnae care who heard us. The first time was silent.

I never told Jas about that first time — couldnae even be honest about that. Just said it was over.

Over? What d'you mean, over?

I'm sorry, Jas.

Fiona . . .

I'm really sorry.

The gulls swooping and diving over a grey sky as we walked along by the brown, murky river. My haunds that cold they hurt. And his eyes that I didnae dare look intae.

Mrs Kaur was kind, phoned and told me to keep in touch. *I mean it, dear. You are always welcome in our home.* I wonder how much she knew then. She was a wise woman who knew her sons. It must of been obvious fae the way I looked at Amrik that there was something up. But if she had known, could she really have been so kind to me?

But then everyone was kind to me, too kind. Janice gied me the *probably best not to get tied down at your age* speech, and Jemma said, *These things happen.* Only Monica blurted out, *Oh that's a shame, Jas is so nice* when I tellt her, then she went scarlet and said, *Of course I'm sure Amrik is nice too but . . .*

But?

Oh what do I know? I just hope he looks after you as well as Jas.

Jemma laughed. *Boyfriends don't look after you, they're for having fun with.*

I guess, said Monica. *But in the long run you want someone you can rely on.*

AMRIK HAD A chipped front tooth, no obvious, just a tiny diagonal space which contrasted with his perfectly even white smile. He smiled often but not often directly at anyone. Over the time we were thegether I watched him smile to hissel as he made a cup of coffee, or stared out the windae, or played the sitar. And he played almost all the time.

I'd of understood if he'd sat and practised, or played specific pieces but it wasnae that; he was always tinkering, footering up and doon the scales, could never leave it alane for a moment. Even after we'd just made love, he'd lie still only for a few seconds afore rolling over and reaching for the instrument, pulling it across tae the mattress on the flair where he'd sit beside me, sheet wrapped round him, playing. The first time I thought it was romantic, lying in bed close by, listening to these beautiful sounds created by his elegant fingers, but I soon realised that it was the sitar he was making love to; he'd turned fae me to something he loved mair.

Only once did I show how I felt, stroking his thigh and saying, *D'you have to play just now? Can we lie thegether for a while?*

He looked at me as if I'd asked him to stop breathing.

I wished I could be as single-minded about my art; I always had tae get in the right frame of mind, think mysel intae what I was daeing. Was it because visual art wasnae as straightforward as picking up an instrument? For a fresco painter aye, but surely lifting a camera was no more difficult than a sitar. Picasso would of reached for a sketchpad and pencil to draw his lover after sex if she happened to be in an interesting light – he'd probably of stopped in mid-flow if he got a good composition. Mibbe I wasnae a real artist.

It was not just Amrik either – the other guys who turned up at the flat were just as obsessive. In the middle of a conversation one would pick up a guitar, apparently idly, another would join in and next minute they'd all be at it. It'd last for a few minutes mibbe, or hours, till someone noticed it was getting dark or they were hungry.

In the beginning I hung around while they were playing, respectful, following the wandering progress of fragmented melodies, till I realised I was invisible, something that came with the flat – no one, not even Amrik, knew I was there unless they wanted a beer oot the fridge or a cup of coffee. I wasnae used tae guys expecting me to wait on them; my brother and Jas werenae like that and I never thought young men in the twenty-first century would be either, but they were engrossed in their music, oblivious to everything else.

Once I made tea, tiptoed round with mugs and chocolate biscuits, but Amrik barely looked at me as I placed his on the flair beside him. If he'd gied me that smile I'd of stayed, it'd of been worth it, but I couldnae bear him blanking me out. Next time the guys arrived at the door I lifted my books and heided for the library.

I spent maist of my time at Amrik's though I was now officially living with my da and the twins. After a few weeks at Janice's, I'd come tae my senses, knew it wasnae fair on them.

You know you can stay as long as you like, Fiona.

Naa, you need your space; you and Angie and Evie and the new baby, when it comes — you're a family.

As I said it I could feel tears starting. A family. Who was my family?

You could always go and stay with your da and the twins.

I don't know, Janice.

Your daddy is trying, Fiona. He really is. He went and asked the guys for his job back and they've taken him on for a trial. He's got a real incentive to keep off the drink. And it would be good for you all to be thegether again.

I sat looking at the fire. It was one of they living flame ones but it was turned aff cause it was July; deid grey lumps of fake coal.

When you start at Art School you can get a place in the residences, or share a flat if you want — it's only a few month away. Why don't you go hame till then?

Hame.

A three-bedroom flat on the third flair of a council block with a rectangle of red chips in front. A ten minute walk fae wur auld hoose but a million miles away. At the entrance to the stairwell were two tubs that had been planted with flowers, but only weeds flourished in them noo; the flowers were twisted dried-up twigs nourished wi deid fag ends. The guy on the ground flair kept a nasty wee skelly-eyed dug and you'd tae dodge its mess when you took the rubbish out to the bins, the couple across the landing wore black leather and painted a skull and crossbones on their front door. Could of been worse. At least there were nae drug dealers or folk having all-night parties. And we were the only social misfits rehoused by the council.

You're such a snob, said Rona, when I moaned about having a whirligig instead of proper clothes lines tae hang the washing out.

No one could accuse Rona and Mona of being snobs.

Fae July tae September I drifted in hauf-lives, between my da's house and Amrik's bedsit, between school and college – I guess you'd of said between childhood and being an adult except I felt as if I'd never been a child yet never would be an adult.

Amrik never came to the house and Da never mentioned him, just asked me to let him know when I was staying over.

Just tell me when you'll no be hame, hen. That's all.

Hame. The box. At least I wasnae sharing with the twins, but the third bedroom was toty, just big enough for a single bed.

Like Emily's, I tellt Amrik.

Cool, he said. *Maybe it'll inspire your poetry.*

I don't write poetry any mair though.

Why not?

Dunno, somehow since I've got mair intae the visual stuff I don't dae any writing.

A lie. I hadnae written a poem since Mammy died.

He leaned on one elbow. Already his attention was wandering

towards the sitar propped up near the bed. He reached for the instrument and pulled it across. The round wooden base pushed itsel against the curve of my hip. Hard, cauld. A shower of golden notes and Amrik was lost to me.

I turned my back, pulled the covers over my heid and closed my eyes. Why did I stay with him? If he was obsessed with the music and I hated him playing it, why be thegether? But it didnae seem like that then – it was as if I had somehow captured this wonderful being, like a selkie, and naturally you couldnae expect them to behave like a human, to be normal like anyone else. So you had tae put up with them. I guess I thought this was the price I had to pay for choosing the fallen angel.

And I didnae have anyone tae tell about it. Only Jas would have understood, and he was the one I could never talk to. I went out of my way to avoid anywhere he was likely to be and I guess he done the same. By now of course he'd know me and Amrik were thegether, but I hoped Jas believed that I'd waited till after we'd split up afore starting anything. Nae doubt he'd make excuses for Amrik too; he was different, special.

And the moments when it worked were special. Looking intae those eyes when we were alone in the quiet of his room, the rare moments when he'd take my haund loosely in his long fingers as we walked alang the street. The even rarer occasions when we'd talk. Amrik barely talked at all. He seemed tae have nae interest in the past, his or mine. The usual ways lovers find out about themselves, the sharing of histories, meant nothing to him, and the future appeared equally uninteresting. He never made plans, drifted, so there was nae point in discussing what we would do, even the next day.

He occasionally commented on things around us, like a bird on the windae sill, a poly bag coiled in a tree, the film we'd seen. Mainly he was silent, not a companionable silence, but a silence that suggested something was going on in his heid which needed his full attention. Later I realised it was – he was working out his music, composing.

One of the few times we had what could of been described as a discussion about anything was when Baz came to the flat. He was one of the musicians who used tae hang round Amrik, a shambling lump of a guy, terminally uncool, with a straggly beard and Jesus sandals.

How are you, Amrik man?

Cool. You?

Aye, me too.

So what's new?

Baz and his band had just signed with a record company.

It's pure wicked, man. Money up front and everything. So, like, we want you to join. Play with us.

Amrik shook his heid.

Aw c'mon, Amrik. Just for this one recording. You can play anything you like – you know like the stuff we were doing at the club last week. You'd be totally, like, free. And you'd get a cut of the profits and all.

I don't do recordings.

After the guy had left I asked Amrik about it. I thought he was holding out for a contract of his ain.

It's not that. I've had offers, said no. I just don't believe in recording music.

How d'you mean?

Music is something that happens. In that moment. It's alive. As soon as you start to record it, it dies.

But you listen to recorded music, on the radio, on CDs . . .

I know — and sometimes it's the only way of experiencing music I might never get to hear otherwise. But it's still second-hand. He picked up the sitar. *I want my music to remain pure.*

I left the flat and walked doon Great Western Road, eyes on the dusty pavements. Folk were sitting outside a bar; the view was of the back of a graffitied wall but hey, they were outside and that's the only place folk in Glasgow want tae be any day it isnae chuckin it doon or minus fifteen degrees.

Pure.

I felt ashamed. A strange emotion in the circumstances since I hadnae done anything wrang, but I felt as if I had. All those hours Amrik spent, as I'd thought, footering with the sitar, avoiding other things – like me – when truly it was the only important thing in his life. His art was so important to him that he turned doon all kinds of recording deals to keep playing in grotty wee clubs and cafés. I could understand what he meant though I'd never thought of it like that. The notes, emerging from the instrument at that precise moment, echoing in that space, whether it was a concert hall with brilliant acoustics or a dusty bedsit. That was the moment – that note was in the moment and, nae matter how often you played it, it would never be that note ever again. Recording appeared to catch the moment, capture it, but it wasnae the same; it was the recording of the moment, the recording of the sound, distorted by the electronic means of recording, sealed in it, killed by it. It was like the difference between looking at the face of your loved one and looking at a photograph.

Pure.

Art.

I had a lot to think about.

*   *   *

Finding somewhere tae think wasnae easy. Amrik could dissolve everything outside hissel as soon as he started playing; wherever he was, whoever was around, he stepped intae that place inside him and the rest was irrelevant.

I wasnae like that. I needed peace and quiet, had tae prepare mysel, no jump fae washing the dishes or having a conversation to daeing my work. I wisht I was different; mibbe it showed I wasnae a real artist like Amrik cause I wasnae as focused as him, mibbe I had to be that obsessed if I was ever gonnae dae anything good. Art School started in a week and I'd done nothing since the fire.

Amrik could have lived wi my da and the twins, wandered fae one house to another and never bothered about it. But when I came back after talking to him, fired up with enthusiasm, determined to really work things out and produce something better, all it took was the first moment in the doorway – the sight of oose on the carpet, the ironing board left out in the middle of the hall, iron still on it, no put away by whichever twin had been using it – and my intentions all fizzled away.

I put my heid round the living room door. Declan was clocked on the settee watching the twins, in full western gear with short skirts, bare legs, cowboy boots and Stetson hats, daeing their routine, twirling and birling as they had when they were wee. The stereo was blaring out a song about someone who'd lost his heart in a Kentucky farmyard and when it finished they collapsed in a heap on either side of Declan, giggling.

Declan was Mona's boyfriend. He wore a trackie of dazzling whiteness, spotlessly white trainers and a pastel coloured polo top wi a designer label. His baseball cap was at a perfect forty-five degree angle and covered a hairstyle so short it looked as if it had been trimmed wi a lawnmower. Mona had met him hinging about the swing park after school. I could never understaund how they'd got to the stage of gaun out cause I'd rarely heard Declan say mair than two words strung thegether. He spent a lot of time smiling admiringly at Mona and grunted when anyone else spoke to him. Although he was technically Mona's, Rona seemed to still be always with them; watching them thegether it was as if the twins were a couple and Declan the hanger-on.

Hi, I said.

Hiya.

I closed the door on them, went through tae my room. In the tiny space I threw mysel on the bed.

THE FIRST DAY of Art School sneaked up on me afore I knew it. I'd meant tae look for a flat or find out about residences but somehow never got round tae it, couldnae get my act thegether.

Da was already in the kitchen. *Want some toast, hen?*

If you're making it.

Usually the morning was a mad scrabble, a trail of crumbs and hauf-drunk mugs strewn across worksurfaces, but he'd set the table wi placemats and coasters, poured a glass of orange juice for me. Next tae my place was a wee package, wrapped in red shiny paper.

Marmalade?

No thanks, Da.

I opened the parcel. Inside was a pack of coloured pencils, the kind you get in Woolies when you're starting school.

He turned, put the plate in fronty me.

Seein it's your first day.

Thanks, Da.

Just a wee thing.

Thanks very much.

When I set off, the pencils were in my rucksack.

I loved being an art student. Loved carrying a portfolio under my airm, wearing paint-spattered jeans and above all walking up they steps every morning to a building designed by one of the greatest architects ever. I loved the ruggedness of it – like a fortress rooted intae that steep steep slope – counterpointed wi the delicate design features. I thought everybody would feel the same, but some folk in my class thought it was cool tae play doon the Mackintosh stuff, make light of the wee square glass panes in the door, the metalwork, the motifs they claimed had all been devalued, printed on teatowels and postcards.

My style was changing too. Insteid of baggy trousers I'd started to wear tighter jeans and I searched charity shops for floral dresses which I customised and wore over them. I tied scarves round my hair and clipped diamante earrings to the lapel of an auld velvet jacket. I was dead chuffed with mysel as I looked in the blotched mirror on the back of the door, getting ready to go out. The turquoise and green jewel colours made my hair look less drab and I'd even started slicking a bit of shiny eyeliner on my lids, using red lipgloss instead of Vaseline. The twins noticed the change with interest but just as much disapproval as they had for my usual look.

Christ, Fiona, you look like some auld hippy.

Check the bandana – you'll be gaun on a demo next.

* * *

136

Monica fingered the edge of my top. *Pretty*, she said. Monica had had her straight shiny dark hair cut in a neat bob and every article of clothing was perfectly clean, pressed and co-ordinated. Now she no longer wore school uniform, she'd adopted a kind of uniform of her ain choosing: white camisoles with neatly fitting pastel cardigans, blue denims and highly polished shoes. You could imagine her wearing a version of this for the rest of her life, daeing the school run in a 4x4, sitting in her office seeing patients. Monica had torn up all the leaflets on weird and wonderful careers and, with her straight A passes, was studying medicine. Her family, of course, bristled with joy. Jemma was back fae Edinburgh for the weekend, looking lovely, with streaks of pinky-gold layered through her hair. We were in Giardini's for the first time since term started.

So how is your course, Fiona?

Cool.

What do you do? Painting? Drawing?

A bit of that. We have classes but there's also a lot of time to develop your ain stuff.

Hang about in bars you mean. Jemma laughed. *Don't gie us that developing your art stuff. I've met loads of art students in Edinburgh and they're the ones that are at every party.*

And you've been in the house studying every night?

The first week was wild. Theresa O'Rourke fae St Phil's — she's in my hall and she was so drunk she fell downstair and broke her leg — had tae be carted aff to hospital. That'd be something, Mon — if your first case is one of your pals with a broken leg.

I don't think I'll get to see a patient for a long time. The first few years is all science, really.

Don't suppose you've been daeing much partying.

Monica smiled. *Not really.*

So apart from developing your art, how are things, Fiona? Are you still going with Amrik?

Jemma's phrase disturbed me. Going with seemed such an innocent way to put it, suggesting that we went on dates and he bought me flowers or sent me a Valentine's card.

We're still seeing each other.

It's just, I didnae know if I should mention it, but I met Jas.

Where?

We got the same train – there was something up wi the Aberdeen trains that day so he had to go via Edinburgh.

Is he enjoying the course?

Seemed to be – he'd only been there a week so I dunno really.

I havenae seen him since we broke up.

Monica looked at me seriously. *Do you really like Amrik, Fiona?*

Of course she does, why would she be with him?

No, I mean, does he make you happy?

It sounded simple. Do you really like him? Does he make you happy? A for Yes, B for No. Tick the box on the quiz in the magazine and work out if you should be with this person. And if you get all Bs, dump him.

It had seemed that simple with Jas at the beginning. Nae doubts. But then Amrik arrived; sweeping in like a force of nature, a great unstoppable wave destroying everything that had seemed so secure, forcing a new kind of reality. One that wasnae cosy, wasnae simple and suitable but somewhere underneath seemed like the only true kind.

But it wasnae just that. When Jemma conjured that picture in my heid – her and Jas sitting on a train thegether talking, just an ordinary day on an ordinary train, scabby seats and a scuffed table in fronty them, their carryout paper cups of coffee, Jas's face, eyes so like Amrik's but the mouth that different – it hurt.

I'd treated Jas so badly that I had tae make it work with Amrik. The only way to wipe out the shame was if something good and beautiful resulted fae my actions.

CHRIST KNOWS WHAT he must of been thinking. I was too much in shock to take in the look he gied me, the glance round the manky room. Deid flies stuck to the bottom of the curtains, oose clumped in corners of the room, Amrik, dishevelled and hauf-dressed.

Amrik had phoned the doctor when I started shaking and got the chills. I was so out of it I hardly registered what he was daeing but afterwards, when I remembered, I was amazed at how calm and insistent he was.

No we can't come in — she needs a doctor, here, now. It is an emergency.

It was like Jas, the way Jas would of done it, no like slow, casual Amrik at all. The one time I saw a brotherly resemblance between them.

Then, as he was haunding back my phone, the pain suddenly cracking my belly in two. Earlier I'd thought I was getting a bad cramp, noo I felt as if someone was tearing my insides out with a Hoover. I tried tae go to the bathroom and my legs wouldnae support me. Amrik put his airm round my waist and we both went.

I was too far gone tae be embarrassed at the flood of red all over my pants, the flair, the toilet seat. Even then, I was still thinking it was some terrible period, when a horrible big disgusting clot came out and there, swimming in a sea of gunk and blood and mess, was something that looked like a curled up wee prawn.

Our baby.

The nurse was dead nice in a matter-of-fact kind of way. Temperature taken, chart checked.

Are you in any pain, dear? Then away tae someone mair in need of attention. I didnae want attention. Just left alane.

The emergency doctor had wheeched me aff tae hospital to get checked up. *Best make sure it's all away,* he said.

I lay on the bed for what felt like ages till a young doctor, her fair hair tied in a pony tail, came and sat on the chair beside me.

Everything seems fine, she said. *No retained products.*
What?
Sometimes after a miscarriage little bits of the placenta can stay inside, cause an infection. Looks fine in your case, though.
Oh.
I'll just check a few details, then you can go home as soon as you feel up to moving. Now, when was your last period?
I'm no sure. They're not that regular.
Looked as if it was about eight weeks. Does that seem right?

Probably. I usually have them every four weeks but sometimes it's six weeks or a couple of months.

That's a pain, isn't it? Mine are like clockwork.

I always know it's about to start when the cramps come. That's what I thought was happening at first then it got so bad I couldnae speak.

So you weren't planning a pregnancy?

No. I'd nae idea I was.

What contraception were you using?

Condoms.

Any time your partner didn't use them?

No.

D'you ever notice one splitting?

No.

I know this has been a shock — not even knowing you were pregnant — but once you've had time to get over it, it's probably for the best.

I stared at her.

I mean if you weren't planning the baby. She looked at my notes. *I see you're a student. What're you studying?*

Art. First year at Art School.

That is so cool. I wish I was creative.

She scribbled something on the form, then stood up.

There's a counsellor in the hospital who talks to couples who've had a miscarriage. You could go along with your boyfriend if you like.

No. Thanks.

Well, if you feel like it later, you can come back. I'm Doctor Harrison. Trudi. Just give me a ring if you need to.

I thought he'd be waiting for me. Sitting there on a plastic seat, ready to put his airms round me, take me hame, wherever that was.

But he wasnae.

The nurse at the reception area saw me come out, look round.

Fiona?

I nodded.

Your friend said he had to go — he'll call you later.

Thanks.

He had to go.

Oh of course he did, his life is so full. Mibbe he had a rehearsal or a gig, or mibbe there was some wonderful tune that came intae his heid he just had to get out, inspired by being in a grotty bathroom with a woman screaming and pouring out blood. Perhaps the sight of his unborn child moved him that much he had to write a raga or a saga or whatever about it.

Or mibbe he just didnae care enough tae stay and wait for me.

I'd never felt so alone. When my mammy died, when my daddy set fire to the hoose, no then. There was always someone else to share the pain; the twins, Patrick, my da. Even when I thought they didnae understaund how I was feeling, at least someone else had experienced the same thing. But me and Amrik were the only folk who'd experienced this, except for a locum doctor who probably thought we were a couple of pathetic irresponsible tramps. Some silly lassie that never even knew she was pregnant till she tossed out the remains of her baby in a manky shared toilet in a grotty shared flat. I sat on the bed in my wee room, put my haunds over my eyes trying to block out the image of that mess.

I never tellt my da or the twins. Just said I wasnae feeling well and wanted to lie doon. I'd nae idea what time it was or how long I'd been lying there when Mona knocked on the door and asked if I wanted a cuppa tea.

Thanks.

She squeezed in the tiny space and set it doon on the bedside table. *I broke open the chocolate gingers since they're your favourite.*

Ta.

Hey what's up, sis? You look terrible.

I looked beyond the wall of make-up, the elaborate hairstyle, the short skirt and pierced belly button, and seen my wee sister who was genuinely worried aboot me. For a split second I nearly broke doon and tellt her everything, but something stopped me.

I'm all right. Must be some bug. I'll be fine if I have a rest.

Well, let me know if you need anything. But shout loud. We're watching 'Tom and Jerry'.

I drifted in and out of sleep as the sounds of cartoon music and the twins and Declan laughing floated through the thin walls. When my phone rang I'd lost all sense of time but the clock said it was 10.30 at night. Twelve hours since I'd been discharged.

Hi, Amrik said. *Are you at home now?*

Aye.

How are you feeling?

If you'd bothered to wait for me, you'd know.

They'd no idea how long you would be and they wouldn't let me on the ward to see you. I thought it was pointless to hang around.

Oh.

Silence.

D'you want to come over? Or should I come round?

Amrik had never been tae the house. Mibbe this was his way of showing it was important.

It's late.
I was at a gig.
Right.
I'll come round if you want.
Voice like honey and cigarettes.
No, I need to sleep now.
Cool. Talk to you tomorrow.

A night of tossing and turning, getting up to change my towel, soaked through with the reddest blood I'd ever seen. Fairy-tale blood like Snow White's pricked finger, but a flood of it. They said at the hospital I would bleed a little. Normal. No need to worry unless it continued for more than a few days.

I always thought medical folk used scientific words, precise delineations.

What's 'a little' blood?

What's 'normal'?

What's 'a few' days? Two? Three? Six?

You could bleed tae death and be carted aff, your dying words, *It was only a little blood for a few days. I thought it was normal.*

I rose early the next morning and started tae clean. First my room, folding up the camp bed and hoovering every inch of the flair, washing the windaes, clearing all the dust that had accumulated while I lived my nomadic existence between here and Amrik's room. I got a binbag and flung in wads of auld papers and school stuff, never stopped till the place was shining. Then I done the rest of the house, bleaching and scouring obsessively.

When I was finished I stood in the shower for ages, letting the water cascade over my heid, my body, every part of me.

I could feel the blood flow between my legs and when I looked doon there was a pinky trail in the bottom of the shower.

The pain started for real the next day. No as bad as the miscarriage but a dull throb and a feeling of unreality, as though my heid was stuffed with cotton wool. I thought I must of overdone it with the cleaning and lay on my bed in the room that now looked like a nun's cell, held a hot water bottle to my middle. I grew too hot, then started to shiver. I don't know how long I lay there afore Mona tapped on the door, pushed it open slightly.

Tea?

No thanks.

She moved a few steps intae the room, knelt doon and put her haund on my heid. *Hey. You're burning up. Whit's wrang?*

Dunno.

D'you want me to phone the doctor?

No. I'll get a cab.

I tried tae stand up. The room swam.

The young doctor with the fair hair was on duty again.

Sorry, she said.

What?

You know I said it was very unusual for an infection to develop afterwards. Well you were one of the unlucky ones.

Oh.

We're going to do a D&C just to be on the safe side.

What's that?

Don't worry, it's totally routine. A tiny scrape to make sure everything's away. And we'll put you on intravenous antibiotics till you settle down, then continue with an oral course. You'll be fit as a flea in a few days.

Do I have to stay here?

Till your temperature is down and you're stable. You'll probably get out later today.

Dreams of dead babies, flying through a grey fog. Bits of babies – airms and legs and heids all floating round by themselves, looking for the lost parts. When I was wee they used tae tell us about Limbo, that place between Heaven and Hell that the deid babies went, the ones who died afore they could be baptised, the ones that never got properly born. I didnae understaund what an unborn child was.

No one talked about miscarriages then. Did Mammy ever have a miscarriage? The gaps between us, five year between me and Patrick, four between me and the twins, then the big space afore the last . . . were they planned, or were there other babies inbetween that never made it through? The booklet they gied me at the hospital says it's important tae talk but who dae I talk to. The twins? My da? Mammy's the only one who could of understood what happened and, though I think of her every day, she feels further away than ever.

Amrik's the one I should talk with. The booklet says no tae underestimate the father's feelings, how some men are really traumatised but cannae face it, cannae talk about it.

Somehow I don't think Amrik is traumatised. If he feels anything it's relief. I've seen him three times since I came out the hospital. He's just the same as he ever was; there's nae special softness in his voice, he doesnae take my airm in a way that shows any recognition of what's happened. They said nae sex for a month in case of infection, so we went to the movies. Some French film about terrorists blowing up a factory. Then a walk in the park. One night he was playing and I sat in the audience, listening to perfect, beautiful, poignant notes emerge fae his sitar. Melancholy and uplifting at the same time. It's amazing how he puts so much heart intae it. Mibbe that's why he has nae heart left over for anything else.

The month was up but I hadnae said anything cause I was still confused about how I felt. But sitting next tae him at the pictures, his elbow on the armrest between us, I felt closer tae Amrik than I had for ages. It was as if something had been washed clean between us in the time of abstinence. There was an innocence about Amrik when he watched a movie that was never there any other time; he opened hissel like a wean lost in play.

Back at his flat, in the silence, bare boards and uncurtained windaes, freezing air. We dived beneath the bedcovers, grabbed each other. When Amrik reached for the pack of condoms on the table, I whispered, *It's cool* and pulled him back intae the warmth.

After, lying with his haunds linked behind his heid he said, *You sure the timing's okay?*

Aye.

Don't want any more accidents.

I'm gonnae go on the pill anyway. Saves all that hassle.

Oh?

Yeah, got an appointment tomorrow actually.

He pulled on his jeans and jumper, his haunds closed round the neck of his sitar.

Cool.

It was a lie, of course. So big a lie that afterwards I was amazed he seemed to believe me. I've never been good at lying, always stammer or look shifty. When we were wee and one of us had done something bad, I was the one the grown ups knew would tell them the truth, no because I'd clype, but because they could tell right away if I was lying. Mibbe he didnae believe me, just heard what he wanted to hear. That way he could satisfy hissel it wasnae his responsibility if anything went wrang.

It wasnae planned. I hadnae went round with the idea that I'd trick him intae getting me pregnant, just somehow that night the words came out. I had tae take a chance, see if it could happen again. It wasnae logical or rational. Like Doctor Trudi had said, really I was lucky. I was in nae position to bring a baby intae the world, especially wi a father who didnae want it, but somehow, my body couldnae bear no being pregnant. I walked about feeling empty, no emotional emptiness, but literal emptiness. Even though I'd never known I was pregnant in the first place, I felt as if I was missing something, that only a baby inside me would fill the awful gap.

The nice doctor tried tae get me to talk, made an appointment for the counsellor, but I never went. I'd work late at Art School then went hame tae my da's or else drifted to wherever Amrik was playing. He'd built up a big following in Glasgow by ths time. Never needed tae advertise, word of mouth meant that no matter how big or wee, how mainstream or out the way the venue was, loads of folk turned up.

At first the audience had mostly been male, often Asian, but as his music became better known, a mair mixed crowd started to squeeze its way intae the sweaty basements and smoky back rooms. Loads of women stood entranced by his playing and by him. Amrik was golden, a saffron halo fae the lights, his fingers producing a round sweet honey tone.

When the playing was over he was surrounded by people,

all wanting a piece of him, but after a while, after a few drinks, he'd make his way over to me, and we'd go back tae his place thegether. I knew it was stupid, but I couldnae help mysel. I was obsessed. No because I was in love with him, but because there was something physical that bound us thegether, something I hated and was disgusted by, but there. I didnae need much, but I needed the wee bits of him that I had.

PATRICK WAS NOW officially Patric. He announced this when he came up tae visit for the Christmas holidays. My da, of course, thought this was hysterical.

Jeezo, son, they'll think you cannae spell. Or you're foreign or somethin.

Patric seemed no the least bit bothered by my da's reaction, whereas even a year ago, he'd of flinched as if he'd been nipped by a wee bit of stone chipped up fae the road. I knew that look well in Patric. He always seemed calm, but you could tell when something upset him by that hauf-twitch at the corner of his mouth. I looked for it while my da was ranting, but it never came. Patric was totally relaxed, smiled as if it made nae difference to him what my da thought. Either he had changed a hell of a lot while he'd been in London, or mibbe it was my da who'd lost his power.

No that he'd ever been a macho man, but somehow since the fire and the drinking, he'd stopped being the da, the adult in the family, and become the one that needed looked after. And Patric, well he was different fae Patrick. No just the superficial stuff, like the clothes, made fae really good, expensive fabrics that were so soft to the touch it took your breath away when you hugged him. No just the fancy watch or the way he spoke, less broad and with an inflection that sounded like someone fae a New York sitcom. No just that he was staying in a hotel even though both my da and me had offered tae sleep on the couch and gie him wur rooms. Something that I couldnae put my finger on.

Efter he'd gone back to his hotel, I sat on my bed in the tiny room, downie round my shoulders. I knew it was stupid to expect him tae be the same old Patrick but everything else had changed that much, it was as if I was constantly at sea, rocking and moving up and doon with nae solid land beneath me. I'd never really thought about how much Patrick had been like that for me; he was the only one of the family who'd stayed the same – reliable, looking out for me. I knew Janice was too but it was different – she was my auntie, I hadnae grown up with her in the same hoose – and anyway, she had enough on her plate and I didnae want tae burden her with my problems.

Next day Patric took me out for a drink. Some trendy place doon Byres Road I'd never been in afore. When I asked for a hauf-pint of lager and lime he made a face. *Oh go mad, Fiona, have a cocktail, or a G&T or something.*

I never know what to drink. I never go tae pubs.

Well, I'll choose for you, will I?

152

He came back with cocktails in fancy glasses, paper parasols stuck in them.

Cheers.

I took a sip.

What d'you think?

Tastes like American Cream Soda — mind we used to get it as a treat?

I'd forgotten. What was in it anyway?

God knows.

So how are things?

So-so. Da seems a bit better. He's no drinking as much, the odd binge noo and again, but I think he's learned a lesson. He's working steady too. But he's no happy. I sipped the drink, sweet and sticky. *And the twins just dae what they like.*

I can see that. But what about you, Fiona?

How d'you mean?

You look awful.

Thanks.

I don't mean it like that. It's just, you look so tired, your hair needs washed, you look as if you put on the first thing that falls out the cupboard in the morning.

I've never been interested in clothes. No everybody's like you.

I don't expect you to be. It's internal. There's something inside you — it's like you don't care about yourself any more.

I wanted tae greet. I wanted to sit in the trendy bar with the cool barman who's really an actor in his spare time and all the beautiful people who look like Patric, and howl and howl till the snotters run doon my cheeks. But I never. I sat, twirling the parasol round and round the frosted glass.

I wanted tae tell Patric but the days went by and he returned tae London with nothing said. I felt as though Amrik had trapped me in a spider's web of shimmering notes, sticky and sweet and addictive. After the miscarriage the web had fragmented, but I still couldnae fight my way out of it entirely. And the desire for a baby, which had come upon me that suddenly, wouldnae go away, no matter how much I tried tae rationalise mysel out of it.

I did try. When I was working or reading a book or just lying in bed, I reminded mysel how impossible this would be if I had a baby to look after. Once I'd finished Art School, when I had a job or met someone else who had, that was the time to get pregnant.

But some nights, lying in my bed on the verge of sleep, it was as if I could sense deep inside my body, my ovaries and my womb longing for a baby. No me, no Fiona, the art student, but my body. And though on the surface the relationship between me and Amrik was casual, there was nothing casual about the way I checked my dates, made sure I seen him the times I thought I'd be most fertile, bought pregnancy tests at the chemist. But nothing happened.

IN JAS'S HOUSE was a box full of Barbie bits. They'd been stored there after the exams, because by then my house was an empty shell. When I'd moved out I left them, but I knew they'd still be there. Jas's ma is allergic to throwing anything out. Now I wanted them back, but dreaded gaun round tae collect them. I wasnae sure what she knew about me and Amrik but she'd know how much I'd hurt Jas by splitting fae him. I couldnae forgive mysel for that, so I could hardly expect his ma to forgive me. And I didnae want to run the risk of bumping intae Jas, hame fae Aberdeen.

But there was nothing else for it, so the next day I found mysel on her doorstep. When she opened the door, at first there was a look of shock, as if she'd just seen a dead person, then a hauf-smile.

Come in, Fiona.

I'm sorry to disturb you, Mrs Kaur.

You are always welcome, dear.

I stood looking doon at the doormat. It had a pattern of tulips, woven in brilliant colours of magenta, orange and green.

I left a box here and I'd like to take it back.

Come in, come in − do you know where it is?

I stepped inside hesitantly. *I think it's mibbe still in the room I . . . stayed in.*

Off you go and see, dear. I'll put the kettle on − you have time for a cup of tea?

The box was sitting where I'd left it in the wardrobe. The room felt quiet, as if it was waiting for someone to come and stay in it and, for a moment, I wished it was me.

In the kitchen there were mugs of tea and chocolate biscuits piled high on the plate.

So dear, how are things. How is your daddy?

I don't know, really. He doesnae say much.

That is to be expected. It is hard, very hard, for him. Tell him to come round and visit. He could come to the Scrabble club with me.

Aye.

I mean it. He and I have things in common, being on our own. But I have had time to get used to it.

Right, I'll tell him.

And your little sisters?

No so little. Mona has a boyfriend now.

And is he a nice boy?

I sipped my tea. It was too hot and I felt it burn my throat. I had tae think for a minute. With his trackies and baseball cap he was just no my type, it was as if he came fae another planet. Rona was right. I was a snob.

Aye, he is, I said. *He's a very nice boy.*

Over the next few weeks I worked and worked and worked with the doll parts, tried everything. Taking photies of them, painting them, arranging and rearranging them in every way possible.

Obvious: A papier-mâché womb with the parts spilling out, covered in red paint.

Subtle: Ghostly grey nets with bits hanging from wires. Barbie Limbo.

The tutor quite liked that one.

As far as I was concerned, it was all crap.

The one good thing was that it kept me occupied. As long as I could obsess over bits of plastic dolls I didnae have tae think about the bits of real baby that had come out of me. Spent every moment possible at the Art School, thrown out by the jannie when he was closing up. No that that was unusual, there were a lot of us obsessives there. Nuala with her beads, tiny ones she laid in delicate roads, interwoven with wee poems, James with his video installations about pandas – though they were in fourth year, clear on their path, their way of daeing things. Maist of the other first year were out partying and when they were working they were playing too, trying different forms and ideas. But mainly drinking, gaun to the movies and talking, talking, endlessly talking about art, about their art.

No me. Why talk about it if everything you tried to dae was crap? Mibbe afterwards, mibbe you could analyse it then, but what was the point in having an explanation for something incomplete, hauf-finished, something that made nae sense?

* * *

Hauf-term arrived and the jannie came round tae chuck the sad obsessives out.

Come on, noo, some of us have got hames to go tae.

Sorry, I'll just be a minute. I knew I couldnae move all my stuff but I flung some paper and pencils in my bag. Mibbe I could dae a few sketches over the long weekend. *When does Art School open again?*

Tuesday morning, nine o'clock. Jeezo, hen, you're a teenager — could you no go out clubbing or somethin?

Da was sitting at the kitchen table wi a dictionary and a bit of paper, writing a list. I looked over his shoulder.

zo, zho, dzo – Tibetan breed of cattle, cross between common cattle and yak

zebu – domesticated ox with humped back, long ears and large dewlap

What you daeing, Da?

It's this Scrabble, hen. They all know these mad words tae use up your letters.

Did you go to the club with Mrs Kaur then?

Aye, it was brilliant. But ah feel like a right numpty. That's how ah'm tryin tae swot up a bit afore Monday.

It's good, but. Gets you out the house.

Gets yer brain workin and all.

Use it or lose it.

Aye. Hey, did you know that en and em are terms used in printing? Dead handy for wee odd spaces on the board.

Cool.

Over the weekend I tried a few drawings but it was useless. Released fae their place in the artwork, the babies began to invade my dreams and I'd wake, lashing with sweat, the pillow twisted and out its case fae God knows how much tossing and turning, chased by babies. Babies dropped fae multistorey buildings, smashed intae brick walls, drowning in glue seas.

I dialled the number Dr Harrison had given me.

She took me intae a wee office, like a cupboard under the stair. Her hair was shorter, blonder.

Thanks for seeing me, Doctor.

It's fine, Fiona. Now, what's the trouble?

I don't know, it's daft.

Anything that worries you isn't daft. Are your periods normal?

Normal for me.

Good. Any unusual symptoms?

No.

So it's more emotional?

I nodded.

Miscarriage is a bereavement, Fiona. You have to grieve.

It's just . . . I cannae get the idea of having a baby out my mind. I know it's daft but I really want to be pregnant again. It's as if nothing else will make me complete.

Are you having sex at the moment?

Yes.

Using protection?

No. That was another thing I wanted tae ask you. Could the miscarriage affect my fertility?

Absolutely not. Listen, Fiona, you need to get clear. If you let your heart rule your head you will end up pregnant and I honestly don't think this is what you want or need just now. She turned to the computer. *I think I should make you an appointment with the counsellor.*

I don't want one.

159

Women find it really helps to talk to someone who's experienced the same thing.

I shook my heid.

Fiona, there's plenty of time for you to have a baby. She put her haund on my airm. *Just give yourself time.*

That didnae stop me going to Amrik's flat that night. It looked emptier than usual; between the drifts of clothing and debris you could even glimpse patches of bare floor.

Tidying up?

Amrik smiled. *Getting rid of things. I think I'm gonna split soon.*

What — go back to London?

Aye. If there's anything you want, just take it.

I couldnae help laughing. *I don't think your stuff would be much use to me.*

That night we made love with a fierceness and passion I hadnae felt for a long time. I knew it might be the last time, my last chance. Lying in the dark, Amrik beside me, I felt a tenderness towards him that I never felt when he was awake. Three days later, when I went round to the flat, he was gone.

Three weeks later, I peed on the test I had unwrapped fae its plastic. It said on the instructions to dae it for five seconds but I left at least ten afore setting the test on the shelf and waiting, my eyes hauf on the test and hauf on the minutes passing on my phone. The red colour seeped through the windae.

'If, after four minutes, the red line remains in the box, you are pregnant.'

The red faded tae pink, then washed away tae nothing.

MONA'S EXPECTIN.

Rona planted a cuppa tea in fronty ma da just as he shouted, *Immoral.*

That's a bit heavy, Da.

Immoral — it's the only seven-letter word you can get fae they letters. God, that was hard.

Da — I'm trying tae tell you somethin.

Well tell me after 'Countdown''s finished. Ah don't try tae tell you things when they daft cartoons are on.

Da, it's important.

He reached for the remote, turned doon the volume, his eyes still on the screen.

Whit is it, hen?

Mona's expectin.

161

Whit, a baby?

Naw, Da, a horse. Of course, a baby.

Jeezo, when?

September.

Christ.

Is that all you've got tae say, Da?

What d'you expect me tae say? She's barely fifteen year auld. If yer mammy was here.

Well, she's no.

Aye she's no. If she was this'd never of happened. Fiona, what're we gonnae dae?

I managed tae get Rona on her ain in the kitchen. *What the hell's gaun on? How come Mona couldnae tell him hersel?*

She couldnae.

Could you no have tellt me first — mibbe we could of broken it to him gently?

Just thought I'd get it over quicker when yous're baith here. Anyway, you're hardly ever around. And when you are you're stuck in that room, moonin over yer art stuff.

She was right of course. A crap sister, how come I hadnae seen what was so obviously gonnae happen.

Anyway, where is Mona?

Out with Declan, shopping.

By the time Mona came hame Da had went out. I hoped it wasnae tae the pub, all we needed noo was for him tae start drinking again. And I done my sensible big sister act, all the while wondering how I could be such a total hypocrite after what I'd done mysel.

How could you dae this, Mona?

Same way everybody does.

162

Don't be like that — could you no have used contraceptives?

Pope says you shouldnae.

Pope says you shouldnae be having sex. Mona, you're only fifteen. And so's Declan. Yous're still at school.

No for long. Anyway, ah hate school.

That's no the point.

So what is the point, Fiona? You tell me — what is the point?

I'm just trying tae get you to be serious about this.

You're trying tae get me to be serious? Ah'm the one that's pregnant. Ah'm the one gettin the morning sickness. Ah'm the one that's gonnae have the baby and look after it.

Aye but will you, Mona? You couldnae look after a cat you're so bloody irresponsible. A baby would get in the way of your beauty routines and your cartoon watching and your line dancing.

You're so fucking smug and superior, Fiona, always have been. What d'you take responsibility for round here? You just come and go whenever it suits you and moan at everyone else for no keeping the place as tidy as you like it. And who are you to look doon on me for line dancing? How come chuckin bits of auld dolls about is mair important than dancing? Me and Rona are the Glasgow and West of Scotland under-16 champions. But to you that's nothing compared to all your artyfarty friends. If we were bloody ballet dancers it'd be different.

She stomped out the kitchen and slammed the living room door. A few minutes later I heard the familiar opening tune of *Tom and Jerry*.

Between the school, the social worker and the ante-natal classes, Mona's pregnancy took up a lot of time. Da, of course, copped out, so I talked to the Guidance teacher about Mona's exams, took Mona tae her checkups and made cups of tea for Miss Starkey, who came tae inspect the flat and decide if it was a suitable environment to bring up this wean. I couldnae figure out how someone who looked about twelve was qualified to know, but she ticked lots of boxes on her form and nodded sympathetically when my da, eyes filling with tears, sais, *If only her mammy was here.*

I bit my tongue. I wanted to say if her mammy had been here this wouldnae of happened, but what was the use. Mona seemed to be neither up nor doon about being pregnant. As the weeks progressed the gap between her microscopic skirt and her crop top got bigger but she rejected all Janice's attempts tae pass on her auld maternity clothes. *Gross,* she said, tossing them back in the plastic bag. The only preparations for pregnancy she seemed tae make was eating mair crisps than usual and wandering round the toon looking at baby clothes with Rona and Declan.

On one of her visits Miss Starkey followed me intae the kitchen where I was making the tea. *Just wanted a quiet word. D'you think Mona is in denial?*

Through in the living room, Mona, Rona and Declan were clocked on the couch, roaring and giggling while Tom chased Jerry round the screen. Mona was bigger noo and had started tae wear longer stretchy tee shirts which clung tae her bump.

What makes you think that?

The doctor had gied me a booklet about miscarriage and there was a section called 'Emotional Effects'. Talked about how the couple had experienced the joy of achieving a pregnancy and anticipating the arrival of a baby. Hardly.

There was a list of all the emotions you might feel. Grief, inadequacy, failure, helplessness, guilt. Tick, tick, tick them all.

Then the green-eyed monster. How you might feel upset

at the sight of pregnant women in the street, TV programmes about babies. Doesnae mention looking at your sister's scan photie, seeing the blurred image of something that looked like a wee monkey staring out at you. Our baby would of been born sometime in May – around the 20th by the doctor's estimate. The book said that the due date was often a diffi-cult time for the couple and it might help to mark it in some way. The couple, of course, would be supporting each other in their grief.

I hadnae heard a word fae Amrik since he'd went tae London. I didnae miss him, no the normal way you miss someone when they're away, like I miss Patric – daeing things thegether, the stuff we'd talk about. What I really missed was the times I'd stood in the darkness at the back of a room, listening to something that moved me beyond everything else.

I'd got used tae seeing Mrs Kaur's blue mini parked outside the house on Wednesdays. The Scrabble club met at the commu-nity centre on Mondays, and a small group played at her house on Fridays but that wasnae enough for my da so Mrs Kaur'd taken to coming round tae ours. Sometimes she was by hersel and sometimes she brung Mrs Grant, a large lady whose hair was a different colour every time you seen her.

The Wednesdays seemed to be a kind of tutorial for my da. They set up camp in the kitchen while the twins and Declan watched DVDs in the living room. When I got back fae Art School I'd make tea for them. Usually they'd be discussing tactics or suggesting how my da could use his letters.

See, Mr O'Connell, if you place 'perish' here, you can make 'he' with the first letter of 'exhale' and also make 'dam' into 'damp'. And you'd get an extra 7 . . . 9 . . . 14 points.

Ah'd never of thought of that.

It's just practice.

Maist of the time they were that absorbed in what they were daeing they never seemed tae notice me floating in and out the room. When Mrs Grant wasnae there, I'd overhear the odd shred of conversation that wasnae about Scrabble.

Is Mona keeping well?

Aye, she's grand. He sighed. *Ach. I just wish . . . if they could of just waited.*

It is difficult sometimes, the young ones. You bring them up with religion, values, hope that will see them through, but the world is very different nowadays.

You're right there. How's yours gettin on?

Amrik — how would I know? He calls me every now and again, tells me he's fine. Jaswinder, of course, is a good boy. I don't worry about him as much as his brother. But that Aberdeen — it's freezing. And I don't know if he is really happy there.

She swopped her letters round on the rack, frowning.

Does he no like the course?

At first I thought it would be good for him to get away. But now I am not so sure. At least you have your daughters round you, Mr O'Connell. That is a comfort.

MAY WAS THE hottest on record for twenty years. Workers escaped at lunchtime fae offices and shops – all they needed was a wall tae perch on or a hankysized bit of grass and there they were with sandwiches or ice-creams, faces turnt tae the heat. Mona and Rona dogged school in the afternoons and went tae the park where students lay wi their books over their faces, kidding on they were studying. Folk smiled at you in the street. Everyone was happy, making the maist of it.

Except me. I spent the whole of May in a high-windaed room in the Art School, working on my end of term piece. There was nae way I could of worked at hame; even without the chaos of the twins and my da, I needed space. In my mind I'd a kind of hauf-vision, ideas and images floating about, and

I tried different ways to put them thegether. I'd cut out photies of pregnant so-called celebrities fae the twins' magazines. Some were tasteful posed shots, on the beach with a fading sunset silhouetting the bump; others, less tastefully, slumped on deck-chairs with unshaven oxters exposed, a peelywally bump like a beer belly. I thought about making a collage wi them but it seemed too obvious. I still had all the Barbie bits but I didnae know what to dae with them either. And I'd a pile of nappies, real cloth wans I'd got fae Janice. They were meant for Mona, but I didnae think she'd be that ecologically aware, and anyhow, I could gie them back later.

Then there were the pregnancy tests. All basically the same, an absorbent bit you pee on and a windae that tells you if you're pregnant. But some have two windaes, others three, some have the control windae on the left, others the right, some are pink and some blue. I took them out the box and counted them. Seven. A nice biblical number but no enough. What would it be like if you had tae try for years like some women? They were expensive – did they buy a job lot on the internet? I'd probably need at least another six tae finish what I had in mind, and my student discount at the Art Store wasnae a whole lot of use. I put my stuff in my locker and heided aff tae Savers.

In the windae was a poster that screamed in big letters, 'May 20th – Red Letter Day – 20 percent off all stock today'. I'd been so caught up in what I was daeing that I'd never realised the date. As I filled my basket with pregnancy tests and walked to the checkout, I felt ridiculous. I wanted tae take them and chuck them all over the shop, gie them out tae folk in the street, saying *Have a nice day*.

After I'd paid, instead of going back to the Art School, I heided round the corner to where there's a big red brick chapel. Inside was dark and cool, empty apart fae a couple of auld wifies wi rosaries. I walked round the outer aisles which had wee chapels placed at intervals. Elaborately carved, tacky, auld-fashioned statues of saints raising their eyes heavenwards – intended as an expression of piety nae doubt but they looked as if somebody had farted in their presence. Eventually I came tae one of St Francis of Assisi, dressed in brown robes, thin haund wi bones sticking out, raised in blessing. A softer face with sad eyes looking straight at me. I put twenty pence in the metal slot, opened the Ikea poly bag of tealights and lit one, as slowly and thoughtfully as I could. I knelt on the hard marble step in fronty the statue and looked at the face of the saint, then intae the candle-flame. I tried tae imagine what this day might of been like if things had been different, envisaged mysel haudin a baby in my airms, surrounded by my family. I could see them all clearly: Da, Mona and Rona, Patric and Janice. The only face I couldnae visualise was Amrik's. He just wasnae there. And neither was the baby. I could see the sleepsuit, the shawl, feel the weight in my airms but couldnae make out a face, imagine its eyes or nose or mouth. I knelt for ages, no praying, just visualising the scene. I wisht I could of cried, but felt empty, no the physical emptiness of longing for a baby – a different kind of emptiness.

A green plastic washing line pegged out with photies of pregnant celebrities, interspersed with nappies on which were scribbled in blue or pink felties, 'It's a boy' or 'It's a girl'. The nappy in the centre had two scrawls side by side, 'It's a bo . . .' and 'It's a gi . . .', the words trailing aff intae a drip as though the pens had given out. Under the washing line, on its side, was a bucket with nappies, bits of Barbies and auld pregnancy tests spilling out. Some of the Barbies had the flexible bits of the tests, the bits you pee on, stuck in their mouths or between their legs. I'd knitted wee hats for the dolls, like the kind premature babies get, but left the knitting tae unravel so there was a tangle of pastel wool all over the flair. Inbetween the bits of doll, wool and tests I'd spilled talc, scattered torn-up vouchers for baby products and instruction leaflets for pregnancy tests.

The title was 'Oh Yes You Are, Oh No You're Not'.

I deliberately didnae tell my da or the twins the dates of the show, but of course Janice always knows these things and mentioned it when she was round, trying yet again to get Mona to take some of her baby things.

I don't want anythin till after the baby's born. It's bad luck.

Suit yourself. But there's a Moses basket and a baby sling all waiting for you.

A baby sling? I'm no using wanny them. I want a pram. A real pram, no a buggy.

You'll need a pram too. But a sling's dead handy for carrying the baby round with you — even in the house when they're girny.

Mona gied Janice wanny her 'in your dreams' looks and returned to the article she was reading, about being a sun goddess.

Janice turned tae me. *I thought I'd go and see your show on Thursday after work, Fiona.*

Is it this week, hen? said my da. *You never tellt us.*

Mibbe we could all go on Thursday, said Janice. *It's late-night shopping. We could see the show, then Mona and me could go and get a few things for the baby. Then we can go for a pizza.* At the words pizza, Mona smiled.

* * *

Janice called the day after the show.

Got time for a coffee, Fiona? I'm in town on a course today and I'll be finished about four. Meet you in Giardini's?

Cool.

How was your course?

Janice made a face. *Boring, they always are. And then when you go back to work things've piled up on your desk. Still, it's nice to get a day in town, specially on a Friday.*

I nodded, stirred the froth on the top of my coffee, wondered when she was gonnae say what she'd brought me here for. Janice was so like my mammy sometimes. She had this way of starting softly, as if she was spreading rose petals for you to walk over, then two sentences in, she shoved the whole lot out the way and the path was clear for the real issue.

Fiona, your installation, your work . . .

Yeah.

You're an artist and I'm not . . .

rose petals, smooth as silk

and I don't mean to draw simplistic parallels between a work of art and the artist's life.

the scent rising, the smoothness caressing your feet.

But

one toe touches hard gravel

Deep breath. Those eyes, brown like my mammy's, turn to me.

Mona's baby is really getting to you, isn't it, Fiona?

jaggy sharpness spikes the soles.

I don't like to analyse my work.

I'm sorry, Fiona. I really don't want to invade your privacy, but I felt very disturbed by it. And I know that's what you meant and good art is disturbing and all that, but it wasnae the art that disturbed me. It was what I felt from you.

I didnae know what tae say. As usual. My life seemed to be full of folk wanting me to say things, talk about my feelings. Nice, kind, sensible folk. The doctor, Janice. If I wanted, the nae-doubt nice, kind sensible counsellor.

I was lucky. This is what they keep telling you is good. Talk. Let it out. Every time there's a disaster or an accident they get teams of counsellors on the job, letting folk talk about it. That was what was so bad about the auld days, they say. After the war all these men who came back, never able to talk about it. Stiff upper lips. And that leads tae all kinds of trauma.

I wish I'd lived then — no I don't mean that — it's just, I don't want tae talk.

Janice is looking at me, kind sensible Janice, who's known me since I was born, who loves me, loved Mammy, who's trained tae understaund these things. Christ if I was one of her clients, nae doubt I'd be pouring out my soul. But here I am, sitting in a café, spooning the remains of the froth intae my mouth, unable to say a word about anything that matters.

Look, if you don't want to talk about it, that's fine. Or mibbe you'd rather talk to someone outside the family. But please, Fiona, if you ever do, you know I'm always here for you.

I know.

Declan had got a book of baby names out the library and he and the twins were falling about laughing over it.

How about Boniface?

If it takes after its ma it'll be moanyface.

Very funny.

Hey Fiona, guess what your name means? Comely, fair.

Aye, right. What are you thinking about calling the baby anyway?

172

If it's a boy, Connor, and if it's a wee lassie either Siobhan or Grace.

I hope it's a girl, then. Connor O'Connell?

The baby's name won't be O'Connell — it'll be Connor Anderson.

You don't have to give the baby Declan's name.

He's the father. You're no gonnae gie us wanny they feminist rants, are you Fiona? I've heard it all fae Janice.

Well, it's true. It's dead sexist that folk assume a baby has to have the father's name.

Yeah and look at Janice's poor wean wi a double-barrelled surname naebody can spell.

You could give the baby your name.

My name'll be the same as Declan's soon enough.

You're changing your name tae Declan's?

We'll be gettin married.

You still don't have tae change your name. Anyway, you're no even sixteen.

I will be in December.

You're no serious, Mona.

Course. Once the baby's born and I'm sixteen, we'll get hitched. A lovely white wedding and I'll be Mrs Declan Anderson. It's nice tae be traditional.

I don't want to shatter your illusions, but it's traditional tae wait till after the white wedding afore you have the baby.

After they went out I sat doon on the settee. They'd left the book of baby names lying, spine bent backwards. I started tae flick through, no really expecting to find it, but there was a section on Asian names. Amrik: God's nectar. That figured. Sweet as honey. But don't try tae live on it.

THE ENVELOPE HAD a plastic windae that the name and address were supposed tae show through. I don't know why they use them for something important like results – hauf the time the letter moves inside the envelope so you don't know who it's for. I was lucky I got it at all – takes our postie all his time to deliver mail which has the exact name, address, flat number and postcode typed on it in enormous letters. Anything the least bit dubious gets left in the close or delivered to the empty flat on the ground floor, presumably cause they don't complain. The guy lives with his girlfriend and just comes round every three month tae check on the place; it's like Christmas when he appears with a pile of letters that have been lying on his mat all that time. I did try tae complain but the postie tellt me he was dyslexic so

174

he fitted the Post Office's commitment to taking on people with a disability.

Anyway, it did get here and not only were the results As all round but there was a letter telling me I'd won a special prize, the chance tae get my work exhibited in a trendy London gallery.

When I phoned Patric, he was over the moon.

You're kidding, Fiona. That is so cool.

It's just a wee exhibition of work by students fae different art schools. I mean it is great but.

It is, Fi.

So can I stay with you then?

Of course – look, why don't you come and stay for a few weeks? I have to work but there's loads you can do on your own during the day and I'll be around in the evening to show you about. It'll be fab.

Patric had flitted again, this time tae a grand apartment building in Bloomsbury – I guessed it must be worth a fortune. He rented it from a friend of a friend. This seemed to be how things worked doon here; someone like Patric, who kept everything that neat and perfect, was in demand fae all these folk who had spare property lying around while they lived abroad or went off on endless business trips. Justin, the friend of a friend, still used a bedroom in the flat but was only there about three or four days every few months and Patric wasnae expecting him till September.

I don't like to use Justin's room, so I'll sleep on the couch – it folds down into a bed. You can have my room.

I can sleep on the couch.

No you won't.

It's a hassle for you.

I've already moved some clothes to a cupboard in the hall. Honest, Fi, it's easier this way. I'll be getting up for work and you may want some long lies after all the partying we'll be doing. I thought we'd have a quiet night in tonight but, break you in gently.

Patric cooked a lovely dinner which we ate in the dining room. There was a table in the kitchen, but the flat had a proper dining room too, with retro wallpaper and modern silver candlesticks. The table was set with a runner in the middle and fresh flowers, artistically arranged.

This is amazing, I said. *It's like a restaurant.*

Patric smiled.

You don't live like this all the time but, do you? Don't you ever flop on the couch and eat something fae the microwave?

Patric lifted his wine glass, twirled it round for a moment and looked at me seriously. *You know, Fiona, I don't.*

I waited for him to go on.

I reckon that's what life is about. Having the best. No just the most expensive, though usually if something's good it is expensive. But having beautiful things round you, wearing good clothes, having your hair cut properly, manicuring your nails.

Some folk cannae afford all that.

I know, Fiona — and I never forget how things were when we were wee. But I remember, even when we didnae have much money, Mammy always got us leather shoes, measured properly. And we always had good home-cooked food.

I thought of the way things were at hame noo, the freezer filled with ready meals, the twins' plastic trinkets littering the house.

And it's about looking after what you've got — nae use having silver candlesticks if you don't polish them. Anyway, let's drink a toast — to your show. Success.

*   *   *

176

Next morning it took me three buses tae get to the gallery. Patric gied me directions for the tube but I hate the London underground. Hate being underground at all, only cope with the Glasgow subway cause it's so wee – even if you go the whole way round in a circle it only takes hauf an hour. But the thought of all they vast subterranean tunnels, the clunky escalators and great waves of folk who always seem to be gaun in the opposite direction, just does my heid in. The buses in London are nice; the stops tell you the destination and how long it'll be till the next one, and with my day pass I could hop on and off as much as I liked. I sat with my wee streetmap, following the route. All the streets you've heard of even though you've never been here.

The gallery was in the east end, which, according to Patric, was the place for the mair avant-garde stuff; the exciting trendy parties and media openings were all out here. It didnae look that edgy to me, too clean and neat by hauf, freshly painted wi big windaes and a fluorescent sign. The street was clean too – nae litter, nae dodgy-looking folk. Obviously cutting edge in London was a bit mair gentrified than in Glasgow.

I hadnae expected to be welcomed with open airms – they're mair used tae dealing with Tracey Emin than some peelywally art student fae the frozen north – but the bored-looking lassie glued to the phone never even said hello, just nodded me in the direction of the gallery. Took me ages tae find the box with my stuff in it, stuck in a corner at the back under a pile of junk, but nothing was damaged and I spent ages getting the piece ready. The space wasnae as good as the one I'd had for the show at hame. All the students' work was in this wee room at the back of the gallery, and the areas werenae marked out properly. One other exhibit was up –

looked like trees made out of bits of broken glass – but there was naebody else there. When I finished I went and stood at the desk till the bored girl eventually turned, put the phone against her breast as if it was a baby, and said, *Can I help you?*

Just tae say I've finished.

Cool. She returned tae her conversation.

The heat hit me as soon as I left the air-conditioned building. City heat, trapped in the grey tarmac of the pavements, intensified, multiplied by buildings all squashed thegether till it became almost unbearable. I was wearing a pair of cotton trousers and a long-sleeved shirt but the skin on my wrists and my cheeks started tae burn afore I'd got the length of the street. It was two o'clock and the pavements were crowded; it felt as if everyone was outside pubs, drinking. I had tae weave on and off the pavement to get by them, hearing fragments of conversations and peals of laughter. Everyone here looks that confident in their summer city clothes, with their mobiles and sunglasses, as if they belong. At hame when it's sunny folk havenae a clue what tae wear, they put on shorts and tops meant for the beach and roll up their tee shirts. But people in London actually have summer clothes for work, wear the kind of clothes you see in magazines and think are ridiculous – city shorts, dresses with tulip-shaped skirts.

I was parched. The bottle of water I'd brought with me was finished and I bought another at a stall. Leaning on a wall outside a hairdressers tae drink it, I smelled the fruity scent of conditioner and shampoo wafting fae the open door. I swigged the last of the water and set off towards the bus stop.

* * *

I know it was really stupid but in quiet moments I'd fanta-
sised about the night of the launch – important folk seeing
my work and being dead impressed, the gallery signing me
up and asking me to dae a show when I left Art School. On
the train yesterday, sitting spread out with my coffee and my
paper, looking out the windae as the green fields sped by,
watching the changes in architecture as we came further south
– the back to back houses of the north, the red brick estates
of the south – I'd felt free, as if the edges of who I was had
started tae blur, possibilities opening up. In the imaginary
story running in my heid as the train tracks rushed past, I
was scrubbed clean of all the messy stuff.

Standing, legs aching, squashed inside a crowd of braying folk
who neither knew nor cared who I was, who never even made
it intae the room which contained the art students' exhibits,
but stayed in the main part of the gallery with the work of the
big boys and girls, mair interested in the canapés and the conversation than they were in art. One guy in a navy-blue suit with
a chin like Desperate Dan shoved his prawn wonton in my face
as he gestured round the walls. *So, you an art lover, then?*

Art student.

St Martins?

Glasgow.

Oh, Glasgow, he said, stuffing the pastry in his mouth in a
oner. *I've heard it's a very sexy city.*

I didnae know what to say but couldnae move away.

So what brings you here?

I've an installation in the other room.

*Is there another room? I came with my sister, she's into art and
all that. I'm just here for the bubbly. Still, I must go and look at
your . . . installation. Is it in the catalogue?*

Dunno. Obviously they kept them for the visitors.

He thrust it intae my haund and I turned the glossy illustrated pages till I found the place. Nae photies, just a list: Title, Art School, Artist.

I ran my finger doon the page. *Here it is – 'Oh Yes You Are, Oh No You're Not'.*

He looked. *Fun title. Pleased to meet you, Fiona O'Connor.*

O'Connell.

My eyesight's getting worse. He squinted. *Nope – look.*

Sure enough, in black and white – Fiona O'Connor. They'd got my name wrang. As the guy left, Patric fought his way back, thrust a drink in my hand. *The fizz has run out, I'm afraid, it's just ordinary wine.*

I took a sip; it tasted flat and dull.

Patric was great, done everything he could to gie me a good time. Lined up dinners, theatre trips, visits tae trendy bars and God knows what, paid for everything. Any normal poverty-stricken student fae the sticks would of been in seventh heaven but I dragged mysel through it.

I had the days to mysel. The first three I spent gaun round galleries; after all, seeing some art would make my trip worthwhile. I checked out all the exhibitions in *Time Out*, drew up a list and set off: Old Masters, photography, sculpture.

At least it gied me something tae talk about at night. Patric and me were rarely alone and hardly ever spent an evening wi the same folk. One night we went tae a Channel 4 party where the waiters were dressed as devils; we drank margaritas and ate food fae an enormous flaming barbecue with 'Abandon hope all ye who enter here' printed across it in red letters. Everyone we met was either a journalist or a director of documentaries. Another night we had dinner with a group of designers and architects in some new restaurant that had opened on a houseboat. Jack and Melissa were married and she was expecting her first baby, Owen and Simon ran a business thegether and wore matching rings.

They were all really nice, but I felt like a six-year-old allowed to stay up late with the grown ups. No their fault. As we nibbled delicious appetisers, I sipped the lovely wine, looked round the picturesque boat with the hanging baskets of summer flowers, felt the slight sway of water beneath us and a fresh warm breeze on my cheek.

Isn't this perfect? said Owen, squeezing my haund. *It's so lovely to meet you at last, Fiona. Patric is always talking about you.*

I looked across at Patric. Lightly suntanned, in a blue linen shirt and expensive watch, he was laughing and his smile was perfect. Patric always had nice teeth but he'd now had the back ones veneered so nae matter how widely he smiled all you could see was a wall of white. The only thing that looked the same as when he was young was his neat fair hair, seemingly unchanged since he was seventeen.

Patric and I used to be an item, Owen confided.

I looked at Simon, head bowed in conversation with Melissa. *Doesn't that make things a bit . . . awkward?*

Oh no, Owen laughed. *It was the most amicable break imaginable. Patric and I both knew it was, you know, as the divine Cole says, just one of those things. And when I met Simon, well, he's the one. But I always think it's so important to keep one's friends. Lovers may come and go — I mean don't get me wrong, Simon and I are absolutely rocksolid and all that — but friendship is what really counts. And we just adore Patric.*

He raised his glass and caught Patric's eye. Patric raised his and looked across at the two of us, smiling his lovely white smile.

*   *   *

181

On the third day I went tae the National Portrait Gallery to see the painting of Emily by her brother. It was in a room with lots of other pictures of Victorian writers, like Dickens and Elizabeth Barrett Browning but they were all professional portraits, formal and highly finished, while hers was a scabby remnant fae a lost canvas. The image was that familiar, fae the paperweight, the postcard, the cover of the biography, but I felt shivery when I seen it in the flesh. It was a lot smaller than I'd expected, the paint cracked and peeling, and I didnae believe the way he'd made the line of her neck that perfect, her dress hingin aff her shoulders. The auld da would hardly of let his daughters sit like that. I mind being fascinated by the picture when I was about thirteen and in the first flush of my obsession with Emily. I thought it was dead poetic tae sit in profile, gazing out the picture, contemplating the vision fae your muse, that you alone could see. I even tried tae practise that pose, using two mirrors to see my profile, pulling my tee shirt aff my shoulder. I mind Mammy coming in when I was daeing it – I was dead embarrassed but she never even laughed, just smiled and put her airm round me. Noo I seen the picture for what it was – her brother's vision of a romantic portrait, rather than a real picture of his sister.

I bought a poster of the painting in the gift shop, showed it tae Patric when I got back to the flat.

I don't think he wanted tae paint them – just didnae have any other models while he was learning.

Patric scanned the reproduction. *It's dead romantic, isn't it? Just how you'd imagine her.* He rolled it up and started to replace it in the cardboard tube. *So did Branwell ever make it as an artist?*

Naa. They wanted him to go to the Art School in London but he never even went to the interview or whatever it was then. Chickened out and crawled back hame with his tail between his legs. Then they set him up in a studio somewhere — they thought cause he was the boy he'd make something of hissel, but of course he never.

I was due tae stay for two weeks but haufway through the first I was desperate tae get back hame and managed to change my ticket for Saturday. Patric tried to persuade me tae stay but eventually gave in.

We'll just need to make sure your last night's a good one. Lionel and Clara always know the coolest places — we'll get a crowd together.

I thought about arguing with him but kept my mouth shut. Why bother if it made him happy. Soon I'd be away on the train, back to my boring routine life in Glasgow. I never needed to go out the house again if I didnae want.

I couldnae be bothered traipsing round galleries any mair. After the late nights I'd sleep in till eleven or twelve o'clock, pick at some leftover food fae the always well-stocked fridge and wander about the hoose, unable tae settle to anything. Eventually the sunshine lured me outside and I made my way through dusty streets to a square where I could sit on a bench in the shade of some scabby trees, eat an ice lolly and flick through wanny Patric's design magazines. They're nice, these wee gardens scattered about London. In Glasgow they're building on every square inch that isnae already built on — bits of wasteground that have laid derelict for years suddenly sprout scaffolding and girders and a month later a hideous block of grey flats have been thrown up. Every week the local free paper runs headlines about yet another attempt tae take over a bowling green or tennis club and build on the land. It's one of the few things that gets my da's goat, drags him away fae *Countdown* or holiday programmes about the Seychelles.

There won't be a patch of green left if these vandals arenae

183

stopped. What the hell are the council up tae, lettin them away wi this? The dear green place they used tae cry it. There'll be nae green left and it's already far too dear tae live here. They've nae right to be selling aff bowling greens. When the city was designed they were part of the plan, so folk living in tenements could have a wee patch of grass to look at.

These squares didnae seem to be under threat. Mibbe in London they had enough buildings but then there never seemed to be enough houses. I'd mentioned this to Patric on a rare night when we stayed in.

It's the demography, Patrick said. *More folk live alone, more folk want holiday homes. And they want space in their houses too — look at this.* He showed me a spread in wanny his lifestyle magazines. *A meditation room, a spa, an office. Bedrooms and living rooms aren't enough now.*

If I move out ma da's, he could put a meditation room or a spa in my bedroom, aka the cell.

Patric laughed. *So you really thinking about moving out, Fiona?*

Dunno. But with the baby coming, there's gonnae be even less space than there is noo.

Will Mona go on living at my da's?

Guess so. I mean she's too young for a flat of her ain. Though she's talking about getting married tae Declan when she's sixteen.

Christ.

I know. He'll probably move in as well. Mibbe you could get your architect pals to design us a mezzanine flair.

Mibbe. But it's time you thought about what was best for you. And it's really time you left, shared a flat with folk your own age.

Patric opened a pack of mixed leaves and arranged them in a glass salad bowl. He drizzled olive oil over them. *Can you pass the balsamic — it's just behind you?*

Patric tossed the salad, mixing the oil and vinegar. *I did think at one stage you might move in with Amrik.*

That was never an option.

You weren't that serious then?

In *Wuthering Heights* there's this scene where Catherine tells Nelly how she feels about Heathcliff, how it would degrade her to marry him. She doesnae know he's behind the settee listening but when he overhears this, he leaves and never gets to hear her say how much she loves him. That's the turning point that changes everything. All because she doesnae know he's there.

And just at that moment, just when I was about to tell Patric what happened between me and Amrik, the phone rang and Patric went through to the other room tae answer it.

Keep an eye on those fishcakes, Fi — watch they don't burn.

When he came back the food was ready and the moment was lost. We never returned to the subject till after the meal, while I was helping him stack the dishwasher.

By the way, Fi, what I was gonnae ask you earlier, about Amrik. It's just that Lionel was talking about going to see him play tomorrow — apparently Amrik's beginning to get a bit of a cult following.

Oh. I bent over, rearranged plates so I could fit in a casserole.

But we don't have to go if you'd rather not. I don't know how it finished between you guys, but if it's not cool, then just say so.

Nae bother, Patric. It's totally cool.

I straightened up, pressed the rinse cycle button and shut the door.

WE MET IN yet another trendy new bar, this time with a water theme. In the centre of the room was a huge pool with a waterfall, fish darting about and water lilies floating on the surface. The waitresses were dressed as mermaids in green silvery frocks with long fishtails at the back and the drinks had cocktail sticks patterned with green and pink flowers.

Lionel was a stunning-looking guy. Patric was six foot two but Lionel towered over him and had wonderful dreadlocks. He had a lovely voice, quite upperclass but wi subtle rhythmic undertones of the West Indies. Clara was a wee woman slightly older than him, mibbe late twenties. She wore a sparkly frock and chatted animatedly, waving her haunds about. Eventually we were joined by Owen, Simon and a couple of other pals. I went to the toilet which had basins like fountains and a pile of tiny green and pink hand towels folded tae resemble water lilies. When I came out I seen Patric and his friends fae across the room, draped artistically round the fountain as if someone had arranged them, glasses in haund, chatting and laughing thegether. They looked like film stars.

We squashed intae two taxis. I was with Patric, Lionel and Simon, speeding through the streets. I was starving. I was used tae having my tea at six o'clock every night, but for Patric's crowd dinner at eight was quite early and more often the restaurant was booked for nine. Tonight we had some nibbles at the bar but were gonnae have what Patric called supper in a restaurant at 10.30. I wondered if I could last out. The taxi drew up and we spilled out on to the hot pavement. In fronty us was an elaborately patterned tiled frontage. Peaches.

The basement was arched like auld railway tunnels, original red brick exposed. It was dark wi nasty fluorescent coloured lights, acid green, yellow and pink, randomly changing fae one to the other. When I'd got used to the gloom I looked around. The crowd were mainly in their early twenties, a few slightly younger. It was a really mixed crowd, far mair so than the Glasgow scene. Folk of all colours and races, some cross-dressed and tranny. Patric's team looked slightly out of place, a bit too well dressed, too cool, like film stars slumming it. And I always look out of place.

Patric thrust a bottle of trendy beer in my haund. *This isnae the place for cocktails.*

I guess.

A bottle of beer is safer in clubs like this — drinks can get spiked. Keep hold of it.

We took up residence against a wall, a few feet away fae

the bar. The stage was at the other end, bare except for a mic and a few sad-looking coloured lights. The DJ played ambient music, trying hauf-heartedly tae get folk up to dance every now and again with something a bit faster, but this crowd werenae moving. They talked and posed; girls giggling and greeting friends like they hadnae seen them for years, guys trying to look cool, phones stuck to their ear. The hum of conversation grew louder and louder and I gied up trying to make mysel heard over it, lapsed intae silence on the fringes of our group. Then the DJ stopped his music and the hum of the crowd became a buzz of excitement.

All right, everyone, the regulars among you will need no intro-duction to our Friday gig, but for those of you who've just beamed down from the moon (That's us, whispered Lionel in my ear, his dreadlocks tickling my nose) *prepare to be impressed, be very, very impressed by the magical music of Amrik Singh.*

It was a weird juxtaposition of the absolutely familiar with the absolutely strange. Watching Amrik on stage, listening tae him play, was the same – but the venue, the folk around me, even the way the London crowd responded, was different. They were quiet but there was less intensity in the way they listened. I thought mibbe I was imagining it; it was the acoustics of the cavernous bar, or the distance fae the stage. But I felt there was something, a quality of listening in the Glasgow crowd, that wasnae here. I stood, unable to lose mysel in the music as I normally did, trying tae work out what it was.

They were wildly enthusiastic, applauded ecstatically after each long exquisite number. The women loved him nae doubt, moving closer, some dancing self-consciously beside the stage.

Wicked, Lionel said when the first number stopped and I nodded, unable tae speak. The others were smiling, showing Lionel by their body language that he'd picked a winner.

Then I realised what the difference was. The London audience loved Amrik, recognised his special quality, but they didnae need him the way Glaswegians did. London love was clean and manicured; after the gig they'd go off and have a lovely supper in an elegant restaurant, or move on to the next club they'd heard was cool, or heid hame tae their trendy apartment, having pulled some guy or girl. But their souls werenae riven apart, their whole beings shattered and put back thegether in a new way. Mibbe they were incapable of it, or just didnae need it, but for the first time I truly understood what Amrik had meant about playing live; it wasnae some theory about his art or the precious musician-talk I'd heard that often. His music was different here because the people were different.

When Amrik finished I didnae know what to dae. Part of me wanted to go over and say hello, but another part would rather scurry aff with Patric and his pals. They'd started to debate whether there was time for another drink or if we should get a taxi to the restaurant when I felt his haund on my shoulder.

Fiona.

Hi Amrik.

I couldnae look in his face.

What are you doing here?

I'm in London for a wee while — I've a piece in a show here.

Cool.

I'm staying with my brother. Amrik, Patric.

Patric shook his haund. *Hey, our names rhyme.*

Different spelling, but. I said. *Amrik with a k.*

Amrik with a k, that was such a great gig.

Thanks.

Would you like to join us? We're going for something to eat.

I was sure Amrik would say no, would disappear intae the crowd afore I'd be able to talk to him, find out his address, but he looked at Patric for a moment as though sizing him up, then said *Sure*.

Even though Patric sat me next tae Amrik we never got a chance to speak properly. As usual everyone wanted a piece of him but even that was different fae Glasgow. Lionel was a theatre director, Clara a dance reviewer; art in all its forms was the backdrop to their lives. Of course Amrik was great but to them he was just one of many great musicians. They wanted to dissect, debate, compare one artist to another, draw parallels between art forms. The conversation would start on music then move in the course of a few sentences tae sculpture or dance.

The subject of recording came up very quickly. Clara asked Amrik where she could get a CD of his music and Amrik shrugged and said *I don't do CDs*.

Can I download it from your website?

Amrik placed a forkful of rice in his mouth and chewed it slowly. When he'd finished, he smiled. *I don't record my music. I believe that music happens in the moment. Recorded music is dead.*

Gosh, that's so zen. Clara took a sip of wine.

Lionel, who had been talking to Owen about some factory in South London that was under threat from developers, turned and looked across the table.

That's such a theatre concept. Theatre happens in the moment — which is why it has so much more impact than film.

Simon interjected. *I won't let you get away with that one, Lionel. Some films have as much impact as theatre — and surely any art form can only be understood by reference to the moment in which it takes place and the person who sees it. Take what might be considered the*

190

most static form of art — a building: a cathedral, let's say, constructed of solid stone. Yet you can visit it on one day then go back the next and experience it in a completely different way.

I could feel the discussion slipping away. It was always like this with Patric's friends, like being in a sea; a serene, kind sea, but the waves rocked you gently fae one part to another. Afore you knew, you were drifting far away fae where you'd started and far away fae where you might want to be.

But what Amrik's saying, about music . . . Everyone looked at me respectfully as they always done when someone was talking, especially me as I said so little. I stumbled on haltingly. *I've seen Amrik in Glasgow loads of times but tonight it was that different and that's cause the folk here are different.*

The viewer or listener of the art form is not a passive vessel, not just a receiver but actually forms part of the work itself, Simon began, and I could feel it happening again, felt the sea shifting, the drift under me and I burst in, interrupting in a way they never done.

Don't you want tae be somewhere the audience really love you and need you, where you dae something amazing for them, rather than in a place where they've got so much stuff you're just . . . I stopped.

Amrik looked round. *Sometimes you feel one note is better or a run of notes has more depth or intensity. You think — ah, that's it — but it's not. If you keep doing the same thing, it becomes stale. If I stay too long in one place my music stagnates and it needs to be alive.*

Alternate slices of avocado and beetroot fanned round the plate, red and green sauce spiralled over them. And in the middle a huge prawn, eyes staring up at me.

I felt hot, the restaurant was stuffy and my glass had been refilled that often I'd nae idea how much I'd had to drink.

191

I stood up and pushed my chair back, stumbling slightly. I walked towards the bathroom, treading very carefully between the tables. The bathroom walls were tiled in brown and the towels lime green. Seventies theme. I managed to get inside a cubicle and threw up in the avocado toilet.

Slumped in the train on the way back next day, I closed my eyes and cooried intae my fleece. My Walkman covered my ears though I'd nae music on; it slightly blotted out the sound of the other passengers and this way naebody would talk to me. Patric had been amazed when he seen I still had a Walkman.

It's like something out the dark ages.

I smiled. *I'm a poor student, remember, fae a family that's been rehoused by the social.*

Cue the violins. He patted my airm. *Never mind, Fiona, I'll buy you an iPod.*

Next time he came up there'd be a wee parcel for me. Patric was like that, never said things and didnae deliver.

It was another roasting hot day but the air-conditioning in the train was daeing overtime and I felt shivery, or mibbe it was after throwing up yesterday. I didnae want to think about it, it was too mortifying. Course everyone'd known what was wrang. When I hadnae returned fae the toilet Clara followed me to cradle my heid and wipe my face with a towel damp-ened in cool water.

She'd taken me back to the flat, too. Patric had offered, but she'd insisted.

A woman's touch, she'd said. *I need to leave now anyway – I've a meeting at ten tomorrow.*

You sure, sis? Patric stroked my hair. *I'll come too.*

Don't be daft – they've just brought your food. I glanced at the leafy concoction strewn with pink peppercorns that passed for a main course but it made me feel queasy again and I turned away.

Okay. I won't be long though. Get straight to bed. Drink some water first.

I will.

I waved goodbye to everyone and got out the door, never daring to glance in Amrik's direction.

I don't know what time Patric came in but he was up afore me next morning, clean and shaved, wearing jeans and another of his lovely linen shirts.

Can you face a bit of dry toast and a cuppa tea?

Okay.

I wasnae up for talking and Patric bustled round, making sure I had everything. He came with me in the taxi to the station, got me magazines and water and a sandwich.

You'll probably feel starving about two o'clock.

He even came in the train with me, settled me in the seat like an invalid.

I'm sorry about last night, he said.

You're sorry — it was my fault.

Happens to us all at some time.

I knew he was right but I couldnae imagine any of his friends throwing up in a restaurant toilet. Or if they did, nae doubt they'd recover and walk out five minutes later as if nothing had happened.

You take care and call me when you get back. And you must come down again soon. Everyone loved you.

He planted a kiss on my cheek then hugged me as much as he could with me sitting and him towering over me. For a second I was enveloped in the cool of his shirt and the subtle scent of his aftershave, then he was gone, waving goodbye fae the platform.

I dozed on and off for maist of the journey, then got a coffee and sat, flicking through wanny the magazines Patric had gied me. Articles about how tae have perfect hair and skin, organise your work and rustle up lovely meals in ten minutes. Photies of all the must-have accessories you couldnae live without. I tossed it aside, curled my legs under me and shut my eyes. It felt that different fae the journey doon, when I'd been full of hope about the exhibition. And seeing Amrik in that environment had been weird, but then mibbe it was just me that was weird. The train smelled stale and the air-conditioning had given up altogether. The folk across the aisle were eating crisps that honked like they'd been flavoured wi vomit. I looked at my watch. By the grace of Virgin Trains, I'd be hame in an hour.

I DID WANT to come hame, but back in Glasgow the summer stretched ahead of me like a desert, dry and dusty and arid.

Maist folk are desperate for the summer, look forward tae those two weeks in the year when they feel human, laid out on a beach or planked round the hotel pool, sun warm on their bodies, but I'd always felt a sense of dread when the summer holiday loomed intae view. I liked school, the routine of it. And even at Art School you still have things you're supposed to be daeing, a place in the world.

But now I'd need tae earn some money. Even though Janice made sure we got all the benefits we were entitled to and had secured every student loan and bursary in existence for me, I still needed tae make as much as possible during the holidays to tide me over the next year. And if I was gonnae have tae leave hame – and I couldnae really see any way round it – then I'd need mair to pay for a flat.

So I spent every hour I could in the supermarket, took on extra shifts: late shifts, early shifts, every shift no one else wanted. I knew when I looked in the mirror what a toll it was taking on me – my eyes looked like a panda's and my skin was breaking out in rough red patches. No enough sunlight or fresh air, food snatched at odd times of the day and night. But my bank balance was building up; I was working that many hours I'd nae time tae spend anything and every week when I put the money in my savings account I felt a warm glow at the thought of being able tae support mysel through the next term. Every now and again Janice would drag me round to hers for a home-cooked meal and tell me I needed to cut doon my hours but she was too busy to sort out my life. And I was that caught up in the treadmill I'd made for mysel that when Monica phoned and asked me to go and meet her and Jemma for coffee, I realised I hadnae seen my so-called best friends for months.

Monica was her usual neat self but Jemma looked like a supermodel. Tall and slim with her hair beautifully cut in subtle layers, she was wearing the kind of cropped trousers that make most folk look daft. Somehow that first year at uni had changed that skinny gawkiness of hers intae slender glamour.

Then there was me. I knew I wasnae at my best; I'd come straight fae work, stuffed my overall in a poly bag and rushed across in the subway without having time to wash my face, but even so. I could tell by the look in their eyes.

It's so good to see you. Monica hugged me and Jemma squeezed my haund as I sat doon.

How's things?

Good, said Jemma. *Passed the exams okay.*

196

She came top of the class, Fiona. But she's too modest to say.

Ach, said Jemma. *It's no big deal.*

Away you go.

Anyhow Monica has even bigger news. Not only has she passed all her exams with flying colours, she's got a boyfriend.

Monica blushed.

Who is he?

A boy on my course. Charles.

I'm amazed you ever have time to see him — you must have that much studying to do.

Oh you know, we go to the library together. And he goes to the chaplaincy at lunchtime. That's how we got talking.

The chaplaincy?

You know the Catholic chaplaincy — they have mass at lunchtime.

When we were at school Monica was the maist devout of us — lighting candles, daeing novenas. Her mother went tae mass every morning afore her work in the family's takeaway, and there were holy water fonts and statues in every room of the house. I wondered if Jemma still went.

The waiter came and I ordered penne amatriciana and a coffee. I'd been looking forward to seeing the others, but I was now beginning to feel a bit spare; they obviously still phoned regularly and met up, were part of each other's lives, while I was an outsider, a shadow left over from some other time and place. No their fault but — mines.

Jemma drained the last of her coffee, put her cup back on the saucer. *So what's new, Fiona? We saw you'd won another prize at the Art School — it was in the free paper. That's fantastic.*

I nodded, didnae know what to say.

What else have you been up to?

Nothing. I've been working in the supermarket every hour God sends.

Monica leaned her elbows on the table, and cupped her face in her haunds. *Fiona, we're worried about you. You look so tired and drawn. You're working too hard.*

Her soft voice was so loving that my eyes started to prick with tears. I swallowed them, looked doon at a trace of sugar on the table.

I'm fine. It's no for long. I need tae get money for next year.

We all do. I'm working and so is Jemma. But you need to relax sometimes too.

Believe her, said Jemma. *Coming from Monica whose idea of relaxation is helping with a soup run for homeless folk or mibbe doing some algebra problems in her head, that is really something.*

Monica smiled. *Very funny. And how is Amrik?*

Amrik and me are . . . over.

I'm so sorry, Fiona. Monica touched my wrist.

It's cool. He went tae London.

And do you have a new boyfriend?

Drifting. That feeling of drifting that had been so strong with Patric's friends in London, came back. I was adrift in a sea, but this time Monica and Jemma were the secure jetty I somehow could not find anchor with. I wanted to, longed to sit there and confess all – Amrik and the miscarriage and everything from start tae finish, but it was impossible. There were too many gaps between us and it was too late to fill them in.

No, I said. *There's no one. But I do have some news.* And I started tae tell them all about Mona and her baby.

One Sunday around the middle of August it dawned on me that Patric hadnae phoned for a while. I was that exhausted by work I'd never realised the time passing. We used tae have a long blether every week or so, but since I'd got back there had only been a few hurried calls fae his mobile while he was on the way somewhere. I needed to hear his voice, reconnect.

It was hauf eleven and my shift didnae start till two. The twins and Declan had left for the town and Da went for a cup of tea in the chapel hall after ten o'clock mass so I'd probably have the place to mysel for a while. It was a bit early to phone but Patric was normally up by now – he usually met friends for lunch on a Sunday so he'd nae doubt be floating around the flat, mibbe in his goonie after a bath, watering his plants, making sure everything was pristine. Anyway, it was worth a try. I dialled his number.

I don't know why I dae it, but I always count the number of rings afore someone answers. At seven maist phones go through tae voicemail but his must of been switched off as it kept on ringing – eight, nine, ten. Then it was picked up at the other end.

Hello.

I didnae answer and the voice said, *Hello* again.

It was Amrik's voice.

I put doon the receiver then a moment later the phone rang again.

I picked it up immediately. *Hello.*

Fiona?

Patric.

Did you just call?

Uhhuh. I thought I had a wrong number.

I was in the bathroom.

Was that Amrik?

Yeah, he's here – we're just about to go for lunch with some of the others.

I never realised you two were friends.

We've been seeing a bit of each other since you introduced us that night at the club.

Oh.

Pause.

So how are you, Fiona?

Tired. Working in the supermarket.

You need a break.

This was the time he'd normally say, *Why don't you come down here for a few days?* but he never. *You should go for a holiday with Monica and Jemma. Get a cheapo flight somewhere hot.*

They're already booked up.

Oh. Well, do something, get away before the baby comes and you get roped into being a nanny. How is Mona?

She's fine.

Great.

Have you had any time to do your artwork?

No, barely time tae sleep.

Listen Fiona, I've got to go now. You don't want to run up the bill. I'm planning to come up next weekend — a flying visit. So take some time off and we'll go out. Talk then.

Sure.

Don't work too hard.

The supermarket has a micro-climate of its ain, different fae anything that goes on outside. Nae matter whether it's chucking it doon or blazing hot, the temperature is set to 17 degrees Celsius, except for the freezer cabinets, fruit and perishable items. The fluorescent lights cast an unnaturally even glow and bland music washes over you, interrupted by annoying announcements. I spent the afternoon and early evening on the till, beeping through items, smiling mechanically at the customers, punctuated by a few spells sorting tinned vegetables.

But while my body was on autopilot, my mind was birling with thoughts of Amrik and Patric with their rhyming names. How could they of become friends? Easy to see how Patric and his pals would adopt Amrik after the night at the gig, how they'd drop by some Friday night and take him out. But his lifestyle was that different fae theirs. For all their apparent casualness there was a high degree of organisation under-pinning their lives. They all worked at real, though glamorous, jobs; while much of their work seemed tae consist of wittering intae mobiles in the street or in cabs, and having lunch and coffees with folk, they did have places tae go and people tae see. And they relied on their phones, texting and emailing and voice messaging to say they'd been held up at X so would be at Y ten minutes late and could they reschedule lunch as they couldnae make it tomorrow but could manage cocktails tonight.

How on earth would Amrik, who didnae possess a phone, barely knew what day it was and cared less, fit in with the precision power-socialising? He'd coincide with them once or twice then fall out their orbit when a new club became fashion-able and they moved on tae another galaxy.

Why was it bugging me that much anyway? After all what difference did it make that Amrik and Patric were friends. I'd never tellt Patric the truth about me and Amrik and for all he knew we might just of drifted apart. Amrik wasnae likely tae tell him – I don't suppose he spent a lot of time thinking about it. But there was something niggling away inside me. It just didnae feel right.

Casual workers never got Saturday aff but I tellt Marie I was gaun tae a wedding. I felt a bit guilty – Marie is really nice, in her late fifties with twinkly eyes, hair dyed jet-black and hairsprayed within an inch of its life. She always looks dead smart with her shoes polished and her uniform neatly ironed. I look hingy, sleeves escaping fae under the overall, hair trailing out fae the elastic band I've scraped it back with. I mind the first day I started, when the big boss manager put me under Marie's care.

Och, Fiona, says Marie, *that gorgeous hair of yours.* She stroked it, tried to push the strands back in. *It's no gonnae gie up easily, is it?*

Five minutes later the curls at the front had all come loose again and at teabreak I was standing in front of the mirror trying tae shove them back when Marie came in the wee cupboard that passed for a staffroom. *C'mere hen,* she said, taking a plastic poke out her handbag. *I nipped out tae Savers and got these for you.*

She pulled my hair tighter intae the pony tail, then lifted the rogue locks at the front and clipped them back neatly with little hairgrips. They were covered with pink and blue sparkly flowers, the kind the twins loved and I thought were hideous.

These'll keep things where they should be. I know your hair is lovely and clean but working in a shop, around food, you've got to be really careful. Don't want you getting into trouble, darlin. Here. She thrust the pack in my haund. *These'll dae for spares.*

I looked at the remaining hairgrips in the pack. *But Marie, did you buy these yourself?*

Och, I was getting some shampoo and I seen them and thought they'd be just the job.

But how much dae I . . .?

Don't be daft, hen.

I started to protest but she closed her haund over mines. *Time we got back tae work.*

That was Marie all over. Always bringing in biscuits she'd had too many of in the house or buying a cake on someone's birthday. Bill, the manager, used to call her the ER; if anyone needed paracetamol, plasters or a safety pin, Marie was the one they went tae. She noticed things too. I was on the checkout when Kathryn, a tall skinny lassie with a pale complexion, came to let me aff. As she sat doon at the till, and started to key in the code, Marie appeared at her elbow and whispered in her ear. Kathryn looked up and nodded. Marie slipped something in her haund and took over the till. As we walked away, I noticed Kathryn walked slowly and her face was chalk-white.

You okay?

Cramp, she said. *My period came on dead suddenly — Marie must of noticed I wasnae looking right — she gave me painkillers and let me take a break.*

After a long lie on the Saturday morning the difference showed in my face — the circles were less pronounced though I still looked drawn and there wasnae much I could dae about the red patches on my skin apart from dab over them wi the twins' make-up. I washed my hair and ironed a flowery top tae wear over my jeans. When I looked in the mirror my hair was all springing up round my heid like a character in the twins' cartoons when they've had an electric shock. I took a scarf, wanny they Indian cotton ones with a gold pattern running through it, wound it round like a headband. It was a bit long but I thought it gied a nice effect, and the hair springing out at the back looked as if it was meant tae be like that.

We were meeting Patric and he was taking us for lunch. My da had put on a tie and a light-coloured jacket I couldnae mind him wearing afore. It hung on his shoulders. Mona and

Rona were in their best jeans with glittery belts and bags. Mona's bump was huge noo and her shiny top barely covered it. Declan was his usual pristine self.

When I came in the living room, Rona pointed at the scarf round my hair. *Christ Fiona, you look like you're about tae clean the hoose.*

I shrugged.

You're like wanny they women in the land army in the second world war, hen.

Didnae know you were that auld, Da.

Very funny – ah was born in 1950 as you well know. I've seen photies of them with their hair tied back wi a scarf wearing flowery pinnies like that.

It's no a flowery pinny, it's a . . .

Never mind hen, you look very nice. He turned to the twins. *Yous all look very nice. Now let's go or we'll be late.*

We had lunch in the restaurant of Patric's hotel, a light and airy place with glass tables and huge displays of lilies. There was a buffet laid out with lovely salads, roast meats and poached salmon.

You can have something hot if you prefer, said Patric when we were all seated, *but I think this is nice on a warm day, and you can always go for seconds.*

Once we'd chosen, I looked round the table. Patric's plate was tasteful; a little salmon, a wafer-thin slice of roast beef, salads of various kinds – bulgar wheat, caesar – laid out as elegantly as the floral displays in the room. My da had solid helpings of roast beef, potato salad, tomato salad and lettuce, all separated on his plate. Mona and Rona took huge helpings of the cooked meats, a tiny amount of tomato with the dressing scraped aff and a daud of potato salad. On Declan's plate was a triangular pile of food which he would nae doubt eat his way through, silently as he usually did. In fronty me was a small portion of everything, not artistically arranged, just there, mindlessly. I wondered if all families were this different. Or did no one else ever look at the way their family ate.

Everyone was on their best behaviour and though Patric ordered some wine my da only had one glass. We talked about Mona's baby, and Patric's work. Anyone looking at us would of thought we were having a nice family lunch out. Which of course we were.

After lunch Declan, Mona and Rona were off to the movies and Da decided tae join them. After they'd left, Patric led me to a table in the windae at the front of the hotel. You could watch the madness of a Saturday in Glasgow, cocooned fae the noise. Patric ordered coffee and the waiter brought us a cafetière.

Patric leaned back in the upholstered chair, crossed his legs.

Da's looking a bit better.

He's awful thin.

Aye, but he ate a good meal. And he only had one glass of wine.

He's no been drinking much recently.

That's good.

He pressed the plunger on the cafetière, poured the coffee. We sipped in silence for a few minutes then Patrick put doon the cup and saucer.

Fiona, there's something we need to talk about.

Shoot.

I meant to tell you about it before but . . . it's not really something you can talk about easily on the phone.

What is it?

Last week, when Amrik answered the phone, and I said that he and I were friends.

Uhhuh.

Well, actually, we've become very close. More than just friends.

At first I was just utterly, utterly confused.

But Amrik's not . . . I paused.

He is. Patric lifted a teaspoon aff the table and placed it in the saucer. *I mean, obviously he's bisexual.*

Obviously.

Patric turned tae face me, took baith my haunds in his. *Fiona, I feel really bad about this. I know that you and Amrik went out for a while but I never thought it was serious — you were always quite casual about it.*

I know. It's no your fault — it's just — a shock.

I mean, you weren't serious, were you?

No.

Clearly, however close they were, Amrik hadnae tellt Patric about what happened. Mibbe he'd forgotten or mibbe, with his total lack of interest in anything other than what was going on at the moment, he didnae think it was important.

Thank God for that. He let go my haunds. *I mean, I know it is a bit . . . well . . .*

I didnae say anything.

Complicated.

Good word. Very good.

I mean, you and Jas, you and Amrik, me and Amrik.

You don't need tae spell it out.

Fiona, are you okay?

I don't know. I really don't know.

You see, if it wasn't important to me I would never have let it happen. If it had been something casual, I wouldnae want to hurt your feelings or make things awkward. You and me have always been so close, flesh and blood. If it had been casual . . .

But it's no.

206

No.

He looked out the windae. *I've never felt like this for anyone, Fiona.*

And Amrik?

I'm not sure — it's early days. He turned and smiled, no the nice wallpaper smile I'd seen so often with his pals in London, a smile that came from inside. *We're just very happy thegether.*

I didnae want to but I had to. I wasnae sure if I was daeing it from pure motives or if the mixed-up mess that was inside me had spewed it out.

Be careful, Patric. I mean, Amrik is . . . well, he loves his freedom.

I don't have a problem with that.

I just don't want you to get hurt.

Patric stood, pulled me up on my feet and hugged me very tightly.

Don't you worry, wee sis. Don't you worry.

I caught the subway home like a zombie, chucked mysel on my bed and lay there, unable to dae anything. The room felt even smaller than usual; I stretched out to the sides and touched the walls without moving. They felt synthetic and if you pushed your fingers hard enough intae them you could make indentations — God knows what material they used tae build these wee boxes. The late afternoon sun stippled the far end of the right wall and I watched a bluebottle chase its shadow across it. The windae was open a crack at the bottom and it kept trying tae escape and failing, buzzing off to the patch of light, perhaps thinking it was another exit. I could not make mysel get up to open the windae and shoo it; my heid was full of its own buzzing insects unable to find their way out.

I tried tae assemble them in some kind of order, line them

up in wee insect regiments but they just stayed in a guddle that didnae make sense. Patric and Amrik, Amrik and me, me and Jas. I lay watching the light fade on the wall, till I eventually dropped off to sleep, waking only when I heard the voices of my da and the twins, returning fae the movies.

How was the wedding?

Marie leaned over me, stuck her key in the till and opened it. A man with a basket full of dogfood drew daggers at her.

We'll just be a moment, sir. Marie started tae bag the money.

Oh . . . I'd forgotten I'd said I was going to a wedding. *Fine. Late night, eh?* She patted my shoulder. *You can go off for your tea in ten minutes, hen. I'll send Jo over.*

During the break I went out for some fresh air, bought a carryout coffee and stood in fronty the wee paper shop. The moment I'd been putting off. I had tae find somewhere to live, couldnae keep staying at my da's after the baby was born. A few weeks ago Miss Starkey had muttered about getting Mona a flat but she didnae want that, at least no right away, and my da wouldnae hear of it. Janice didnae think it was a good idea either. *I think Mona needs security and family round her at this time.*

She kept dropping hints about me sharing with other students, gied me cuttings about student flats.

They've got these modern places now, Fiona. Your own flat but with other folk around, security doors and everything. Something like that would be really nice.

I don't think so.

I'd seen the ads too. Urban student living. Purpose-built blocks thrown up on wasteground on the fringes of real areas. With fako names. I passed one on my way to the Art School each day, surrounded by tenements and multistoreys – they'd called it Ciao as if it was a restaurant or something. The ads were full of photies of trendy – but not too trendy in case it put off the mas and das who'd be paying for it – young folk all laughing thegether. Hopping in and out of each other's Ikea-furnished boxes.

Janice didnae gie up easily. *What about the residences?*

They only have places for first years.

Oh well, you'll just need tae look for a flatshare. She laughed. *Actually it's quite exciting. I can still remember the first time I moved into a flat.*

If I was gonnae dae it this was the best time, afore everyone came back for the start of term. The windae of the shop was plastered with ads, some neatly word-processed, some barely-literate scrawls. I scanned through them, made a list of possibles and put the paper in my pocket. I'd call them after I finished work.

CLYTEMNESTRA IS EATING only yellow foods this month: egg yolks, sweetcorn, yellow peppers, lemons, grapefruit, butter and saffron rice.

I'm balancing my chakras, she says, pulling her messages fae a Somerfield bag. *My therapist thinks my aura is lacking in yellow.* She took a Polaroid snap fae her backpack and haunded it to me. Her sat staring at the camera with all these swirly patterns round her, as if a wean had scrawled on it wi felties.

Look, she says, pointing. *Too much blue here.*

Clytemnestra isnae her real name. She used tae be Caroline; that's the name on the official mail that drops on the doormat made of ecologically sound something or another that sheds jaggy hairs all over the place. She's a lumpy lassie wi bad skin and stringy hair, and it's her flat, well her parents bought it for her when she came tae uni. They live in Kent and she was supposed tae be gaun tae Edinburgh but ended up in Glasgow.

There's five of us; Eric and Sanj are engineers and Nicole is a music student at the RSAMD. I managed tae pass the interview with Clytemnestra even though I'm no a vegetarian. She even made me a cup of nettle tea.

There's something about your presence, Fi. It's like, the flat is a canvas, an abstract painting, an apparently random pattern of colours and shapes. But if you take the blue and make it green, it just doesn't work. Or if the shade of orange doesn't balance the purple — well, you'll understand, being an artist.

I hadnae a scooby what she was on about but she seemed harmless and, anyway, she was gonnae be my landlady, so I had to be polite.

Are you an artist too? Did you no say you were studying Languages?

She chucked the teabag in the orange bin. *Society is too caught up with putting us in little boxes — you go to Art School so you're an artist, Nicole goes to the RSAMD so she is a musician. It's just not a holistic way of life.*

Uhhuh.

I follow the Artist's Way. Have you read it?

No.

You should, Fi. I'm sure you'd find it illuminating. It's about nurturing your inner artist.

Right.

Even though Clytemnestra sounded as if she was talking pish maisty the time, what she said about the folk in the flat made sense when I got tae know them a bit. There was certainly a balance of energies between us. Eric's a wee guy with cropped dark hair who works out till his muscles are like gnarled old tree trunks, Sanj is smiley and laid back and Nicole is tall and elegant looking, dead intense about her music and deadly quiet about everything else. Where I fitted in I'd nae idea but Clytemnestra obviously seen me as the missing link.

My room was the smallest but even so it was about four times as big as the box I'd been sleeping in at my da's. Tenements feel bigger; the high ceilings and tall windaes make space and light, especially since we're on the top flair wi a view across hauf the city. The living room was massive and the kitchen big enough for us to eat in. The only downer was that the 'ideal location' in the advert turned out to be just round the corner fae where our auld house was. So, even though it took longer, I always went the other way, unable tae face passing it.

It was weird sharing a flat with strangers but we rubbed along fine, barring the odd argument about using up all the hot water or whose turn it was tae buy milk. I guess all flatmates have these ridiculous conversations:

Eric: (accusingly) Why is the cheese on the bottom shelf in the fridge?

Me: Does it matter?

Eric: I think it's better if we have some organisation here. Cheese on the top shelf, other stuff in the middle, vegetables in the bottom, milk and juice in the door.

Me: Oh, cool.

Eric was positively militaristic about the kitchen and got really pissed about food being out of place in the fridge. He bought a large bottle of anti-bacterial cleaner and placed it accusingly in the middle of the kitchen table.

I was laid back about replacing the spices in alphabetical order, but couldnae bear the bathroom being dirty. I couldnae understaund how someone who checked the fridge thermometer every day seemed unable to turn round after he'd used the toilet and realise it needed cleaned and that the green stuff in the bottle shaped like a duck was for that purpose. Or that it wasnae very nice to have tae clean someone else's hair out the plughole. The twins were dead messy too, but somehow it was different when it was your ain family.

I moaned about it to Janice one day. After letting me rant for a while about Eric, she said, *What about the others?*

Nicole's all right. Clytemnestra's idea of cleaning is burning joss sticks. And I don't think Sanj would notice if you redecorated the entire flat while he was in it.

Why don't you all sit down and talk about it? You could be responsible for cleaning the bathroom and Eric the kitchen. And the others could do something else. It's best if everybody knows where they stand, otherwise you can end up with a lot of resentment.

She was right, of course. I'd already started to seethe with hatred towards Eric every time I seen his razor on the side of the bath, nasty wee hairs stuck tae it like beasties, and I'm sure he felt the same way about me when I placed Paprika on the shelf after Turmeric. So we had a big, clear-the-air session one night, decided who done what, then went out to the pub.

Next morning I found Sanj sitting at the table with a big sheet of paper and a packet of felt-tipped pens. He looked up at me and smiled,

Hi. What colour d'you want to be?

Sorry?

What colour? For the list.

List?

Of chores. I'm gonnae write out who does what and stick it on the wall and I thought I'd do it in different colours. Pick a colour. He waved the felties at me. *Any one except lilac. It's no working.*

I looked at the pack. It was one of they cheapies you get in Bargain Books, in a clear plastic pack, colours spread out in the order of the spectrum, with grey, brown and black at one end.

Or red. I thought Eric should be red.

How?

Well he's kind of red, isn't he? Direct, go for it, active.

I'd never thought of Sanj paying any attention tae what people were like, let alone what colour they corresponded to. I was intrigued.

So what colour d'you think I should be?

I think, essentially, you're a green person.

I laughed. *You sound like Clytemnestra. What is an essentially green person?*

He took the green feltie out of the pack and started to shade the corner of the paper with it, giving it his full attention.

Green's like nature. Trees and leaves and all that.

I had a funny feeling, slightly shivery inside, close to tears. The only bit of nature I felt like these days was jaggy nettles. Then I noticed something.

Sanj! Where d'you get that paper?

He kept on colouring in the corner.

Out of that big folder thing you left in the hall.

That's the best cartridge paper I can afford – could you no of used a bit of scrap?

He looked genuinely surprised. *Sorry. I'll buy you another bit if you like.*

You couldnae stay angry with him.

It's cool. Want a coffee?

I filled the kettle at the sink. I'd put three pots of geraniums in the recessed windae sill – red, pink and white. Maisty their petals were still curled up, like rolls of tissue paper. I pulled off a few dead heids and rubbed my thumb across a leaf, fuzzy like peach-skin. The scent filled my nose, making it tickle.

I turned round. Sanj had finished shading the corner in green and was drawing red wiggly lines round the side of the page.

What colour are you, Sanj?

Lilac. That's why the lilac pen is done.

So you cannae be lilac.

I can still be lilac, but the marks I write won't show up on the page. So . . .

So . . .

I won't have to do any chores.

I threw the teatowel at him.

MONA WAS DUE in a couple of weeks and, as the time grew closer, the baby dreams returned. There were recurring ones of a baby wrapped in a shroud-like cloth and once I dreamed about the white coffin, floating away doon a river. Sometimes the dream was of the face of Janice or Mammy, a face filled with joy then crumpling tae grief in slow motion. I'd wake, sweating, rubbing my eyes to try to escape the image. But this morning, waking with a start, the face was still there, a real face, and a haund shaking me awake.

C'mon lazylumps.

Rona, what you daeing here?

Your flatmate let me in, wan wi the funny name.

Clytemnestra.

Whatever.

Suddenly the cloudy dream-fear shrank and sharpened to a real fear and I clutched Rona's airm. *Is Mona OK?*

Course she is, she's doonstairs — you don't think she's gonnae climb three flights unless she has to, dae you? Ah've been trying tae phone you but you never replied. We're gaun intae toon so we thought we'd drop in.

My phone's charging. What time is it anyway?

Ten.

You're awful early for a social call.

Mona cannae sleep too well the noo. Anyway, no everyone keeps student hours.

Rona sat on the bed. *We just wanted tae let you know about the baby shower.*

Baby shower? Mona's been refusing tae buy anything for the baby cause she said it was bad luck.

Well, I guess she's changed her mind then. Janice offered tae have it at her house. The morra night. You comin?

Course I am, but it doesnae gie me much time tae get her a pressie.

Rona turned on her way out the door. *Well, you could always finish aff wanny they baby hats you knitted for thon mad thing you done at the Art School show.*

The baby shower was a strictly all-female affair so Mona arranged for Declan tae keep my da company. As soon as he arrived Da led him intae the kitchen where the Scrabble board was set out.

I cannae play Scrabble, Mr O'Connell.

I'll teach you, son. You'll love it.

Rona had roped me intae decorating Janice's living room. *You're the wan at Art School — at least you could dae somethin useful with it for a change.*

217

She haunded me a couple of bags filled with pink and blue streamers and balloons with cutesy teddy designs on them.

And nae funny stuff – don't want tae come back tae a room fulla broken Barbies.

I pinned the streamers round the walls, tied bunches of balloons in the corners and covered Janice's long coffee table with a white plastic tablecover. It looked a bit bare so I placed some of Evie's teddies on it. One of them was a white bear with a black bowtie, who had a melancholy wee face – no the kind of teddy you'd gie a wean. I looked at him and he looked back, and all the fear and panic I'd been trying tae keep locked inside me, surfaced.

Janice came in fae the kitchen where she and Rona were preparing food.

That's nice, Fiona. We'll need more seats in here but we can get some from the kitchen when they arrive. And there's big cushions and a beanbag in Evie's room.

Janice, I said. *Can I ask you something?*

What?

Did you have a baby shower?

No my scene, really.

I don't mind Mammy having one either.

It's usually just the first baby. I think she had one for Patrick.

Do you no think it's a bit . . .

What?

I dunno, too much like a celebration, when you don't . . .

I didnae want tae say the words, felt as if even saying them out loud would be a horrible curse on Mona.

Janice put her airm round me. *I know, I know. Sometimes I get scared too. But we have to assume it'll be all right, it'll be wonderful. And I think that's what Mona's daeing.*

The doorbell rang. *Can you get that, Fiona?*

Mrs Kaur stood on the doorstep, a couple of huge bags in her haunds. *I hope your auntie won't mind but I thought she might like some food.*

Thanks very much. Come on in.

She started tae put plastic containers on the kitchen table. *That's wonderful, Mrs Kaur, really kind of you,* said Janice.

Rona opened one of the boxes. *Samosas — yes!*

There are a few more things in the car.

She wasnae kidding. It took us two mair trips and the boxes were piled up all round the kitchen. Between Mrs Kaur's food and the stuff Janice had got, it looked as if we had far too much, but when the guests arrived, it was just as well because there were far mair of them than any of us had expected.

I never realised Mona and Rona had asked so many of their pals, said Janice, while we were in the kitchen pouring drinks. *I hope this Cava doesnae run out.*

I'll nip out for more, said Angie.

We were all squashed intae the living room — on seats, on cushions, on each other — when we raised wur glasses and Janice said a toast tae Mona and the new baby. Declan's ma and auntie, Mrs Flanagan, Mrs Jackson, Jean and Betty were there, with what looked like hauf Mona's class at school, as well as Mrs Kaur and a few of Janice's friends. Evie had been allowed tae stay up late and given the job of helping Mona to unwrap each present. Angie refilled glasses as the parcels were opened, each one passed round, greeted appropriately.

Aw, would you look at that? Isn't that gorgeous? A babygrow, a pack of muslin cloths, a cup and bowl wi Peter Rabbit on it, a tiny silver bangle.

Mines was the last to be opened. I'd shoved it to the bottom of the pile when I was decorating the room. When she pulled it out the wrapping, Mona squealed. *Oh my God, Fiona – did you make this yoursel?*

A white shawl, crocheted in an elaborate pattern.

It was Rona gied me the idea. After that crack about the hats I thought of making something really nice, really traditional for the baby. I'd nae idea if Mona would like it – she'd probably think it was dead auld-fashioned – but I knew we'd had a christening shawl my granny made so I'd rushed out tae get the wool and spent the whole of yesterday and hauf the night on it, crocheting away till my haunds ached.

Mona fingered the shawl, placed it against her cheek.

It's dead soft.

Special wool, meant for newborns.

She put her airms round me. *Thanks, sis. It's cool.*

A week later Mona went intae labour at four o'clock and the baby arrived at six. Nae drugs apart fae gas and air. Mona'd had her heart set on an epidural but the midwife said the baby was coming so fast there wasnae time.

See this is what nature intends, dear. A young healthy body like yours, all that dancing you were telling me about, and it just pops out.

And there she was. Eight pound two ounces with dark matted hair and eyes like the ocean. Skin so soft I was feart tae touch her, my haund felt that rough against her cheek. Grace. She couldnae have had any other name.

In the hospital, in her wee white sleepsuit, in the plastic box they called a cot, she looked like an alien, dropped fae some distant star ontae our planet. A miracle. She seemed tae have nothing to dae wi Mona or Declan or any of us, was part of some vast plan of the universe we couldnae understaund. But once she was hame and the weeks passed, an even bigger miracle started to happen. We all changed.

First it was Mona. I'd never admitted it tae anyone else, and only hauf to mysel, in my meanest moments, but I'd assumed Mona would be a fairly crap mother. In fact I'd sometimes imagined me taking over the motherly role, looking after the baby when Mona got sick of it, like the kitten the twins had begged for years ago that got run over when they let it out on the road.

But fae the first day they came hame, the white shawl wrapped round the pair of them, Mona just knew how to be with this wee person. She held and changed and rocked her with such confidence, talked baby-talk tae her wi nae embarrassment. She even breastfed, apparently without any of the hassles I'd read about in the baby magazines.

Miss Starkey was well impressed. *A natural mother,* she said, putting away her clipboard to dangle the baby awkwardly.

Every baby should have a team of adults to look after them. With Rona and Declan always there and Declan's folks and the rest of us often around, Grace never lacked attention.

Then there was my da. The baby seemed to have wrought a magic transformation on him. He watched her insteidy *Countdown*, danced her up and doon, his muckle haunds haudin her secure. Patric flew up fae London to join in the adoration. He had tae go back the next day and seemed distracted, though happy.

Sorry we won't have time to go out for a drink, Fiona — I've got loads to talk to you about. Next time.

ART SCHOOL STARTED back in October. I'd kept on a few shifts at the supermarket every week to make sure I could afford the flat, but that left me plenty time tae get back to my work.

It was hard but. For a whole summer I'd done nothing, never even thought about what I'd dae. The 'Oh Yes You Are . . . ' exhibit hadnae been sold by the gallery (hidden away in the back room it would of been a miracle if anyone had seen it) and at the end of the month I got a call from Bored Girl whose name I discovered was Jessamine.

Will you be popping in over the next few weeks?

Don't think so.

Don't you come up to town much then?

'Town' presumably did not mean Sauchiehall Street or the Buchanan Galleries.

No. It's four hundred miles away.

Oh, right. Well d'you want us to parcel it up and send it to . . . Glasgow?

The way she said it made it sound as if Glasgow was on the moon and she was unsure if Parcelforce delivered there. In the end Patric agreed tae look after the box, which was a relief as I'd nae idea where I'd keep it. I didnae want tae start cluttering up my room at Clytemnestra's when I'd only just moved in.

The room was a blank canvas. No that I work on canvas, but still. Painted white, even the floorboards, with only a bed, an auld wardrobe and chest of drawers, which had been painted white too. Nae curtains, but the flat had the original wooden shutters. Janice bought me a fluffy bedspread in mossy green which was the only colour in the room. Peaceful. I put my stuff away, had nothing out on the surfaces, hoped the emptiness would gie me inspiration. But it didnae. My mind was empty too.

One day, after footering about at Art School, I came hame and took out the album that held photies of all the work I'd done. I flicked through, examining them, hoping I'd get some idea of the next step. All the books claimed there was a progression in an artist's work; one thing led tae another, there was organic development, change and growth. I didnae have a scooby about all that but I knew one thing. Nae mair Barbies.

With only the vaguest of ideas in my mind, I started to collect shoe boxes. I went round to my da's and rummled about, made mysel open his wardrobe, though it felt as if I was prying. His only box held good shoes, stiff and new, for Sundays and special occasions, and I replaced them carefully in the tissue paper. I could get some fae the twins who never put anything away in boxes anyway.

For weeks, as the piece slowly developed, I hardly looked at anything except to weigh up whether it could work in some way, and in the flat I kept picking up things that might be useful. Eric went mental when I took the top aff the washing up liquid.

Sorry, I need it for my artwork.

We need it for doing the dishes.

It still works without the wee bit at the top.

Yeah, but it pours in too fast, you end up using twice as much.

Clytemnestra came in on my side but. She had it in her heid that anything I did was because I was an artist. Nae doubt if I'd started drinking the washing up liquid it'd be because I was an artist.

Fiona's an artist, Eric, she said, pronouncing the word 'artist' in that precious way. *We're so lucky to have the opportunity of living with an artist, seeing how the creative process works. I think it's worth putting up with a few little inconveniences, don't you?*

Eric grunted. He obviously didnae think that but it was her house after all.

Each box represented the front room of a house with a hedge protecting it. The first one worked out quite well but the hedge at the front was rubbish – I'd made it out of scrunched-up tissue paper and it flopped all over the place. Then I remembered the wee hats I'd knitted for the last piece. The texture of the wool would make a nice contrast wi the card and plastic. Angie had recently started knitting since it had become trendy. Last time I seen her she was making an enormous furry jumper for Janice.

Gwyneth Paltrow and Kate Winslet do it on the sets of their films. You know, when they're hanging around.

Bizarrely, Angie took a keen interest in the lives of young women film stars. Gwyneth and Renee and Kate. She could always tell you what diet they were on and which designer label they dressed their weans in. I couldnae figure it out – Angie was definitely no the frivolous type.

But she let me go through what she described as her stash, and I picked out oddments of wool. She was right – it was therapeutic, though I wasnae knitting jumpers or even something for the baby. After a day at Art School I'd sit on my bed knitting hedges out of green wool and covering the furniture I'd made out of matchboxes.

I was just as besotted with Grace as everyone else, but I found it hard to be natural when there were other folk around. They seemed tae coo and baby-talk so much easier than me, their fingers were not clumsy when they changed her nappy or wiped babygunk aff her cheek. It was only when she and I were alone thegether I felt at ease. Sometimes I'd take her out in her buggy – just me and Grace, gaun through the park. I kept up a running commentary about the flowers and trees, while she cooed away tae hersel. One day in November when the sky was cloudless and the trees swayed wildly in the wind, I sat on a bench with the buggy beside me. I looked at Grace's smiley wee face and something inside me cracked. Tears ran doon my face.

I wish it was a special moment of being at one with the universe but it wasnae. It was shame. In that moment, looking at Grace's innocence, I realised how awful I'd been. Who was I judging Mona and Declan? Who was I, thinking I was better than them? What had I done with my life compared to what they had, producing this perfect being? I wanted to start over, be cleaned out.

I wiped my eyes on the corner of a crumpled tissue. I'd nae mirror so I hoped there wasnae any make-up or smudges on my face. Though I still went to mass on and off, I'd no been tae confession for ages, no since the time I'd copped out, no since Amrik. I had a lot to say.

I set aff doon the hill, a lump still screwing up my stomach, but feeling if I could only get tae confession, everything would be all right. I knew it was on at St Clare's afore ten o'clock mass the morra but I didnae even want to wait that long. Mibbe I could go and ask the priest – they would gie you confession any time if you asked – but that was a daft idea, too complicated and embarrassing. Naw, I'd need to go the morra; I'd just try tae hold this ray of hope inside till I could really, truly start over.

I pushed the pram towards the gate, paying nae attention to the crowds of folk attracted intae the park by the un-expected weather. Then I heard a voice say, *Fiona.* I turned and there he was, Jas.

It was barely a year and a hauf since we'd seen each other but he looked different, thinner in the face and with a solitary white hair growing among the black, just above his left ear.

Is this Mona's baby?

You heard?

Ma said she'd had a wee girl.

We stood staring into the buggy, something to look at that saved us fae having to look at each other.

She's lovely. He bent doon, held out his finger which Grace grasped firmly. She stared at him, as if she was summing him up.

How old is she?

Ten weeks.

Such lovely eyes. What did they call her?

226

Grace.

That's nice.

I bent over and settled Grace's dummy in her mouth. *Are you back hame for the weekend?*

I try to get back every two or three weeks unless I've an assignment due. Thought I'd catch this festival of light thing in town as well. How's your da?

Better. The baby's made a huge difference to him.

That's great. She's really a lovely baby. Say congratulations to Mona.

Sure.

We were standing in the middle of the path at the front gate. A woman in a wheelchair weaved her way round us.

I think we're kind of blocking the entrance.

Yeah. We moved over to the side a bit, still hesitating. I didnae know what else to say.

I think I'd better go. Ma will be expecting me.

And I better get Grace hame.

See you.

In the heat of the moment, overcome by Grace's innocence and the light in the park, it had seemed like a good idea, but at nine-thirty next morning on a hard wooden pew in a gloomy church hoaching wi statues, it didnae seem that hot.

The only other folk waiting were a wee wifie in a rain-mate, an auld guy in a sour-smelling sportsjacket and a mum with two wee boys. I kept my eyes downcast, and tried, really tried, tae conjure up some sense of how I'd felt yesterday but I was numb. Worse than numb – stupid. When it came my turn to go in I almost got up and left but the wee wumman dunted me in the ribs and I found mysel in the confessional afore I knew it.

227

Bless me father for I have sinned. It is nearly three years since my last confession.

I'd written it all doon last night in case I was overcome with emotion. But I never felt anything as I went through my list:

I missed mass many times, I slept with a man many times, I felt hatred for my da, contempt for my sisters, I was selfish, I hurt other people, I lied . . .

When I stopped there was a small silence. Then an unfamiliar voice, high-pitched, thin.

My child, your father in heaven is rejoicing that his lost sheep has come back to him.

I still felt nothing but mibbe it didnae matter, mibbe it was daeing it that was important, no the feeling.

Can you say an act of contrition?

I stumbled out the words, stumbled out the box, out the chapel, blinking intae the grey light of a November street.

I DIDNAE EXPECT the light festival to be up to much. Glasgow's always putting on festivals but Edinburgh always manages to dae it bigger and better; there's something feels haund-knitted about the way we dae things. Mibbe all the folk that know how tae run them get snapped up by Edinburgh and we get left with the has-beens. Mibbe it's because Glaswegians cannae seem to go anywhere without leaving trails of sweetie wrappers and fast-food packages lying around behind them. Or that we don't know how tae dress. Or talk. Or something. Anyhow I'd no been that fussed about gaun tae the festival. But that night I found mysel round at my da's trying to persuade him and the twins to come.

What is it anyway, hen?

They've lit up all these buildings in the toon so you can walk round and look at them. There's exhibits as well, wi sound and motion and that. And a café in the City Halls.

Nae answer.

It's free.

I thought that might get my da interested but he said, *Sounds a bit arty for me.*

Da, it's just a chance tae walk about and see the architecture of Glasgow in a different way. You're the one always gaun on about how we don't appreciate wur ain buildings in this city, keep knocking them doon.

I resisted the temptation, never very far away, to add that he had almost contributed to the destruction of one of Glasgow's buildings.

He turned tae Mona and Rona. *What d'yous think, girls? D'yous want to go? Take the wee one tae see the lights?*

Don't be daft, it's baltic the night, said Mona. *Anyhow we're taking her in tae see the Christmas lights in George Square next week.*

You could see them the night.

Aye but the shops'll be shut.

That's the idea, so you can go and see the buildings.

Naa. Why don't you phone Janice — sounds like the kind of thing her and Angie will be intae.

But Angie and Janice were gaun tae a party. I'd either have to go on my ain or sit around watching *The X Factor*.

I'll see yous the morra, okay.

Fine, said my da, turning the volume up. *Mind you wrap up warm, now.*

It was as if the city had been reborn. Families, couples, people on their ain, all just walking, looking round them, laughing and pointing out the illuminations. Cars had been rerouted and, insteidy the hum of traffic, voices rang out intae the cold air. It was wonderful, what they'd done. Some buildings changed colours as you watched, others had a detail lit up, something you'd never normally notice. My da was right about folk in Glasgow – we never see what's round us. So much of the beauty of the buildings is high up and we're scurrying about at ground level, looking intae shops, heiding tae work. Like insects. But the Victorians who built Glasgow were proud of their city, wanted all the fancy stuff – columns and capitals, statues and gold leaf. I snapped away with my camera, hoping that at least some of the effect would come out with the flash, though I didnae hold out much hope. Then I turned the corner of the street that led along to GoMA. The front was all lit up in fluorescent green and they'd roofed the spaces on either side with tiny star-lights. I laughed out loud when I seen it, then felt stupid in case folk around thought I was mad.

The big event of the festival was about tae start and I made my way up the steep hill beside Strathclyde Uni, following the crowds to the viewing area on a piece of wasteground. There was a group of oldies at one side of me, and they moaned about how it was supposed tae start at eight o'clock and how come they never had any seats. I squeezed past them, stood at the back, high up so I could see better.

Doon below, at the bottom of the hill, was the contraption. You couldnae call it anything else – it was like something fae an auld Frankenstein movie, a machine made out of bits of metal and parts of engines, kind of like a train with big funnels. Even at this distance, it was enormous.

It began. Noises, at first like wee toots, then louder. A guy in a fluorescent suit, some kind of safety thing, was climbing around on it, twiddling stuff. By controlling the flame he could make different tones come out the funnels. He played tunes on them, turned the flames different colours. Fireworks went aff in time with the music, colours and sounds in rhythm and harmony, the guy running round the installation working it, calibrating everything. Like a DJ works the decks, works the crowd, samples and puts the music thegether, so this guy done with the light, the music, the machinery – everything working as one. Amazing.

I became aware of someone standing closer than a stranger would of. Jas. Out the corner of my eye I could see him. We never spoke or moved, just stood there watching, listening, experiencing, side by side.

The final part was a huge explosion of colours that zoomed and swooped intae the sky, accompanied by loud bangs and shrieks. A moment's silence then the crowd started tae move. Jas and I stood – I think neither of us was quite sure what to dae. Then I heard the voice of wanny the auld guys.

Well, that wasnae up tae much, was it?

Naw, says the auld dolly next tae him. *Nothing much really happened.*

I looked at Jas and we both burst out laughing.

He came closer, whispered in my ear. *True enough, no much happened. Just twenty minutes of explosions, sound, lights, fireworks all in synchronicity. Wonder where they've come fae – Beirut?*

I whispered back. *And they could of been at hame watching 'Celebrity Come Dancing'.*

We started to walk doon the hill thegether, part of the massive crowd of folk. It was cauld, but sharp and fresh, and I was wrapped up well so I didnae mind the nip on my cheeks.

It's weird how lighting makes such a difference tae the buildings.

I feel like I'm no in Glasgow, said Jas. *Naa, that's no right – it looks different, but it feels like Glasgow underneath.*

I walked beside him in silence for a moment. It did feel the same even though everything else had changed.

Must be the smell. No 'Glasgow's Miles Better' but 'Glasgow Smells Different'.

Jas laughed. *Aye, like the subway. My da always went on and on about that. How when they done it up in the seventies it never smelled the same afterwards. I used to think he was such a saddo.*

We reached the junction of Ingram Street and stood, hovering. Jas had on a thin jacket and his haunds were in his pockets. I had a leaflet with a plan of the light installations and Jas nodded at it. *Can I see?*

He placed his finger on the map. *Look, we're here.* He moved so we were staunding side by side under a streetlight, wanny they new ones that casts a natural light instead of the eerie orange glow that makes your face look blue. *That's this corner.* His elbow touched my side, muffled by layers of fleece. *And there's something along here.* He bent his heid and the side of it touched my forehead, just as it had in the library that first time we kissed. Then he straightened and pointed alang the street.

The Ramshorn Kirk is stark and gloomy, in keeping with the rows of solemn gravestones ranged at the back. But tonight the garden was starred with light, bushes and trees sprinkled wi glitter. As we walked round, the lights changed colours. You'd move towards one and it suddenly leapt at you. The lights washed over the trees; as one set went aff another went on, waves sweeping fae blue tae green tae pink.

A wee girl skipped along the path in fronty us, hauding her daddy's haund. *We're in fairyland!*

Aye, hen.

Jas said softly, *Fiona, look up.*

233

Usually the city sky has a cloudy cover which muffles the starlight. But tonight it was a vault studded by stars with a perfect crescent moon like a sliver of ice, riding high in the darkness.

They'd set up a café in the Candleriggs but Jas and me drifted towards the west end. At the junction of Byres Road we stood, Jas cupping his haunds over his mouth and blowing on them.

You gaun back tae Aberdeen the morra?

I think I'll hang on and get the early train back on Monday.

Oh — right.

He nodded, looked round. *Got time for a hot chocolate?*

So what's Aberdeen like?

Baltic.

Worse than the night?

That's what caught me out. Glasgow always seems warm by comparison so I never put on enough layers.

Global warming.

I guess. But it was great for the festival — too cold to rain.

Having a festival outside in Glasgow in November is really brave. Or stupid.

It was brilliant but. He stirred the froth of his coffee. *So how's your work, Fiona?*

Dunno. Hard tae say really.

Ma said you won a prize. It was in the free paper — she reads it from cover to cover, says it's the only way you ever find out what's happening in Glasgow.

I was surprised Mrs Kaur mentioned me to Jas.

I got to show my work in a London gallery.

Cool.

I guess.

234

*I mean you should be winning prizes and all that — just they
don't always go to the right folk.*

*I'm no sure they got it right with me — I'm trying tae get this
thing finished the noo and it's driving me mad.*

*Divine discontent. Who was it, Michelangelo or someone said that
— the artist is never satisfied with their work.*

It's no just that, but. See the installation the night—

Jas put doon his cup and turned to me and it was the old
Jas — animated, like when he used tae talk about Shelley or
photography. *It's awesome how the guy made everything work
thegether — light, sound, technology — like an old car that needs tae
be coaxed into life by someone who knows it. There's always a risk
something'll go wrong and it'll fall flat. He has to be in tune with
it, be with it — every time he does it, it'll be different.*

And no just because the audience is different. I stared at the
bottom of the mug where the remains of the chocolate had
solidified.

What you thinking, Fiona?

Wish I could dae something like that.

Why not?

Don't be daft.

I mean it. You can dae anything . . . if you really want to enough.

I looked at him. *What about you, Jas? D'you still keep up your
art?*

*Never really have time. I mean I still take photies but it's no the
same. It's just a way of remembering.*

Jas walked me back to the flat where we said goodbye casu-
ally, like pals who would see each other around.

I couldnae sleep but tossed and turned then finally got up,
wrapped in a blanket, and looked out the windae. Stared
across at the bit of wasteground with its fringe of scabby trees

and bushes. A frozen puddle of water glowed blue and violet in the lights fae the streetlamps. I kept thinking about the light installations, the way they had made the city a different and lovely place.

My wee boxes were nearly ready for the end of term show and there was only a couple of weeks left. I'd nae clear sense of how I could take the half-formed ideas and feelings that had arisen inside me tonight, use them to make something better. It seemed too big somehow, like trying tae keep a tiger inside a pillowcase.

I went back tae bed, blanket still wrapped round me like a shroud. I shut my eyes and kept gaun over and over in my heid every detail I could remember of the light show. I knew I should relax, try to let go so I could sleep but every time I did an image of Jas came over me and I must not think of him.

IT WAS CRAP. Everyone else said it was good but to me, smouldering with all these ideas about art being alive, being about change and risk, it was static, dull, predictable.

A row of shoe boxes, the interior of each done out like a pensioner's living room, with beige carpet and wallpaper. I'd tried real wallpaper but the pattern was too big in proportion to the room so I'd used lining paper, painted neat regency stripes and faint geometric patterns on it. The furniture was made out of matchboxes and bits of plastic. I'd upholstered chairs in scraps of fabric, crocheted tiny antimacassars and tablecloths, used washing up liquid tops for cups. Each room had a TV made fae a matchbox, and on each was a different image: a football match, a garden, a woman's face, an advert for washing powder. There was no one in the rooms.

The only bit I really liked was the hedges which ran along the outside of each room, like one of those hauf-doors they have in stables. Some were in thick luxurious wool, others funky yarn wi glitter or ribbons woven through it – I'd even knitted one out of wire. I'd struggled for ages with a title, a sure sign that there was something unclear about the work. Eventually I called it 'Hedging'.

We were having what was called a peer-group assessment session by a group of students in my class, supervised by the tutor. Because I'd had the exhibition in London folk expected something special from me and I think he was disappointed. But they're no supposed tae be judgemental – their role, as it says in the handbook, is to lead each student to the development of their unique talents, to nurture and bring out the inherent qualities of each piece of work, rather than using alien criteria.

Very low-key compared to your other work, isn't it?

I guess.

Anyone else like to comment?

I like the hedges, said Mihaila. *So suburban. It's neat – something which is meant to give the householder privacy actually reveals them to the viewer.*

Yeah, added Paul. *And there's no one in the house, only a TV on. More of that urban alienation stuff you did with the Barbies.*

All very positive. The tutor smiled like a primary teacher whose class had performed well in front of an inspector. *But, if I might suggest something? Your little knitted chairs and furniture?*

Uhhuh.

I can see what you're doing, of course.

I'm glad someone can.

But they're so neatly made that they're in danger of eclipsing the irony rather than pointing it up.

How d'you mean?

If you make them a bit rougher round the edges, do them with less precision, then we can see them as art rather than something a real granny might make for her grandchild's doll's house. D'you see what I mean?

Knitting is only art when it's done badly?

He laughed. *Have I walked into some hornet's nest of feminist reclamation of craft, Fiona?*

I just don't see what you're getting at. I don't think this is my best work — mibbe it's something I need to dae on the way to something better — but I really don't see how knitting badly will give it more artistic credentials.

Actually, Fiona, I wrote a monograph on this very subject — the relationship between art and craft. I'll lend you the book if you like but the gist of it, as I'm sure you'll know anyway, is that for craft to be art it must be done with a knowing, self-referential eye. Your granny making a tapestry chair cover patterned with the Mona Lisa because she thinks it's nice is not art, but an artist using the Mona Lisa as an iconic reference in her own work is.

I knew I'd pissed him aff but I was so mad.

I'm sorry, I said. *I didnae mean to be rude.*

It's good to get angry at criticism, Fiona, all part of the healthy debate and dialogue which keeps art alive. Have a think about what I've said and we'll meet again in January. I liked what you said about this being a step on the way to a bigger and better project. I like your honesty, I think it's part of what makes your art so vibrant. Now, let's look at your sculpture, Jason.

I was mad, but no at what he'd said. I was mad at myself, mad that this crap I'd produced was even being taken seriously. My granny used tae crochet chair covers, knit clothes for dolls — it was her taught me tae knit. Chair covers and dolls' clothes were leisure pursuits to her; during the time her ain family were growing up she'd had tae spend hours knitting jumpers for her man and her weans – Mammy, Janice and the two older brothers who'd emigrated tae Canada years ago. There was nothing ironic or self-referential about her arthritic fingers flying over the stitches, one eye on *Coronation Street*. The wee covers the tutor thought I'd made too perfect were pathetic compared to what my granny could dae wi her eyes shut. As for the cardboard boxes that served as houses, my grandpa would of made them in wood with beautifully dovetailed joins. Even my daddy made us a doll's house when we were wee – out of a kit just – he wasnae the craftsman my grandpa had been but he'd laboured for hours over it, painted and wallpapered it, even redecorated it when the twins spilled juice all doon the walls.

Patrick and me used tae spend hours playing with that house, moving the wee dolls in and out, sitting them round the table for their meals, putting them tae bed at night. My da never thought it was right for Patrick to play with it, used tae try to get him away. *Come and have a wee kickabout in the back court, son.* But Patrick wasnae interested and only the twins ever wanted to play footie. I wondered how much of a disappointment we were tae my da. Clearly Patric wasnae the son he'd expected to bond with, but then we werenae his ideal daughters either. I was too weird, too arty, and for all he loved wee Grace it was hard on a man so deep-doon conventional to have a daughter pregnant at fifteen.

It was easier for Mammy. She could accept us for who we were, seemed tae understaund who needed a bit of freedom and who needed to be kept on a tight rope, knew when she should speak and when tae let us be. Mibbe that's part of being a mother, no a father, or mibbe it was just her nature. And I'll never know cause I cannae ever ask her now. Somehow

240

her dying has robbed me, no just of the times I've had with her but of times to come, when I could talk to her like an adult. But then look at what Da had lost. Mibbe we were too hard on him after all.

MONA AND DECLAN got engaged at Christmas, no long after the twins turned sixteen. Declan was at college noo, studying catering, but he'd a part-time job in a hotel and had saved up for the ring. Declan's parents took us all out for a meal and I took photies. Mona's favourite was of her and Declan, with Grace on her knee, her ring in full view of the camera, so I made a large print which she framed and hung in the living room, next to the others of Grace. Afore the fire there were loads of photies, a wall of them where you could read the story of our family from Mammy and Daddy's engagement and wedding through the baby photies, school photies, first communions, all the formal occasions. Mammy kept albums of snaps too — holidays, maistly — us making sandcastles, or her and Da having a glass of wine in the sun at a beach café. I preferred them to the posed ones. We seemed mair real in them, just better looking, less peelywally versions of wur real selves. But there werenae that many – this was afore digital cameras made it okay to take endless snaps in the hope that one would turn out good.

There were nae photies of the memories I wanted to preserve; us sitting round the table having tea, playing in the back court wi a tent made out the washing line, a doll's tea party with water slittered everywhere.

But what difference would it make – they'd of been destroyed in the fire too.

Afterwards Janice had given my da a few of her snaps of Mammy but, though he looked at them privately, he never put any up in public. That different fae Jas's house where a photo of his dad was displayed prominently, flowers in front of it like a shrine.

Patric came up for Christmas but Amrik stayed in London. *He's gigging three days solid,* said Patric. He poured a few drops of bleach in the sink, filled it with cold water and swirled it round. *I think I might go back for the New Year.*

To London?

He nodded.

The smell of bleach caught the back of my throat. If Patric did go away for the New Year it would be the first time ever. And in our fragmented lives I kept hauding on tae every bit of continuity there was.

D'you have tae?

No, I don't have to but . . .

He pulled out the plug and the water glugged away.

* * *

243

In the end, Amrik came to Glasgow. Patric was tentative about it, walking on eggshells round me.

You don't need to see each other, Fiona. Unless you feel okay about it.

I didnae know how I'd feel. But if Patric and Amrik were serious, I'd need tae get used to it.

Patric brought Amrik round for the bells at my da's house afore they went aff tae some trendy party thegether. He'd asked me to go wi them but I don't think he was too disappointed when I said no. Which made me feel sad, cause it was the first time in my life I'd felt Patric didnae want me to be with him.

Da had already had a few too many afore they came round.

Have a whisky, son, he said. *Fiona, get Patric's pal a whisky, hen.*

No thank you, Mr O'Connell, said Amrik.

Is that cause you're a Muslim?

No Da, Amrik is Sikh.

Sick, that's a good yin, said my da. *Rhymes an all. Amrik is sick. Have a wee whisky — it'll make you feel better.*

Da . . . I said pointedly.

Sorry, son, nae offence, nae offence.

None taken, Mr O'Connell. In any case I do not practise Sikhism now.

Ah mean ah'm no a racist, you know, ah couldnae care less what colour anybody is. Fiona'll tell you. That lassie's only ever had two boyfriends and baith of them were Asian. And did that bother me — no it never did, well you know ah'd of preferred if they'd been Catholic Asians, but.

Rona came intae the living room. *Mona and Declan are on their way — had tae change Grace at the last minute but they should be here afore the bells.*

That's good. Rona, meet Patric's pal.

Amrik put out his haund. *Amrik.*

Amrik and Patric — hey that rhymes — just like me and my twin sister — Mona and Rona. And Fiona — sort of.

Amrik nodded.

Have you no got a drink yet, son? Fiona, get the boy a drink. If you don't want a whisky what'll you take? A beer? A lemonade?

I went in the kitchen, opened the fridge and pulled out a beer. Patric followed me. *I'll strangle him,* I said.

It's cool, said Patric. *Bells in ten minutes.*

What d'you want?

I brought some wine — it's over there.

Patric helped me take drinks through. My da continued to try tae engage Amrik in conversation. *So what is it you dae doon in London, son?*

I'm a musician. I play sitar.

Zat right? Fiona, thon guy you went wi for a while — Jas's brother — did he no dae that too? What was his name, hen?

Amrik.

Aye, Amrik. He looked from me to Amrik and the penny dropped, but just at that moment Mona, Declan and Grace arrived in a flurry of wet coats and baby paraphernalia.

Just made it.

Amrik, this is Mona, Declan and Grace. This is Patric's friend.

Hi.

What d'yous want tae drink — only five minutes tae the bells.

I'll have a vodka and coke — and a beer for Declan.

When I returned everyone was squashed round the living room. As I handed out the drinks, my da said, *Is there no a bit of shortbread in the hoose, hen? It's no the New Year without a bit of shortbread in your haund.* I went back in the kitchen, piled some on a plate and gied that out as well. There was naewhere tae

245

sit so I stood at the kitchen door while Da adjusted the sound on the TV to watch the countdown to the bells. Some TV presenter muffled in scarves, with Edinburgh Castle in the background and folk shouting and waving in the street behind her, then a messy join to Big Ben and the countdown to the bells. Three, two, one.

Declan kissing Mona then Rona. Mona and Rona hugging each other, then me and Declan. I came out of the squash to see Patric hugging my da first, then Da's stunned face as Patric turned and kissed Amrik full on the lips.

My da must of been too shocked to say anything and after the bells there was such chaos – a phone call fae Janice and Angie, Declan phoning his ma, Grace waking up and needing fed – that the moment passed.

After Patric and Amrik had left for their party, Mona, Rona and Declan put on their coats.

Are you coming with us, Fiona?

I shook my heid, though the last thing I wanted was to sit in the hoose.

Naa, I'll stay and look after Gracie if you like.

It's cool, we'll take her with us. Mibbe see yous later if you're still up.

So there we were, me and the da, clocked on the couch with folk in tartan frocks and sashes birlin round in fronty us.

D'you no want the sound up on that, Da? I said.

Ach, I'm no bothered.

Will I make us a cuppa tea?

Dunno hen. D'you want one?

I didnae want anything but I thought it might be a chance to get him tae stop drinking, put some food inside him.

I returned fae the kitchen wi a tray of sandwiches, teapot and two mugs.

I poured the tea out, put in milk, one sugar in his, and stirred. He took a sip and put it doon. *Hot.*

Have a sandwich, Da. They're your favourite.

My da loves sandwiches with disgusting fishpaste in them.

Thanks, hen. He took one, nibbled a corner then replaced it on the plate.

Fiona, did I just see what I thought I did?

I nodded.

He sighed. *I don't understaund.*

I thought you knew Patric was gay.

He never said.

Aye but he's twenty-five and he's never had a girlfriend.

I never had a girlfriend till I was twenty. And I never brung a girl hame till I met your mammy and we were gonnae get engaged. Folk didnae.

I know, it's different now.

Too different. I'm a dinosaur, hen. Extinct. If your mammy had been alive, it'd of been different. She'd of known. She always knew — whatever was happening with yous weans, she understood.

I know.

But I don't understaund. I mean I know it happens — but watching your son kissing another man, well, it made me feel sick inside.

I took his haund, squeezed it. I couldnae say a word, because, deep doon, for very different reasons fae my da's, it made me feel the same. I'd thought I was cool about Patric and Amrik, could haundle it. But when I seen him and Patric kissing, everything went blurred. No because they were men, that wasnae the issue — but because I just didnae want him tae be with my brother.

*   *   *

247

When the phone went I thought it'd be Mona or Rona to say they were staying over wi Declan's folks.

Da roused hissel fae his dwam in fronty the TV. *I'll get it, hen. Hello?* Suddenly Da sounded a lot mair animated. *Happy New Year to you too. It's Mrs Kaur.*

That's nice, I said. He blethered away and I went intae the kitchen, started to clear away the dishes and food.

Fiona, he called me through to the living room. *Mrs Kaur wants to speak to you.*

I took the receiver.

Hello.

Hello Fiona, I just wanted to say happy New Year.

Happy New Year to you too.

Are your sisters with you just now?

They're out at a party — it's just me and my da in the house.

Like me and Jaswinder.

Oh. I paused. *That's nice.*

Would you like to speak to him dear? I'll pass you on.

Thanks.

I could hear her saying something in the background then Jas's voice, clear as if he was next tae me.

Happy New Year.

You too. Pause. *You hame for the holidays?*

Aye.

Having a nice time?

Quiet.

Me too.

My da was signalling something at me. *Look, I think my da wants to speak to your ma again.*

Okay. Well, have a good holiday.

You too.

See you.

I put my haund on my da's shoulder.

I'm away tae bed noo, Da.

Right, hen.

Don't stay up too long.

I'll no.

In the room that used tae be mines but was now Rona's, papered with posters of skinny women and guys wi six-packs, I lay awake for what felt like hours. I tried tae read and it did make me feel sleepy but when I put the light out my mind returned tae endless birling.

I only seen Patric once on his ain during the holidays, when we went out for some fresh air the day after New Year. It was miserable; puddle-grey sky that kept threatening but never actually did rain. No much open apart fae the supermarket but in Byres Road you can always find a café and we sat in the wee one next the chippie, cosy and steamy wi damp coats and the smell of frying food.

Are yous ready to order?

I could murder a bacon roll, said Patric.

Didnae think you ate things like that any mair.

I don't usually, but. He looked at the menu. *Can I have a bacon, egg and tattie scone roll and cup of white coffee, please?*

Sure.

Me too.

Patric looked round. *I've no been in here for years – didn't they used to have a picture of fishing boats over there?*

He redecorated a few months ago. Actually I've no been in since. Used tae come here with Jas sometimes.

That's the first time I've heard you mention his name since you split. D'you never see him now?

No. I did bump intae him a month ago, but.

The waitress arrived with our coffees. *Rolls are coming in a minute.*

Ta. Patric took a sip. *Good coffee.* He replaced his cup.

Fi, I wanted to talk to you about Amrik.

What about him?

Are you okay, about us?

I told you I was.

I know, but it's different saying it and seeing us together. My da was a bit . . .

What d'you expect? He never even knew you were gay.

Course he did.

Did you ever tell him?

Not in so many words but I assumed.

Assumptions.

Assumptions?

Jas always used tae rant about them. It's assumptions that cause all the trouble. You assumed he knew because all the signals you were giving out showed you were gay. And that's fine for me and Janice and all the other folk that assume that some people might actually be gay. But my da hasnae a clue. Then you start kissing Amrik in fronty him.

I guess I've been away too long.

You're lucky. Some fathers would have punched Amrik.

What about you, Fiona? I cannae help feeling you're hiding something.

Like what?

You tell me. As far as Amrik is concerned, you guys hung out a bit and had a nice time, then moved on.

So?

So why do I get the feeling that's not how you see it?

I don't know.

250

Fiona, I'd do anything not to hurt you.

I know. And I know you love Amrik.

I do.

So that's fine.

But I need to know, Fi. Is there something else, something more, between you and Amrik? Even if he didnae think it was important, did you?

This was the moment of truth. I could tell Patric about the miscarriage and it would be up tae him. The weight I was carrying on my shoulders, the responsibility of no hurting him, worrying whether I should let him know what Amrik was really like – all that would go. Patric would know the truth. He could decide whether tae stay with Amrik or to gie him up for my sake. Mibbe it wouldnae even be a conscious decision. Surely when he heard how badly Amrik had behaved to his wee sister, he'd fall out of love for him. Could you really love someone once you knew things like that about them?

And what would I feel then? If he left Amrik because of me I'd be even mair responsible. If, sometime in the future, he blamed me for lossing the love of his life?

I looked intae Patric's steady blue eyes. *D'you really want the truth, Patric?*

Of course I do.

I took a deep breath, treading the fine line of my decision. *For once and for all, there is nothing between me and Amrik. So just be happy thegether.*

A grin spread across his face, an old Patrick grin. He put his haund across and held mines. *I'm glad, sis, really glad.*

They say that the second Monday in January is the most depressing day of the year. There was this article in a paper left lying in Giardini's, saying that after Christmas and the New Year everybody gets fired up with their resolutions, then after a week at work, miserable weather and finding that nothing is any different, they get depressed. No depressed exactly, but a bit flat, scunnered with life. I knew the feeling. Things seemed tae be happening to everyone else but the only thing in my life that could absorb me, stop me feeling as if I was luggin mysel round like a giant suitcase – my work – just wasnae working. All these great ideas about making art that was of the moment, and I couldnae figure out a way to dae it.

Then there was Jas. After seeing him at the light festival I'd tried no tae think of him, but the phone call at the New Year had disturbed me. Did he want to talk to me or was he just being polite? And I wondered how much he knew about Amrik and Patric, and whether it had been as much of a shock to him as it had to me.

MONA AND DECLAN, *you have asked the Church to confer the sacrament of baptism on your child.*

Evie tugged at my sleeve. *What's a sacramnent?*

An outward sign of inward grace, replied my da afore I had time tae answer. *Shoosh the noo, darlin, we'll explain it after the priest's done his stuff.*

Evie sat entranced while Father Donaghy took a light fae the Easter candle and tapers were lit and passed round the congregation. Rona and Declan's brother, Aiden, were godparents and they stood with Mona and Declan while we all renewed our baptismal promises. Wrapped in a white shawl, Grace looked round at all the adults as if she knew exactly what they were daeing. Even when the priest drapped the

253

water on her heid she only gied a wee cry, of surprise it sounded like, mair than anything else.

Did the priest wash me when I was a baby? Evie whispered.

I placed my fingers over my lips and shook my heid at her and she turned back to the show.

Mammy had wanted Janice to get Evie christened but Janice thought it'd be hypocritical.

We're thinking of having a naming ceremony. Just in the house. After all I don't go any mair and Angie's not Catholic, so why would we get her christened?

It's for Evie, but.

I still don't see the point.

Lots of folk get their baby baptised even though they're no regular churchgoers.

Aye, but it's just an excuse for a party.

I didnae mean it like that. She took Janice's airm, looked her in the eye. *It's a blessing, a very special one, and I think everyone needs all the blessings they can get.*

Janice hugged her, and they held each other for a moment. *I'm sorry, Geraldine — I just cannae.*

Da had hired the function room of a nearby hotel, and we sat at tables loaded with sandwiches and party food, while young girls in white frilly pinnies served us tea and coffee. An older waitress in a black frock came round tae take the drinks orders. I was glad Mrs Kaur was sitting at our table as it meant my da was less likely to go overboard.

Evie wandered over with a mini-pizza in her haund. *Auntie Fiona, can I sit at your table?*

Sure, Evie. Have you finished all the pizza at yours?

Not yet. She knelt on the seat next tae me. *You said you'd tell me about the sacramnent.*

What do you want tae know?

Everything.

I turned to my da. *Da, you started this, talking about sacraments.*

He put doon his sandwich. *A sacrament is very special. The priest does something on the outside, like putting the water on the baby, and something special happens on the inside.* He turned to Mrs Kaur. *Is it the same in your religion?*

There are special ceremonies for things like marriage, naming a child. And of course the langar is very important.

What's that?

We bring food to share after the service at the Gurdwara — anyone can come and eat it. It shows that all people are equal in the sight of God.

What kind of food?

All kinds of things. It's very nice.

Sounds a bit better than a cuppa tea and a biscuit efter mass, eh?

You should come one Sunday.

Evie had been eating her way through all the pizza on our table and now it was finished she was ready to restart our conversation.

The sacramnent . . . the baptising. Did I get that?

No Evie, you had a naming ceremony.

At first Da had refused tae go. *Look Geraldine, ah've stood by and said nothing while she set up hame with a woman, then had a baby by God knows who, but I'm no condoning some heathen nonsense insteidy a proper christening.*

She might change her mind in the future, Bobby — I hope she does. But if we start gettin all judgemental on her there's a lot less chance she'll have Evie christened.

So he went. We all did. But it was weird. When you go to the chapel, there's a way of daeing things, a tradition. Even if you don't believe in it, you're part of something bigger. But all of us staunding round their living room while Janice held the baby and Angie recited some poem they'd made up and got us to put flowers in a circle – well it was a nice idea but it was embarrassing. Cause they were trying tae make it mean something when it didnae.

I tried tae change the subject. *What happens at the naming ceremony for babies in Sikhism Mrs Kaur?*

We have special prayers. And the baby will get its first kara, the steel bangle that Sikhs wear.

See there's lots of different ways to give a baby their name and your mammy chose a naming ceremony for you.

Evie finished chewing. *I don't want a naming. I want to get a sacramnent.*

I knew what I wanted too but I still couldnae work out how tae make it happen. Usually I hated saying anything about what I was planning; I liked to go underground, think, try things out till I got something that worked. But this piece required skills I just didnae have.

At first I tried my ain sweet way. Got bits of wood at B&Q, put them thegether with glue and nails. Useless. I thought about taking a woodworking course but they all started in September and when I phoned up there was nae spaces.

They're very popular, always get booked up the first week, the woman said.

* * *

I stood in *Toys'R'Us*, in fronty a huge Victorian doll's house, open at the front to reveal the maids in the attic, the children in the nursery and the lady taking tea in the drawing room. The furniture and dolls were hideous plastic stuff but the house itself was a solid wooden structure. I examined it carefully to see if it could be adapted to what I wanted. The basic shape was right but the price tag said £159.99.

Mona, Rona and Declan stood behind me with Grace in her buggy, sound asleep.

That's gorgeous, isn't it? said Rona. *She's a bit young for it but.*

I'm looking for something to help me in my work.

Mona made a face. *You're obsessed wi toys, Fiona. First Barbies, noo a doll's house.*

It's no . . . What was the point of trying to explain? It sounded stupid when you said it out loud, probably was stupid anyway.

I thought when you went tae Art School you'd learn how tae paint pictures.

That's part of it.

Anyway, said Mona, *we won't need tae buy Grace a doll's house — her daddy can make one for her.*

Her daddy? I looked at Declan, who said nothing but smiled shyly. *Can you dae woodwork, Declan?*

Aye, learned it at school.

He's won prizes for it.

That's great.

I did think of getting a trade in it, know, carpentry and that, but there's nae apprenticeships, it's a lot easier tae get jobs in the catering trade.

This was the longest speech I'd ever heard Declan make.

He's dead handy. You should see the unit he made for his ma's bedroom; exactly the right size for the space between the bed and the

wall, fitted in wee shelves for her book and her specs and the remote.
Even stained it tae match the bed.

Cool.

Anyway, said Mona, *we're gonnae get a coffee – coming?*

It took me ages to pluck up the courage tae ask Declan to help, no because I thought he'd refuse, or even because I dreaded Mona's reaction – though I did – but because I felt a huge wave of shame surge through me every time I thought about it. Every noo and again Declan and me would be alone thegether in the living room when the twins were daeing some mysterious twin thing in their bedroom, and the sight of Declan, his placidity and good humour, opened up this enormous cavern of guilt.

All the time Mona had been with Declan I'd practically ignored him. Since Grace had come alang, I'd been mair aware of his good qualities; that stolid patience which made me impatient while he hung around Mona showed itself as a beautiful virtue when I saw him unfazed by a young baby's grizzly and apparently unstoppable crying. Declan would walk up and doon wi Grace on his shoulder far longer than anyone else could ever be bothered. I'd started to gie him his due, but had never tried tae find out who he was or what he liked – never even thought of him having a particular talent or skill. And now, when I needed that talent of his, how could I suddenly ask him to help me? Eventually, after a couple of weeks, I knew there was nae way round it so when Declan was helping me wash up after tea I blurted it all out. And he said, *Sure, when d'you need it for?*

With Declan started on the woodwork, I could concentrate on the furnishings. I drew sketches, made furniture from matchboxes, plastic, card and anything else I could reclaim;

knitted and crocheted, glued and painted till I'd got it right. I ignored all the stuff the tutor said about being ironic and leaving things unfinished or deliberately scruffy. Even got a book out the library about making furniture and costumes for doll's houses, pored over the detail of it till I figured out my way of adapting the proper techniques. It was as true as I could make it – the only parts that were scruffy and un-finished were the parts that would of been that way in real life.

I stayed as late as I could at Art School every night, grab-bing a sandwich or some pasta at Giardini's, then working on. I went back to the flat only in time for a cuppa tea, shower and bed. Sometimes there'd be someone in the living room watching a DVD but I hardly seen any of the others. I'd thought flat-sharing would be like a family except mair fun, but we were like planets orbiting in different paths, just every now and again finding ourselves near one another.

One night I came back about ten tae find Clytemnestra in the kitchen, concocting some mush out of mung beans and alfalfa sprouts.

Hey, Fi. Gosh I haven't seen you about for ages.

I've been working late at Art School.

The muse flowing?

I guess. I just keep working anyway.

I must talk to you about this some day – you know, the creative process and all that.

Oh, sure. I opened the fridge for some milk. Stuck tae the door were cards wi words on them, arranged in squiggly lines:

who sees purple balance

green scale

psychedelic black

red

259

I pointed. *What's this?*

When someone comes into the kitchen they can change some of the words and make a new poem, building on the first one. Collaborate. Have a go, Fiona — the box is beside the toaster.

On the lid was printed 'An Artist's Poetry Kit'. I pulled words out the box, spread them on the counter: best, then, do, fiery, impression, monument, chisel, symbol. *What on earth is 'latex' daeing in here?*

Clytemnestra giggled.

You know, Fiona, I was thinking it would be fun to have a party on Saturday.

Cool.

It's my birthday, well actually it's not the day on my birth certificate but you know I was a premature baby. She paused as if this was a publicly known fact, the kind of thing you'd be embarrassed not tae know, like the date of Bannockburn or something.

Oh.

Six weeks early — I was tiny. She made a shape with her haunds about the size of a mouse. *My therapist's encouraging me to celebrate the date I should have been born. See I'm Aquarius but I should have been Aries and there's such a big difference between the signs it's like my psyche has its wires crossed.*

Oh well, any excuse for a party.

What's this about a party? The front door opened and Sanjeet clattered across the hall and entered the kitchen.

I'm having one on Saturday, said Clytemnestra.

Cool. Hey, you picked a good weekend to come down, mate.

Just behind Sanj, Jas hesitated in the doorway.

This is Jas — Clytemnestra, Fiona.

Hi, said Jas.

Hi.

260

I've told Nicole about the party and she's going to bring some people, but I haven't seen Eric for days. Nicole says he's been staying over with his new girlfriend.

Sanj was at the sink filling the kettle. *I seen him today down Byres Road. He's got a job as one of those charity muggers.*

Charity muggers? Clytemnestra looked blank.

You know, they come up to you with a clipboard, try to get you to sign a direct debit for some charity. The sight of Eric's hairy legs in baggy shorts made me want to run a mile. And the way he was smiling at people. Sanj mimed a hideous rictus. *God knows how he got the job. Who's for tea and who's for coffee?* He set out four mugs on the counter. *Clyte, d'you want one of these herby things?*

No thanks, Sanj.

Jas? Fi?

Tea, please.

I should head, Sanj, Jas said.

Have a cuppa coffee, man.

Jas looked at me, then, hesitantly, sat doon at the table.

Sanj planted the mugs in front of us. *So, Fi, how's the art coming along? Fiona's our resident artist, Jas.*

Jas looked at his mug. *Fiona and I were at school thegether.*

Cool, said Sanj.

I turned my mug round and round. *How d'yous two know each other?*

My cousin is on Jas's course in Aberdeen. We met when I was up there one weekend and, you know, now when Jas comes home . . . we hang out. When he's no studying. Works too hard. Like you. Sanj swigged his coffee. *Were they all like that at your school?*

What d'you mean?

Workaholics.

Well there's no chance of anyone calling you that, Sanj, said Clytemnestra.

261

Nope, replied Sanj. *Everything in its place. Work is all very well but you have to chill.*

Jas finished his coffee. *And I have to go.*

I'll get that DVD out my room for you, said Sanj.

Jas stood up, nodded at Clytemnestra. *Nice to meet you. See you, Fiona.*

You need to change something in the poem before you go. Clytemnestra handed him the box of words. Jas sorted through them, laying words out on the table. When Sanj reappeared he put the box doon, lifted his jacket fae the back of the chair.

I hope we'll see you at the party Saturday, said Clytemnestra. *Any time after ten, okay?*

I'm no sure. Jas heided out the door.

He'll be here, said Sanj, following him.

Look at this — nice. Clytemnestra placed the words Jas had chosen on the fridge, under the original poem.

I smear passion on my canvases
approach concrete that shimmers.

I lifted the mugs, took them over to the sink and placed them in the soapy water.

THE HARSH LIGHT of the close glared at me as soon as I opened the door. I sat on the stone stair, resting my cheek against the smooth wall tiles. The cold seeped through me but I didnae care. I wanted to cool doon, escape from the suffocating heat and smoke and mass of warm bodies inside the flat. My throat was sore from talking over the noise of music.

Things had started quietly; a few of Clytemnestra's dippy pals fae the chanting group sitting round on cushions in the living room sipping white wine. When Nicole brought some folk back after a concert, dressed in penguin suits and black frocks, the room looked surreal as if a black tie do had got mixed up wi some hippy convention. Around midnight Eric arrived with a gang of rugby-playing types who filled the kitchen with loud voices and beer cans, then Sanj showed up with a crew fae the pub. One of the guys was a DJ so the music and dancing started in earnest.

I'd practised in my heid what I'd dae if Jas turned up, alternating between gaun up to him with a casual, *How you doing?* or waiting to see if he approached me first. I'd taken extra care about how I looked, putting a floaty top over my jeans and winding a piece of chiffon round my hair, even wearing a pair of glittery shoes I'd got at the Mela. But when he arrived, I just felt shy and awkward, and there was a pain in my stomach which might of been from Clytemnestra's punch. I was squashed in a corner between Elvira and Hannah, who were discussing the merits of reiki as opposed to aromatherapy massage.

What kind of massage d'you prefer, Fiona?

I've never had a massage.

They recoiled in horror as if I'd said I'd never had a shower.

You must let me give you one, said Elvira. *I'm training so you'd count towards my practice. I'd only charge you a tenner.*

Thanks, I said. *But I have sensitive skin.*

See, that's why reiki is so good, started Hannah.

'Scuse me, I think I'll get a drink.

The door of the flat opened and Jas came out. *Great minds,* he said. *Can I join you?*

I moved along a bit to gie him room.

It's mental in there.

Too stuffy.

We sat for a minute in silence then he looked at me and said, *Nice top.*

Got it out a second-hand shop. I don't know if it's really seventies but it looks it. I held out the sleeve which was fluted and hung doon like a mediaeval lady's. Jas put his haund out and touched it. I felt my face flush.

Someone spilt red wine on it but.

Shame.

I guess it'll wash out, I said and hauf-turned towards him. Our heids were touching, his forehead and mines, his thick shiny hair against my scarf, the fabric slipping doon over my eyes as we turned tae each other and our lips touched. Almost no a kiss at all so light and soft it was, mair like a butterfly kiss where you flutter your eyelashes against someone's cheek – the touch so gentle you can hardly feel it. Us moving slightly apart tae look in each other's eyes but so shy that we looked away again almost immediately, easier tae sit side by side only our heads touching. Then he put his airm round me and bent his heid and this time we kissed properly, softly but deeply, then came apart and looked, and this time he smiled and so did I.

The rediscovery of love is like looking out at the back court tae see snowdrops growing on a piece of wasteground at the bin shelter. Nature goes through periods when everything is buried, nothing visible above the earth, but underneath something's happening. The bulbs must of been there all the time, deep underground, waiting, but you never knew.

So it was with me and Jas. As subtle and as delicate as snowdrops.

We were that shy with one another at the start. I wasnae even sure we had actually got back thegether the night of the party cause all we done was sit on the steps in silence for ages, till wur bums were numb and cold, then Jas said, *I better go, Fiona. This is too . . . Anyway, I'd walk you home if you didnae live here.*

265

I wish I didnae tonight. This is gonnae go on for hours.

Look, I'll phone you the morra, okay?

Right.

No too early.

He bent over, kissed me lightly on the cheek and was gone.

When he called and we went for coffee on the Sunday afternoon, it was like friends. He never kissed me when we met and we never held haunds walking alang the road. We sat outside in the April sun and it was nice but suddenly I didnae know what tae say. I didnae want tae chat about the party or what Jas was daeing at uni. It was too much like how it used tae be, but so many miles had passed between us. Jas jiggled his leg against the metal table. He dropped his teaspoon on the pavement. I looked at him as he bent to pick it up, the line of his hair so neatly cut and shiny, the back of his neck dark and smooth. I wanted to reach out and stroke it but my haund would not move.

Later we went to the park and sat on the grass under a tree. Blossom flittered doon and stuck to wur hair and clothes. Jas touched my wrist. I grasped his haund firmly and rolled over close, leaning on my elbows, facing him. He pulled me doon and kissed me, then I nuzzled my nose against his.

It was only after Jas went back tae Aberdeen that we started to talk and even then, only about what was happening, nothing about the past. But we'd talk on the phone and text, and as the weeks went by I started to feel closer to him. I was still working hard at Art School and looked forward to getting messages from Jas when I stopped for a break. I usually went tae Giardini's for a coffee around three and felt as though Jas was with me, as I sat in the windae, texting him. Jas's texts werenae like anyone else's; he was still addicted to Shelley and he'd stick in bits of poetry. He never used text abbreviations – insisted on punctuating everything and putting in capital letters.

It was during one of our phone calls that I explained the installation I was planning.

I just don't know if it's possible, but. I mean how can I isolate one section and no damage the rest?

I'm sure it can be done. I'll have a think about it afore I come down. Hey – d'you have the dimensions on you?

Waiting for Jas at Queen Street Station the next weekend, my stomach was in knots. His train never got in till one o'clock so I'd planned to get a long lie, make up some of the sleep I'd lost over endless weeks of working late nights and early mornings. But I was awake at seven, unable to drop off again. I kept thinking about us, hoping that this weekend there'd be some kind of breakthrough. At the party, it was right that things had been tentative, but noo, after all the messages and phone calls, I wanted to move forward.

When I seen him walking along the platform, I wanted to rush over and hug him, but they have these ticket barriers so there's a guddle of folk clogging up the exit and other folk panicking, pushing their way on to the platform, scared they'll miss their train, and machines beeping and folk having to go back. By the time he finally got through we did hug, but his bag got in the way and somehow it wasnae exactly how I'd imagined it.

As we heided towards the subway Jas said, *What d'you want to do?*

Let's go back to the flat.

I knew as soon as I opened the door it felt different, as if the house was holding its breath. I'd banked on it being like this, just the two of us. On Saturday afternoons the others were often out somewhere.

It's massive, said Jas, dropping his bag in the hall. He spread his airms out. *There must of been a million people here the night of the party, you could hardly breathe.*

Aye, it is big. My room's the wee-est but even it's huge.

I opened the door and took him in. We sat side by side on the bed, no touching, just an inch apart. I wanted to grab him and pull him doon on the bed with me but we just sat and he put his haund on mines. Then he said, *I've brought the thing for your installation – d'you want to see it?*

So we looked at what he'd made and talked about it, and I made us coffee, then Jas said, *I better get round to Ma's. Want to go for a meal tonight? I could meet you later.*

I was wondering if you wanted to stay here . . . the night?

He stared at the kitchen table, an old wooden one with deep furrows and cracks in it, the kind of table that should be scrubbed and oiled and looked after but in our flat just got stained with spilled drinks and littered with crumbs.

Then he looked up. *I don't think it's a good idea, Fiona.*

His face was gentle and open, but I felt as if I'd been punched.

He spoke slowly, measured his words. *It'd be very easy . . . but I don't think it's the right thing just now.*

What d'you think is the right thing?

I think we need more time. To talk, to be thegether, to see how things work out before we go further.

Though his face and words were calm I could feel, across the space that divided us, the heat of the fire he was trying to subdue in hissel.

I know that sounds dead sensible, but it's . . . I wasnae sure how tae go on, to find the right words. *When I was wee, at primary,*

I was in the nativity play one year as the back of an ox. I couldnae see anything, couldnae hear properly and I could only feel the world through this great muffle of material. And that's how I feel now. I know there's something out there, I know there's something between us but I cannae feel it, I cannae break free of this big thick costume I'm wearing. We're sitting here on either side of a table and I don't want to be — I want us tae be close.

Jas stood up and came round to my side, pulled me to my feet, put his airms round me. As we held each other I thought he was gonnae change his mind, he kissed wee dry kisses on my face and my foreheid. Then he came apart fae me and said, *I know, I know. I want us to be close too, but so much has happened . . .*

I know it's my fault. I know.

It's not your fault, Fiona, things happen.

But Amrik . . .

I don't want to talk about Amrik.

But how can we move on without talking about Amrik? What I don't understand is how come you're no even angry at him or me?

I cannae be angry. I love you both. Don't let's say any more. Let's just give it time.

I WAS WORKING in the studio when Shazia appeared.

Hi Fiona? I'm Nadia's sister.

Nadia was wanny the other students. She'd tellt me her sister was trying to break intae PR and was looking for students tae practise on, but I'd forgotten.

I have a degree in marketing but it's so hard to find a job and you need to be prepared to, you know, just seize opportunities. So I'd like to publicise your event. Free of course — you'd just pay for printing costs and so on. I guarantee I will get a fantastic audience.

I looked at her, speechless. Shazia was slender with dark shiny hair tied back in a pony tail that swung from side to side as she talked animatedly. She was wearing a carefully pressed red blouse and neat jeans with very pointy shoes poking out from under them. I'd of thought she was the kind

270

of girl who could get a job in marketing by snapping her long, beautifully manicured fingers.

Listen, Shazia. Nae offence to you – I'm sure you'd dae a great job, but I don't want a big fuss. I don't know if it's even gonnae work. It might be a disaster – it's a huge risk.

That's what it's all about isn't it? You could have played safe with paintings or whatever. But you've chosen a risky medium so why not make your risk worthwhile? If it fails, it fails – a smaller audience will only make it less embarrassing, not less of a failure. And if it's a success, don't you want that to be in front of the biggest possible audience?

There was nae doubt, this lassie was in the right job.

Mona, Rona, Declan and Grace sat at the front of the audience with my da and Janice. Since Declan had helped make the house I couldnae avoid telling them about the event, but I hadnae banked on it becoming a family outing. I'd tried to persuade my da no tae come but he insisted on taking the day aff work, and Patric had flown up too, bringing Amrik.

Behind them stood a handful of students and a couple of lecturers – my tutor and an external examiner – as well as a few other folk I didnae recognise. I hoped Shazia wasnae too disappointed with the turnout. She'd put flyers in local offices and shops, the Drama School and even the Dental Hospital – I guessed the two guys in white coats were on a break from there. In the leaflet she'd persuaded me tae write, I'd credited Declan for help in making the house, so Mona was happy and kept showing it to everyone, telling them he was her fiancé.

Jas was at the back with his camera, and he smiled at me reassuringly. I smiled back but all I wanted tae dae was run away. All these months I'd been fixated on my ideas and dreams, on my art, on bringing all my obsessions thegether intae this one-off piece of work. But noo, my family ranged on plastic seats in this scabby room, all I could think of was how this would appear to them.

I'd put a screen in front of the installation, like a curtain in the theatre – Shazia wanted drama. At ten past one I took the screen aside to reveal a metal table on which stood the wooden model of a tenement building, five feet high and open at the front like a doll's house. Two flats on each landing, the close stair in the middle. I'd painted the landing windaes with a floral design and smeared them wi Vaseline to gie a veiled effect, cause of course the windaes in the close are never cleaned properly.

There was a neat wee auld-lady flat on the top right; two figures sat on chintzy armchairs, hauding cups made out the washing up liquid tops. Opposite them was a student flat, with purple walls and a glitterball suspended fae the ceiling. It looked great and was dead easy – aff a keyring I'd bought in a cheapo shop. One of the students was on the phone, a plastic toy mobile of Evie's stuck to his ear. The ground-flair flat had several fat figures, stuffed wi auld tights, squashed on a settee in fronty a television showing an ad for a burger – just as well the Flanagans hadnae come too. The second-left flat had cream walls and a rust-coloured settee on which sat a man with a tiny can in one haund and a piece of rolled-up paper with a red tip in the other.

Above the house was a screen on to which was projected a video, very grainy and blurred. I'd got two other students to help me make it; I filmed their shadows, then touched the images up with the computer. A skinny guy wi a shock of hair waved lit matches in the air and appeared tae set fire to something above his heid. Then a figure in a long skirt rushed

272

in carrying a bucket and threw it over him, putting out the fire. As she did so a voice repeated, *Branwell is a hopeless being he is a hopeless being he is a hopeless being,* then faded out.

The audience shuffled in their seats, nae doubt wondering if this was it, and, if so, what all the fuss was about. It was Mona noticed it first; I could see her stiffen as she spotted the glow on the end of the bit of paper held by the figure in the second-flair flat. The speck of light grew bigger until it became a flame; Jas had figured out a way of using a flint and spark tae start the fire so it would look spontaneous. I still didnae know if it would take properly and I held my breath at the tension until the flame dropped on the carpet; it went up instantly and the whole flat was blazing. There was an intake of breath fae the audience and folk at the front moved back slightly. I'd used petrol on the interior surfaces of the flat and it bleezed away, flames creeping out and charring the edges of the walls.

It seemed like a long time, but really it was only a few minutes afore it started tae fade. I could see some folk were disappointed – the guy fae the paper shop on the corner nudged his pal and nodded in the direction of the exit – obviously they'd of preferred pyrotechnics. But everyone else watched as the fire in the flat burnt itsel out without damaging the rest of the building. It had worked.

As the blaze died doon and the audience began to relax, the video appeared again above the house. The guy set the curtains on fire, the woman flung water over him but this time the voice at the end said, *Mr Brontë has a horror of fire Mr Brontë has a horror of fire don't tell papa don't tell papa.*

A skitter of clapping started tae make its way through the audience, growing louder and louder till it was proper applause, with some of the students shouting and whistling.

In the front row Mona, Rona and Janice looked stony, and my da sat with his heid in his haunds.

I took a step towards him but Shazia took my airm and steered me to where a big guy in a creased suit and a wee wumman in combats and hiking boots were standing. *Local paper and online art mag,* she whispered.

So, the guy said, waving at the installation. *All very interesting, but what makes this kind of thing better than a painting?*

I opened my mouth and shut it again. I'd nae idea what to say. *I don't think it is better. It's just, this is what I do.*

He scribbled away.

So where is the art in this, then? It says in the leaflet you didn't actually make the house.

I think you'll find, Shazia interjected, *that it's very common for contemporary artists to use assistants to carry out their design ideas, just as they always have. In fact Leonardo and Michelangelo didn't actually paint every . . .*

I did make all the furniture and people.

Don't you think that's more 'Blue Peter' than art?

I don't see what you're getting at.

Look, don't take this personally . . . eh . . . Fiona. I'm being devil's advocate here for the sake of our readers so, to put it plainly, where exactly is the art in you setting fire to a nice doll's house that someone else made?

It's symbolic. It's the context . . .

So, if some kid in a baseball cap sets a doll's house on fire, they're hauled off for community service but if you do, because you've been to Art School, it's art?

I . . .

Fine, Fiona, I've got what I need here. Can you stand in front of your thingy so Terry can take a photo.

Shazia pushed me towards the piece and Terry moved me

274

about till he got what he wanted. All the time the other journalist, the one that looked like she was about tae walk the West Highland Way, was at my elbow.

Fiona, if you don't mind, I'd like to ask you about the symbolism of the piece, the relationship between the video and the burning house? I'm a big Brontë fan so I guess it's meant to be when Branwell set the curtains on fire and Emily put the fire out, yeah?

That's right. Shazia thrust a leaflet at her. *You'll see that it's mentioned here but of course the artist doesn't want to explain things in too clearcut a fashion, wants to leave room for ambiguity and making connections . . .*

Thanks, but I'm most interested in why you chose to parallel the two, Fiona. Does the tenement have a personal meaning for you as an artist or is it a political statement about the isolation of our lives? One flat goes on fire and the rest of the building carries on as if nothing had happened. Is this a comment on the isolation of modern life as opposed to the more community-spirited Victorian days?

I don't think the Brontës were all that much part of a community – they were very close as a family but they never really went out of their own circle that much.

Have you always been interested in the Brontës, Fiona?

Yes.

That's great, I'll leave you to it. Well done, though – you've a glittering career in front of you, I'm sure.

I picked my way through students who were hanging around, examining the piece, working out how the fire had been contained in the one flat. A few folk tried tae speak to me, but I went to where my da was still sitting in exactly the same position. Rona had a protective airm round him, while Mona, and Declan, holding Grace, stood as if to shield him from prying eyes, though in fact no one paid him the slightest bit of attention. I was shocked when I seen the look Janice drew me. She was the one who'd always supported me. But lines had appeared round her nose and lips, and the pupils of her eyes lasered me with their intensity.

How could you, Fiona?

Rona said nothing but glared at me and pulled her airm tighter round my da.

I didnae mean tae . . .

Janice got up and moved a few paces, spoke in a low voice so Da couldnae hear her words, but her voice was so incisive there was nae mistaking her tone.

I don't know what you meant, but are you so caught up in this art stuff you've forgotten what you owe to your family?

You've always tellt me to be true to mysel, Janice — you always went your ain way.

There's a difference between going your ain way and stabbing someone in the back.

I mean you were always open about Angie and everything even when it might of hurt people's feelings.

Get a grip, Fiona. You're comparing me being honest about who I am and how I live my life, with this juvenile showing off you label 'art'. If you had to do something like this why ask him to come and see it—

I didnae want him to . . .

She kept gaun. *Can you imagine how hurt he must be? How embarrassed, how ashamed?*

I looked round. All I could see was the back of a jacket, the top of a heid, hair grey and slightly thinning. Then the heid unwound itsel fae the trap of Rona's arm, the figure straightened and rose up fae its seat. Da put one haund on Janice's airm and one on mines. *Leave the lassie alane,* he said.

She's only telling the truth after all. There was a blank weariness in his face, his eyes softened by tears.

You done good, hen. He patted my airm and was led away like an invalid, Rona and Mona on either side.

THE RIVER WAS stagnant in the heat with nae visible movement; green and brown with big round slabbery white bits floating, as if a giant had spat intae it. We stood on the bridge and stared at the dull surface. On a day like this it should be lovely tae stare at the river, flowing and sparkling, frills of leaves reflected in the water, but the Kelvin looked like the congealed surface of a pan of stock that needed skimmed. It never really looks clean except when it tummles and races after heavy rain, but even then you're mair likely to see a poly bag or an old shoe being swept alang than you are a fish. Even the ducks were stupefied by the heat; two of them squashed thegether side by side on a rock.

They're this year's babies, I said. *Look how big they've got.*

Aye, Jas pointed. *See that greenish patch on its heid catching the light — looks as if it'll be a male.*

D'you think they're happy?

Jas laughed. *Mibbe no the day — too hot — but in Glasgow, with all the rain we get, they should be the happiest ducks in the world.*

Nearly every day I pass by here, watch them grow. And it seems as if everything's the same, one wee stretch of manky river.

Jas took my airm. *You need a change of scene. Now you've finished the artwork why don't you come up tae Aberdeen for a visit?*

I'd like that.

Cool. Next weekend, after my exams are over. Now, let's go and get an ice-cream.

I'd a meeting with my tutor next day and I was dreading it. When I keeked round his door he barely glanced at me, just waved in the direction of a chair and continued with his emails. After what seemed like ages, he clicked the mouse and the screen changed tae a Miro design. He swivelled his chair round to face me. *So, Fiona — how d'you feel about yesterday?*

His face was deeply lined; he had a house in Spain and spent the summers there. He'd obviously been quite handsome when he was younger — the photie on the website was carefully posed and he looked about thirty-five — but the sun damage and the reddening of his cheeks caused by fondness for wine and whisky made him look nearer fifty close up. I knew I should tell him what he wanted to hear about the technical success of the piece, the symbolism, the audience reaction and what I might of done differently in hindsight — all the stuff that was supposed to be part of the reflective process they were always telling us was crucial for an artist. I minded the words in his first lecture. *We're not here to teach you to make art — if you want to learn that go to evening classes* in watercolour painting or macramé — we're here to help you become artists.

I said, *I feel like crap, actually.*

He threw his heid back and laughed. Then he lifted a paint-brush on his desk and twirled it round, stroking the bristles. *Can we be a little more specific?*

I shrugged. *I thought I was here tae find out what you and the external tutor thought of it.*

He leaned back in his seat. *Fiona, you know as well as I do that moderation is an integral part of the artistic process, not just something added on at the end. Otherwise, why not have the lecturers standing holding up bits of card with numbers on them, like the judges of 'Come Dancing'.* He put the brush down and looked at me.

Well, the fire worked, the way I'd hoped . . .

Whether it works technically or not isn't really the point.

I didnae say anything, watched as he linked his fingers, pressing his palms thegether. He'd podgy smooth skin, gnarled round the joints.

If the whole building had gone on fire then the observation I presume you intended to make about isolation and communality of urban life would have been a different one. Instead of being isolated in his wretchedness, your little man's misery would spread to his neighbours, destroying their worlds — you'd make exactly the oppos-ite point you set out to make but that is as valid a position as the other.

I couldnae take this any longer.

Dae I get a mark or something for this?

He took a sheet of typed paper from the printer, folded it in two and stuck it in a brown paper envelope which he held out to me. *Fiona, you seem a bit upset today but sometimes it's like that after a show — why don't you come and discuss this with me*

later when you've calmed down. Before the end of next week though
— I'm off early on sabbatical.

Jas was waiting for me in Giardini's.
  What did he say?
  Oh, a lot of pish.
  You need a coffee.
  I placed the envelope on the table in front of me. It was damp and the paper stuck to the formica slightly. When Jas got back fae the counter he lifted the envelope and wiped it wi a paper napkin. *You no gonnae open this?*
  I don't care.
  Aye you dae.
  Okay I dae, but . . .
  Is it your da?
  I've never seen him that upset except about Mammy.
  It's no nice to hurt your family but an artist cannae be constrained by that.
  An artist mibbe. If I'd produced something that was worth hurting him, mibbe. But setting a doll's house on fire? Mibbe I was just recycling my feelings.
  That's not all it was and you know it.
  I still don't think it was worth it. Janice was furious with me. And she's always supported me being an artist.
  It doesnae mean she's always right. Look, drink your coffee afore it gets cold.
  I took a sip; it was creamy, slightly sticky on my tongue.
  Look at Shelley.
  What about him?
  He never bothered about what his family thought, he done what he thought was right.
  And look at the trail of devastation he left behind him.

But look at the poetry. And Emily Brontë — did she sit about worrying whether her da liked 'Wuthering Heights'?

I'm nae Shelley. Or Emily Brontë.

How d'you know? You've no even opened the envelope to see what they say about it.

I looked at it, lying beside the plate, damp around the edges and with a trail of crumbs across it.

Jas, you wouldnae even study literature or art because your family wanted you tae be a pharmacist.

He put his haund on mines. *Fiona, I'm perfectly happy studying pharmacy.*

You could of went tae Art School.

Aye great and then there'd be two of us sitting here, angst ridden. Gies a break. He grinned. *And for God's sake are you gonnae open this envelope or do I have to do it myself?*

The comments, from baith my own tutor and an external moderator, were embarrassingly good. They praised it up to the skies and read intae it things I'd never even thought of. The only bit they were less enthusiastic about was the references to Branwell and Emily which they described as 'over-icing the cake'. But they'd gied me an A and said it was being considered for a prize and a travel bursary.

I'd be lying if I said it didnae make me feel a bit better but there was still a lump in my throat. And I knew it wouldnae go away till I talked to my da.

Mona was in the kitchen making toasted cheese while Grace slept in her buggy.

I'm surprised at you comin here after yesterday.

Gie it a rest, Mona.

He's been like that ever since we got back. She nodded through tae the living room where my da sat, as usual, on the settee.

He's been like that for the last three year, Mona.

Don't try tae justify what you done.

I'm no. Just let me deal with it.

Declan too, all that work on the house and you set it on fire.

Mona . . .

She snorted.

Mona! I gestured at the grill where smoke was beginning to emerge.

Oh Christ!

Just as she pulled it out the smoke alarm let out a high-pitched wailing. Grace woke and started to cry. Mona turned tae me, *Noo look what you've done!*

I switched the alarm aff and went through tae the living room.

What's up?

Smoke alarm. It's okay. Mona burned the toast.

I was just having a wee nap.

Aye, so was Grace.

I sat doon beside him. *Da.*

Aye hen.

Da, about yesterday.

Ach, ah'm sorry.

You're sorry?

Ah didnae mean tae greet. Couldnae help it.

It's me who's sorry. I didnae mean tae hurt your feelings.

You never.

Aye I did.

Ah was just proud of you, that's all.

Janice thought . . .

Ach, Janice is great. But she's like your mammy, always trying tae protect folk. Look, hen, ah know hee-haw about art, and even less

283

about modern art. But sittin there wi all they folk round about, watching somethin you made . . .

I was beginning tae get well confused. Had he no realised what the installation was about, how it had been inspired?

But the fire . . .

Fiona. Ah'm mair ashamed than ah can say about what ah done. There's no a day goes by when ah don't look round this hoose and think about it. There's no a night goes by when ah don't talk to your mammy about it. Ah know that sounds daft.

It's no.

It is, but ah don't even care. He turned round, took my haund in his rough sandpapery one. Ah used tae think I was an okay guy. Ah wasnae the greatest but ah worked and supported yous, left the day-tae-day stuff to your mammy. Then all of a sudden she's gone and it's doon tae me. And ah made a mess of it, a big mess. Ah might of made an even bigger mess if it hadnae been for Janice and Mrs Kaur. She's a great wee wumman, Jas's ma.

Janice tried tae talk to me about it yesterday, tried tae gie me all the art no being just a copy of life stuff. Ah'm no daft, Fiona. Ah know the wee guy wi the fag was me — you even gied him a jumper like mines. But it was the truth. And nae matter how much we don't like the truth, we have to face it.

He put his haund on mines, nodded towards the kitchen. Away and see if Mona's rescued thon toasted cheese, hen.

THAT NIGHT JAS and me wandered in the Botanic Gardens. It was still hot, too hot – felt as though the sky would explode if it didnae rain soon and bring relief. The park was mobbed; folk laid out on the big grassy slopes, making the maist of the unusual Glasgow heatwave – even wee toddlers out way past their bedtimes. We heided alang the path that led tae the Arboretum where there was mair of a breeze. We lay on the grass, watching leaves ripple across the clear sky.

I arranged for us to meet up with Amrik and Patric later tonight. Amrik's playing in the café. Jas leaned on one elbow and looked doon at me. *If it's all right with you.*

I looked intae his eyes, so clear and clean, minding the first time I'd done so.

Is it cool with you, Jas?

285

Course. There's nae point in pretending. Stuff has happened and we've all been hurt. But now, this is how it is.

My da was talking about that the day. How we need tae face the truth.

Jas nodded.

I sat up. *Jas, how can you be so . . . good?*

Jas threw back his heid and laughed. He giggled so much he put his haund on his side. *Oh God, that is sore, don't make me laugh.*

It's no funny.

It is funny. Saint Jaswinder. Mibbe the Pope'll canonise me – I could be the first Sikh Catholic saint.

I don't get it.

Fiona, don't you think I wanted to strangle Amrik when you two went off thegether? Don't you think I wanted to strangle you too? It's only natural. But things worked themselves out and now Amrik has found Patric and you and me are back thegether. It's good.

But . . .

Amrik is my brother, Fiona. I love him. Patric is your brother. And you can forgive your brother anything.

Truth. Facing the truth.

They were all happily facing the truth. Except they didnae know what it was. If I went alang with this, I'd be hiding the truth for the rest of my life. And if I pulled the truth out intae the light? Jas said he could forgive Amrik anything. But could he forgive me?

I had to speak tae Amrik alone and my chance came that night. When we met in the lounge of Patric's hotel for a drink afore the gig, Patric and Jas went up to the bar thegether. It was very busy, crowded with businessmen on a convention. While they waited to be served, I sat with Amrik.

I have to ask you something, Amrik. It's important.

Shoot.

Do Jas or Patric know about the baby?

The baby?

Our baby.

Amrik took a deep breath. He reached across, brushed my haund lightly with his then withdrew it. *Fiona, there was no baby.*

I had a miscarriage.

You had a very heavy period which contained the remains of an unviable . . . foetus.

His eyes were so dark I could read nothing in them but his voice, though firm, was not unkind, merely factual.

I was pregnant.

He shrugged.

I was.

Fiona, I know it was a very upsetting time. I'm sorry. But it's not the worst thing that has happened to you. You're a strong woman. You have to move on.

That's not the point.

I lowered my voice as Jas crossed to us.

Becks okay, Amrik?

Cool.

Sorry this is taking so long.

When he left, Amrik moved to the seat next to mine. *What is the point, Fiona?*

The point is — dae Jas and Patric know?

I've never talked to either of them about it. Have you?

No.

So they don't know.

But they should know.

Why? Everyone seems quite happy the way things are.

But it's all based on a lie.

That's a bit melodramatic.

Patric thinks you and me had a casual relationship.

Amrik shrugged. *There can be different perceptions of a relationship.*

And Jas doesnae know about it either.

Fiona, if you want to tell them of course I can't stop you but I think it'll just make things more complicated than they need to be.

They should know the truth.

What is the truth Fiona?

Patric and Jas appeared carrying drinks. *That was a nightmare,* said Patric.

Standing, watching Amrik through the haze of spotlights. Familiar, subtle phrasing, notes that bent and quivered then came back to the truth of a pure sound. Amrik, calm and impassive as usual, within his music. I guessed that was Amrik's only truth.

Amrik and Patric flew off tae London the next day and Jas returned tae Aberdeen. Once they'd gone I felt like someone left behind after a disaster. My life was littered with debris, all of my ain making. First I had tae decide what to dae with the remains of the house installation. My tutor wanted me to keep it and rework it for some future exhibit, but I didnae.

It's meant to be of the moment. As soon as you start trying tae keep it and use it for something else you lose its significance.

I disagree, Fiona, but I'm glad you're thinking along these lines. Last week you were doubting the worth of your art altogether. He smiled. *Which is, of course, one of the marks of a true artist.*

But even though I didnae want to reuse it, I didnae like tae dump it – Declan had worked so hard on it. I packed it all up in a box and left it in storage at the Art School. Mibbe later on he could fix it up for Grace.

The other debris was emotional. Even though Da had said he wasnae hurt, Mona and Rona treated me with contempt when I went up to the house and Janice hadnae phoned since last Thursday. I'd hoped it was her when I got a text on Monday but it was Shazia to say there was something about me in the local free paper. I heided round tae my da's, reasoning that the mair I seen Mona and Rona the mair likely it was they'd just forget about the whole thing.

They were all round the kitchen table, newspaper spread out in fronty them. Da looked up.

Fiona, you've got a whole page in the paper, hen.

'Local Lass Fires Up Art World' was the heading and my heart sank when I seen the journalist was Mr Devil's Advocate hissel.

But instead of an investigative piece on the horrors of modern art, ninety per cent of the page was taken up with a photo of me standing looking awkward in fronty the installation and the tiny paragraph said virtually nothing apart from the fact I was at Art School. It did mention Declan's role, however, and Mona seemed tae have completely forgotten how mad at me she'd been.

Ah'm gonnae cut this out and save it for Grace when she's older. She'll be that proud her daddy's in the paper.

Take a copy for your scrapbook, Fiona. My da lifted a pile of newspapers. *Ah took all these fae the close when we seen you were in it.*

Thanks, Da.

Mona finished cutting round the article and laid it flat on the worksurface. *Want a cuppa tea, Fiona?*

Restored to the bosom of my family, I sat in the living room with Mona and Rona wittering on about Mona's wedding plans. I was barely listening when Rona shook me. *Wake up, Fiona.*

Sorry.

Noo all this art stuff is finished, can you fix a time tae come wi us tae get the dress fitted?

What dress?

Are you daft or something? Your bridesmaid's dress.

I thought Rona—

Of course Rona's a bridesmaid, but I've two sisters – you don't get out of it that easy.

Thanks.

Anyway, said Mona, *it's the only way we can make sure you don't turn up like some auld hippy.*

She kept her face straight for a moment, then she and Rona started to giggle. I shoved Rona and Mona and we collapsed over the end of the settee, all of us laughing thegether.

I WENT UP tae Aberdeen the next weekend. It was a wonderful day, sun beating doon and a breeze blowing stiff aff the sea.

Thought you said it was baltic up here.

Don't be fooled, it's only doing this in your honour.

We wandered alang the seafront, gulls wheeling and skraiking above us in the cauld blue. Then we sat on a patch of grass, looked out to where the bluegreen water became grey, at the endlessness of the ocean.

Jas, I said. *There's something I want to talk to you about.*

On you go.

I don't know if I'm daeing the right thing but — it's about me and Amrik.

Fiona, I don't need you to . . .

291

I need to tell you. I took a deep breath. *When Amrik and me were thegether, I had a miscarriage.*

I could sense, rather than feel, the tension stiffening his body.

It wasnae planned – I never even knew I was pregnant. I thought I was just having a bad period and then the doctor came and I'd to go tae hospital. And that was what it was.

Silence.

I looked at him and he looked out tae sea. I sat, giving him time to take it in, waited for him to say something, anything. I was prepared for anger or shock or even for him to just walk away, unable to take it. That was why I'd told him now, this afternoon, while there was still time for me to get a train back hame if everything fell apart.

You slept with Amrik.

You knew.

No, Fiona. Actually, I never.

But, I thought . . .

So did I. He turned to me. *And you carried his baby for . . . how long?*

They said eight weeks.

Eight.

He put his heid in his haunds, sat like that for what felt like ages. Then he looked up again, stared intae the distance. A patch of cloud sailed in fast, close tae the horizon, white bits flaking aff it like blossom.

It must've been awful for you, Fiona.

I nodded.

He looked round. *I know I said we have to look at things as they are. But I think I'm gonnae need some time.*

The weather turned on the way hame in the train. Clear east-coast skies wi birlin white angel clouds giving way tae lurkin grey battleships, and by the time the train reached the outskirts of Glasgow it was dreich and drear. My heid was stuffed up and my stomach, which had been tied in churning knots throughout the journey, dulled tae a solid lumpen pain. I'd went over and over it as the scenery flew by in a blur, wondering what he was gonnae dae. The ball was in Jas's court. If he couldnae cope with what had happened, that was us, finished.

And if I'd just kept quiet, as Amrik had said, everything would of been fine.

But I knew in my heart that it wouldnae. However awful things would be without Jas, the alternative was living with an unspoken lie for the rest of my life. And lies are like weeds; left too long they creep round healthy plants and destroy them.

It was a week afore I heard fae Jas. A week of trailing my misery round with me through the boring, routine stuff that was my life in the aftermath of the show. Before it there'd been such a build up; every waking minute spent preparing, thinking, working on this artwork, then suddenly it's done and you realise you've nae clean clothes, or food in the fridge, while all the stuff you've ignored is sitting waiting for you. In spite of everything, that was what I still admired about Amrik, his ability to just coast through it all. But then, when things got too much hassle for him, he just disappeared.

I wondered how he and Patric managed thegether – Patric with his neat and perfect life and Amrik, floating about paying nae attention to anything except his music. On the surface they complement each other cause Patric loves taking care of the practicalities. But in some strange deep-seated way, Patric is like Amrik. He doesnae get attached tae things, moves on.

Like never owning a house, just living in someone else's. He makes it his ain for a while, then when he's had enough, he leaves. Sure he could afford to buy something but that would be too permanent. The only things that have any permanence in his life are us, his family.

When Jas did get in touch it was very low key, not at all how I'd expected. At night in my bed, I'd run through the scenes of what would happen when he finally contacted me. In version one of my fantasy, he wrote a long letter explaining why he could never forgive me, in version two he declared undying love. Instead, there was a text saying he'd be doon the following weekend and could we meet for a coffee.

Sitting in the front windae of Giardini's I watched him walk up the road fae the subway. I'd always thought Jas was handsome but no stunning like Amrik; Jas's attractiveness was that he was always animated, talking intently, waving his haunds about. But observing him when he didnae know I was looking, I realised how he was changing as he grew older. The lines of his face seemed mair defined, but he still had that softness about him, a gentle presence. He waved when he seen me, smiled. I wanted to hug him but as he came in a woman wi a buggy was leaving and he held the door open for her. Then he sat doon and said, *Hi, how are you?*

Fine. How were your exams?

Okay, I think. Won't know till July, but.

Right.

Pause. Deep breath. Reality time.

Fiona.

Our knees were three inches apart but it felt like miles. I was waiting, waiting for him to say *I'm sorry but*, waiting so hard I was sure he'd said it already and I blurted out, *I understand.*

What?

294

I know. I spoiled everything.

A finger touching the back of my haund, so briefly it could of been my imagination.

Fiona, that's no it. Look, I want to be completely honest.

I nodded.

I know it must of been terrible for you – I cannae begin tae imagine what it was like. I've been gaun round and round in circles all week, trying to work it out. And I think I'm getting there. He paused. *But it's hard to come to terms with . . . that you and Amrik . . .*

You mean, you cannae forgive me.

I hate that word – as if I was better than you. If you want forgiven, go tae confession, Fiona. It's no my place to forgive you.

I looked at him, thinking, this is it, this is it, this is the last time I will see that dark shiny hair, will hear this voice.

All I can do is stop blaming you.

He looked in my eyes.

I could feel the tears bubble up. Jas put his airms round me, whispered intae my hair. *Oh Fiona, I cannae just snap out of it right away. But I want to, I really do.*

I gulped back my tears. *I know. I'm sorry.*

He pushed my hair back fae my foreheid. *And please, stop saying you're sorry.*

WHEN I LOOK back on the time between that day and Mona's wedding, it feels like a wee safe bubble in my life. For once, nothing much was happening, at least nothing I needed tae think about.

I'd moved back in wi my da — I was gonnae come back after the wedding anyway tae save some money, but the twins suggested I done it earlier.

It'll be a laugh, said Rona.

Probably the last time we'll be thegether, said Mona.

You can have your room back, added Rona. *Ah'll go in with Mona and Grace.*

It was mental, us all squashed up thegether, but it felt good.

Jas was in Glasgow for the holidays, working in the shop. I was back in the supermarket but I didnae need tae dae as many hours as last summer – I'd been awarded a bursary which meant I'd be okay when the new term started. I actually had spare time to help Mona and Rona with the wedding preparations and catch up with Monica and Jemma. Da was happy and everything seemed settled.

Me and Jas seen each other maist nights, sometimes went for a meal or to see a movie, other times we'd just walk and talk in the park. Or we'd spend time in the calm of his place or the madhouse that was my da's. It was nice. I know it sounds pathetic but that's what it was like. Jas was the same as he'd ever been but there was another layer to him, a greater strength and solidity that I was just beginning tae know. And when we kissed and held each other, even though we never went any further than we ever had, it felt deeper, mair passionate. I settled intae the relationship, no thinking about the future.

Mona looked lovely in her white dress wi puffed sleeves and a skirt like a meringue. Her hair was in an elaborate twist, looped and crossed like a Celtic knot. Me and Rona had identical frocks in turquoise, long skirts that were too narrow to walk in comfortably and a neckline that kept falling aff my shoulder, but Mona was happy and that was what mattered. My hair was pinned intae a net like a mediaeval maiden's, hair-sprayed so the rogue curls couldnae escape. Declan was wearing a kilt, as was his brother, Aiden, the best man. It was a made-up tartan, purple and turquoise and blue. *Modern,* said Mona.

She'd wanted my da tae wear a kilt too but he put his foot doon for once.

A morning suit is what the father of the bride should be dressed in.

And he looked surprisingly elegant in it, with a cream tie and shiny black shoes.

Jas amazed me by turning up in full Highland dress, including a sgian dubh.

It's a traditional Sikh tartan, he tellt Mona who believed him for hauf a minute afore she and Jas burst out laughing.

Father O'Hara done the ceremony, much to Mona's disgust. She'd taken a shine to the new wee priest who was a big fan of Grace, but he was away.

I just hope he doesnae start talkin aboot the missions, she said.

But even Mona was pleased with the service. The altar was decked out wi lilies, the chapel full tae bursting and what wi the cantor's resounding soprano and Father O'Hara's sermon about young love and walking haund in haund wi God tae build a family there was barely a dry eye in the place.

Da had planned tae hold the reception in the parish hall but Patric stepped in and insisted on paying for a fancy do in the hotel where he stayed when he came to Glasgow. Apparently he was well in with the owner due tae some business deal he'd arranged with one of his London friends so he got it for a great price. This helped soothe my da's pride and Mona was over the moon. The meal was fantastic and the function room elegant and airy but I think the hotel management didnae know what hit them when the evening guests arrived and the dancing started. It was all very sedate at first, with Declan and Mona and my da and Declan's ma on the flair for the waltz, but later on some of the twins' dancing pals, all fake tan and floral frocks, done a display. The only person who never danced was Amrik. Patric had suggested he should play the sitar but Amrik refused. *Thank God for that,* said Mona.

I was watching my da teach Jas's ma the finer points of the hokey-cokey when Jas came up behind me.

East meets West. The city council would love this — some kind of cross-cultural box they could tick there.

I know.

Let's creep off.

We cannae, it's rude to leave afore the bride.

She won't be leaving. Mona and Declan are staying here the night.

I still don't think we should go.

They'll be at it for hours yet. Come. I want to show you something.

I was intrigued, of course, couldnae figure out why Jas would drag me away fae my ain sister's wedding party.

There were taxis waiting outside the hotel and Jas led me intae the first one. *It's a surprise,* he said and gied the driver a piece of paper. The guy nodded and set aff.

There was nae surprise as the cab sped alang familiar streets. I thought for a minute Jas was gonnae stop at his ma's house but we went past it and when the taxi turned the corner near the park I knew.

Jas, why are we . . .

Just wait.

He led me in the close and up the familiar stair. It was the first time I'd been there since that night I'd run all the way here and found it boarded up. Since then I'd never even had the courage tae walk alang the street, let alone return to the house.

I knew every tile: the missing one outside the Flanagans' house, the crack in the border tile on the first landing. Mrs Jackson had painted her door green and the Flanagans had a new doormat wi a picture of a dug on it, but apart fae that everything was the same.

There was nae sign of smoke damage and the door looked

better than when we lived there as it had been revarnished. Jas unlocked the door, let me go in front of him intae the hall. The boards were bare, the walls newly plastered. An unshaded bulb hung fae the ceiling, casting bright light intae every corner.

Jas?

He led me through each room, one by one. The flat felt huge without the crush of furniture and people; light flooded fae the uncurtained windaes. When we entered the kitchen I gasped – all the units had been ripped out, the pipes and electric wires were exposed.

What's happening? How did you get the keys?

My uncle knows the builder who's doing it up. The guy who bought the flat after the repossession never lived in it and a few month ago he started to do it up. This is as far as they've got.

I walked across to the windae, looked out to the back court. *Feels dead strange. The same house, but so different.*

When I was wee I used tae play with the weans who lived in the flat across the landing. Because it was on the other side of the close all the rooms were the opposite way round and the furniture and carpets were different fae ours – it had always made me feel unsettled.

Jas, what's gaun on?

The flat is for sale.

Jas held out the key. It lay shiny and bright on his outstretched palm. I closed his fingers over it. *Jas don't make jokes, it's no funny.*

He turned, paced across to the door and back to me again, kilt swaying fae side to side.

I'm sorry, Fiona, I'm an eejit, I'm daeing this the wrong way.

He put his airms round me. The metal buttons on his jacket pressed hard intae me and my hair started tae unfankle fae its net. *I love you.* He stepped back, took my haunds. *It's like, whatever else has happened, I've always felt this way about you. Like that line of Shelley's – 'I am not thine, I am a part of thee.'*

Jas, I . . .

I want us to get married. Please don't say anything, I'm no asking for answers – it's much too soon. I just want you to know. Before I tell you about the house.

There was naewhere tae sit that wasnae covered wi a thin film of plaster dust so we stood in the living room as he explained.

My da owned a property that he let out. Ma couldnae be bothered with the hassle – she decided to sell it and split the money between me and Amrik. I hoped we could use it for a deposit on a house eventually, once we'd finished studying.

Then my uncle heard about a flat that was getting done up, said the owner was going abroad to work, might do a deal. Nae harm in having a look. He dropped off the key this morning just as we were about to leave for the church. It was only then I found out it was your house. All day I've been thinking about it, trying to work out what to dae. I couldnae wait, Fiona. I had to bring you here. It's like it was meant.

I didnae know what to say, just looked at Jas's eager face. I felt that my legs would collapse under me if I stood much longer. I couldnae take it in – it was all too fast, too confusing.

I'll need time tae think, Jas. I put my haund on his airm. *Let's get back to the reception.*

We arrived just as everything was fizzling out.

Where have yous been? asked Rona. *You just missed Mona throwing her bouquet. Caitlin caught it. And it could of been you.*

Never mind.

After we'd said our goodbyes to Mona and Declan, Jas

made sure his ma got a taxi. Then we stood on the steps of the hotel watching folk pass by, enjoying the warm evening.

D'you feel like talking? asked Jas. *We could go for a walk if you like.*

No in this, I said, tugging at the skirt of my frock. *Anyway, I think I need a bit of time on my ain, think things through.*

Sure. Jas took my haund and we started to go up the steps towards the hotel entrance. All of a sudden it hit me – I knew what I had to dae. I stopped, let go his haund. *Jas, wait here – I'll be back in five minutes.*

Patric had booked hotel rooms for our family and some of Declan's relatives. I rushed upstairs to the room I was sharing with Rona, changed intae my jeans and shoved a few things in a bag. As I was locking the door she arrived.

Leave it, Fiona. I'm just gonnae fix my make-up and the light in that toilet doonstairs is terrible. She looked at me. *Did you have to change? You looked nice.*

I'm going out with Jas. I paused. *Rona, don't worry if I don't come back to the room the night, okay?*

Like I'd be shocked?

See you the morra.

In the dark the flat looked mair familiar than it had in daylight. The light of the streetlamps softened its bareness and made the plastered walls look like pink marble. On the way I'd got the taxi to stop at my da's, packed a rucksack while Jas waited for me. I opened it, took out a blanket and spread it on the living room flair. We sat side by side, leaning on the wall opposite the windae.

Jas put his airm round me. *This is cosy.*

Don't get too comfy.

It took a while to persuade Jas to leave me alone in the

flat. *I cannae,* he said, when I'd explained what I wanted to dae. *It's no safe.*

I'll be fine. There's a better lock on the door than when we stayed here and there's neighbours around. This is something I have to dae.

When he left I went intae the room that I used to share wi the twins, curled the blanket round me and lay on the flair, looking out at the trees. This was the first time in my life I'd ever spent the night alone in any house. In spite of what I'd said tae Jas, I felt a bit nervous, listening to the creaks and squeaks as the building settled doon intae night, but there was comfort in the familiar tenement noises; the sounds of a tap running in the flat upstairs, lights being switched off below, folk getting ready for bed.

I was wide awake. I wrapped the blanket round me like a shawl and walked through the empty rooms. Would this be the first night of many I'd spend in the house again, or was it a kind of farewell? When I'd had the notion to stay here, I'd decided on impulse, with some vague idea that the house itsel would provide answers.

But there were nae ghosts here. I remembered things that had happened, ordinary things like us having breakfast or watching TV, but they were memories I could of had any-where. It wasnae like visiting the Brontë parsonage, where you could feel so strongly the presence of the family who'd lived there. However much I wanted, I couldnae call up the spirit of Mammy, call on her wisdom to help me decide, as if she was alive. I had to rely on the spirit inside me, the one she'd helped tae shape and form.

I stood on a creaky floorboard and the sound shattered the silence. This house had never been silent. And if Jas and me got married and had children, it would be filled with noise again.

303

For Jas it seemed simple.

If you want it, it's ours, he'd said. But, even if we bought it, done it all up, decorated it the way we wanted, could it ever really be ours? How would my da feel about us living in the house that had been his hame? I didnae think I was ready to get married so soon either – I wasnae like Mona who dreamed of walking doon the aisle in a white wedding dress. Of course I loved Jas, but I was overwhelmed.

I watched the moon creep into view in the uncurtained windae; three-quarters full with misty trails across its surface. I opened my rucksack and took out the copy of *Wuthering Heights* I'd brought with me, turned to the familiar passage.

'Whatever our souls are made of, his and mine are the same.'

In the twenty-first century we don't live like this, with a great love, with a passion as vast as the ocean and pure as the stars. We are tentative and conditional; all the get-out clauses are written fae the moment we set eyes on someone. We don't believe there is one person for us – we try out partners as we send for things on the internet, knowing we have thirty days to return them. No one expects to get married without living with their partner, or at least sleeping with them, and if it doesnae work out there is always amicable, civilised divorce. Makes sense. In our age we recognise the truth of human nature; our society accommodates it.

Jas isnae like that.

But even though he can swear to be always loving and faithful, what about me? When we were first thegether I thought I loved Jas and we'd always be happy, but one sight of Amrik and I dumped him. Could I trust mysel no tae rush off with someone else again? I hoped I'd learned something from what happened with Amrik, but suppose that's how I am — mibbe I'm just that type of person and Jas isnae. Even though he thinks he only wants me, he'd be better aff wi someone like hissel, someone faithful and loving.

Outside, in the long summer night, the sky was dark blue above the familiar shadowy trees. I reread the words of Cathy's testimony. Deep, fine, moving words.

But look at what happened in *Wuthering Heights*. Cathy and Heathcliff separated, only reunited in death, and as for Shelley and Mary — they had their share of problems too: unfaithfulness, dead babies, tragedy.

But they still believed, they had an ideal. I knew that however improbable it seemed, I wanted to live my life by an ideal: nae compromises, nae conditions. And I couldnae imagine daeing that with anyone but Jas.

Four Years Later

THE MORNING SUN flickers through the room, light dappled by the trees outside. I'm alone in the flat, painting the room that'll be our baby's when he or she is born in three months' time. I bend over my bump awkwardly as I sweep the brush near the skirting board to outline the golden fish – I've already stretched high tae paint stars on the ceiling though I'll no tell Jas I stood on a ladder while he wasnae here.

It's a year since we got married. Doubly married, with Catholic and Sikh services. I got all jittery afore it – I'd lived here by mysel for three years and got used to my ain company – part of me dreaded having tae share my space. But I end up missing Jas when he's at work, looking forward to his return.

I still love spending time alone, working in the room

I used to share with the twins, now a studio with white walls and shelves full of objects waiting to be turned intae art. Mona can hardly believe it but. *I hate it when there's naebody in the house,* she says. No much chance of that in hers. With a bit of financial help from Patric, she and Declan got a big flat where they live with my da, Rona, Grace and the new baby, Kieran. Janice has had a son too – James, who's three – and Mona watches him two days a week. Rona has a boyfriend who spends hauf his time there and Mrs Kaur and Declan's family are close by.

When I first came here it was strange for me too, never having lived alone in my life. I loved the feeling of space and light and freedom, but it took me a while tae feel that the house was mine, to reconcile the echoes of the past life with the new one that was beginning tae unfold. Often, when it was very quiet and still, I found mysel thinking of Mammy, and I'd put my heid on the table, greet.

Patric and Amrik are still thegether. Still in London, still moving on whenever the mood takes them. Last year they lived in a Georgian house in the east end – the owner had tae go abroad for a year so Patric looked after it. The guy had done it up and furnished it exactly as it would of been in the eighteenth century with candles for light and a wee bath you filled wi hot water fae a jug. *You have to come and visit, Fiona – you'll love it, living like the Brontës.* It looked brilliant wi the candles and wood fires and all that, but of course Patric had showers at the health club and they ate out maist of the time. Amrik, with his disregard for his surroundings, was perfectly at hame there but I think Patric was happy enough tae move on to their next place, a huge modern apartment overlooking the river. He's still working on hauf a dozen projects at any one time, heavily in demand for all kinds of styling work, while Amrik continues to pursue his music in his ain way.

Since Art School I've divided my time between teaching two days a week and my ain work the rest of the time. I've had commissions and sold stuff, even got shortlisted for a big prize. I've nae idea how much I'll be able to dae after the baby comes, and that scares me. But that fear isnae as great as the feeling that overwhelms me when I feel the baby move, delicately, like a butterfly brushing the inside of me.

I find mysel working in pastel and chalk, avoiding sharp objects and harsh colours, gaun quiet and still inside. I know all that will change – I mind all the other babies in the family – the huge fuss and noise and mess each one created. Mona's unbearable now, lording her superior knowledge of mother-hood, phoning me tae chat endlessly about contractions and teething. But it's cool. She's my sister after all.

I finish my painting, look round the room. One side is filled with the mural; fantastic fish swim in a silver sea and birds hover round a tree with turquoise and lilac leaves. The other walls are emulsioned in soft white, blank spaces to be filled by the future. Above the mantelpiece there's a picture of the Guru alongside one I painted, of Our Lady. It won't ever form part of a show – it's too personal, hasnae the irony that would make it real art in the eyes of folk like my tutor – but I think Mammy would of loved it.

Mary, in blue jeans and a white tee shirt, is hanging out the washing in her back court. I know she'd of had dark skin and eyes but this madonna has a peelywally west of Scotland complexion and eyes that hover between blue and green. Jesus is dark-skinned, lighter than Jas but no much; he's haunding her the pegs and they're smiling at each other.

I wash my brushes in the sink in my red kitchen, sit at the

wooden table with a cup of tea. I imagine Jas in the shop, making up prescriptions with his long, beautiful fingers, speaking seriously to a customer about contraindications, joking with another in Punjabi. I look out the windae at the trees where a bird is cheeping and chattering as birds dae.